MARGARET MANCHESTER

The Lead Miner's Daughter

Historical Romance

First published by Mosaic Design and Print,
Middleton-in-Teesdale 2020

First edition

This book was professionally typeset on Reedsy.
Find out more at reedsy.com

To the memory of my mother, Sheila Adamson, whose stories of her childhood on a Weardale farm inspired me to learn more about the people and the history of the dale.

Acknowledgement

Firstly, I would like to thank my husband, Alec, for his patience and understanding while I was writing this book, and for reading and commenting on my early drafts. I could not have completed it without his support.

I am very grateful to my sister, Linda Brown, my in-laws, Leslie and Annette Manchester, and my friends, Ian and Pam Forbes, for proofreading this book and giving feedback on it. Their comments on the plots and characters have been invaluable.

The front cover photograph was taken by Gary Lintern, who specialises in night-time and underground photography. His model was Emma Hutchinson, daughter of my friends, Jacky and David. Thanks to Peter Jackson at Nenthead Mines for providing the location for the photograph.

The back cover photograph was taken by Linda Brown. It is a view of Weardale taken from Crawleyside, Stanhope.

Finally, a big thank you to Judith Mashiter at Mosaic Publishing for her advice and for all the work she has done to get this book into print.

Chapter 1

The morning was misty as Mary set off for the lead mine at Killhope. As she walked down the steep slope from Fell Top towards the valley bottom, she looked down at the washing floor, which was a hive of activity. The master washerman was telling off a young boy. The boy's head was down, his eyes glued to his feet. The other lads worked hard, with shovels, buckers and rakes, separating the lead ore from the other minerals that had been hauled from the mine.

As Mary crossed the bridge over the burn, light rain began to fall. By the time she reached the washing floor, the scolded boy was back to work, and the master washerman's full attention was on her.

'Sir,' she said. 'Are there any jobs going here?'

'Who for?'

'For me, sir.'

The master washerman laughed and laughed as though he'd heard the funniest joke ever. When eventually he stopped, he said, 'For you lass – no!'

His answer was so resounding that she didn't even think

about arguing her case. She couldn't see why a girl wanting to work there was so funny. She was stronger than she looked, and she could work hard. Why couldn't lasses work there as well?

With his blunt rejection, he had humiliated Mary in front of the men and boys working above ground at the mine. They had all heard what he'd said, and she could feel their eyes on her back. Even the blacksmith had left his hearth to find out what was going on outside. He stood in the doorway of the smithy staring at her. Mary could hear the master washerman chuckling to himself as she walked away with her head held high, her cheeks red and her eyes glassy with unshed tears. She wanted to run, but she wouldn't give him the satisfaction.

A young, fair-haired man descended the steps from the mine office, and their paths crossed beside the stables.

'Excuse me,' he said, removing his cap. 'I heard what he said. Don't take any notice.' Shaking his head, he said, 'I pity the poor lads that work for him.'

'Aye, me too.'

'So, you're looking for a job, then?'

'Aye, I need to find something.'

'Our neighbours down at Westgate are looking for a lass to help in their house. It's on a farm and they're decent people. Would that be any good for you?'

'That would be perfect. Thank you. Who should I contact?'

'I'll write down their details for you.'

The man pulled a notebook and pencil from his jacket pocket and started to write. He tore out the page and handed it to her. The note read:

Mr & Mrs Peart

Springbank Farm

Westgate

'Thank you. That's very good of you. I'll write to them as soon as I get home.'

'Good luck!' He smiled and walked over to his horse and cart.

Mary watched him stroke the bay horse's neck and whisper something in its ear before he climbed up onto the cart and drove off towards the bridge. She reread the note, folded the paper and walked briskly back up the hill to Fell Top. She couldn't wait to tell her sister.

* * *

As Tom Milburn walked back to his horse, he smiled to himself. He couldn't believe he'd met a bonny lass and at the mine of all places. He was sure he hadn't seen her before, but that was hardly surprising because he didn't get up to Killhope very often. He hoped she would take the job with the Pearts at Westgate because if they were neighbours, then he'd be more likely to see her again, and he would like that very much.

'That was a nice surprise, wasn't it, Bobby, lad?' he whispered into his horse's ear. He smiled to himself as he walked round to the cart and stepped up. Taking hold of the reins, Tom set off for home feeling much happier than he had for quite some time.

* * *

Mary and her sister, Annie, had just finished writing a letter to Mr and Mrs Peart when their father, George Watson, burst through the door. He took off his work boots, removed his wet jacket and hat and hung them on the back of the door, and then he turned and looked directly at Mary.

'What were you thinking, lass?'

Mary stared at him wide-eyed. Her father worked underground, and she hadn't thought he would get to know about her visit to the mine, but obviously, he had.

'A man is supposed to provide for his family. You've embarrassed me by turning up at Killhope like that and asking for work behind me back. I'll tell you something lass, no daughter of mine will ever work on the washing floor while there's a breath left in my body! That's no place for a girl down there.'

'I'm sorry, Father, I should have asked you first.' She paused before saying, 'You do know we can't pay the bills though, don't you?'

'Aye, I know that, but the whole world doesn't need to know. How does that make me look? Like I can't look after me own, that's what.'

'Me and Annie were talking earlier. We think we should bring John home. He can be weaned now. We could look after him here and we won't have to pay his wet nurse anymore.'

'John...,' George murmured as though he had forgotten his youngest son existed. He sat down, and his shoulders slumped.

'It's time he came home, Father. It's nearly five months since Mother died.'

'Aye, if you think so. It'll be you two that'll be looking after him, anyway. Is our William back from school yet?'

'No, he must be playing out. He'll be back when tea's ready.'

Mary moved to hide the letter that sat on the table behind

her and said, 'By the way, I heard there's a job going at Westgate. A farmer called Mr Peart needs somebody to help in the farmhouse. Do you think I should write to him?'

'Why not?' said George resignedly. 'At least that's better work for a lass than the washing floor.'

Mary turned to Annie, and they smiled knowingly at each other.

George Watson borrowed a pony and trap from a neighbour to take his daughter to Westgate. As they set off from Fell Top, Mary looked back at the house she had called home. It had been crowded at times with only one room downstairs and one upstairs, but she had fond memories of her childhood there. The stone cottage with its small plot of land was nestled on Killhope Moor. The open expanse of fell around the smallholding was pitted with quarries and mines, and sheep grazed on the coarse grasses that grew on the boggy peat soils, along with rushes, mosses and heather. Mary's favourite time of year was late summer when this upland landscape was transformed into a sea of purple, and the gentry came to shoot the grouse. Today, the rugged hills were green and peaceful.

They reached the valley bottom and joined the road that meandered down the dale, crossing backwards and forwards over the river on its way. Looking across at her father, Mary wondered what he was thinking. He'd hardly said a word since they'd set off.

'Father, I know you're not happy about me going out to work, but me wages will help out at home and you'll need less food with me living-in.'

When George turned to his daughter, she couldn't read his

expression.

'It just doesn't feel right sendin' a lass out to work.' He shook his head. 'The Watsons have lived through some hard times before, but we've never had to send our women out to work.'

'Lots of girls work these days, at least until they get married, and there's not much chance of me meeting a man up at Killhope, is there?'

'What about Hughie Jackson?'

'There's no way I'd marry him - he's horrible! He used to bully me at school.'

'Jim Simpson?'

'Jim's nice enough but he's getting on a bit. He must be thirty-five, at least, and he hardly has any teeth left. No, I wouldn't want to marry him. Maybe I'll find my future husband at Westgate,' she said.

'Don't you be gettin' too close to any young lads down there.'

Mary laughed.

'I mean it. There are a few decent lads about, but there's plenty that'll take advantage of a bonny, young lass like you. Just be careful.'

Her father had called her bonny. Was she bonny? Nobody had ever said so before. She had always felt plain next to her younger sister Annie, who had golden hair, green eyes and a lovely smile. Mary's dark auburn hair framed a pale face with hazel eyes that seemed to change colour depending on her mood. Everyone said she looked like her mother. She missed her mother.

Hannah Watson had died from an infection shortly after John's birth. When the doctor had visited her, he'd said that there was nothing left to do but pray, but prayers hadn't worked. Her mother had died, anyway. Mary felt a lump form in her throat.

'What's the matter, lass? It's not too late to go back if you've changed your mind.'

'I was thinking about Mother.'

After a brief pause, her father swallowed and said, 'Aye, it was hard when she went, but it was God's will so we have to accept it.'

George and Mary continued their journey down the dale passing through several villages on the way to Westgate. Both were lost in their thoughts until, up ahead, they saw a horse and cart standing sideways in the road, completely blocking their path. George pulled up the pony.

Mary thought it looked like the horse she had seen at Killhope, the one belonging to the man from Westgate who had told her about the job at Springbank Farm. She saw a young man sauntering towards them. His walk was self-assured, and he whistled a jolly tune. As he got closer, she could see him more clearly and was disappointed to see that it wasn't the man from Killhope, after all. She had hoped to tell him that she'd got the job and that she was on her way there now.

Mary noticed that this man was tall, and he had dark brown hair, with large brown eyes to match. He wore a striped shirt that was open at the neck, moleskin trousers and leather clogs. As he approached, he said, 'I'm sorry, we won't be long. I've just blocked the road off while we move the sheep into this field.'

George nodded and sat patiently as he watched the sheep move like a wave up the road towards them. A woman and a collie dog herded them towards the gate.

The man turned towards Mary, surveying her with those

beautiful eyes, and then he smiled. He had a lovely smile, and Mary's cheeks flushed. He winked at her and went back to guide the sheep through the gate. Mary wondered who he was and watched him until the sheep were safely secured in the field.

Shortly after they set off again, George turned the pony onto a farm track. A newly-painted sign read 'Springbank Farm'. They were almost there. Mary could see a chimney over the brow of the hill, and, as they climbed higher, the house gradually came into view. The farmhouse was a large, double-fronted Georgian building, two storeys high, and Mary considered it very grand indeed.

As they pulled up in the yard, George said, 'Well, this is it, lass. This is goin' to be your home for a bit. You know where we are though if things don't work out.'

Mary nodded and stepped down from the trap, saying, 'I'll be alright. I'll come back up to see you as soon as I can.' As she reached for her small bundle, he leaned forward, and, in a rare show of affection, he kissed her cheek.

Turning to face the house, Mary saw a middle-aged couple, who she presumed to be Mr and Mr Peart, coming to meet them. Nervously brushing the dust off her skirt, she waited for them with her father by her side. They all took it in turns to shake hands while Mr Peart made the introductions.

'Would you like a cup of tea before you head home, Mr Watson?' asked Mrs Peart.

'No, thank you. I'd better be goin'. It'll be dark by the time I get back. Thank you for takin' her on.' Looking at his daughter, he said, 'She's a good lass, our Mary.'

Mary blushed at the compliment.

George tipped his cap to them all and climbed onto the trap.

He turned the pony around in the yard and set off for home.

Watching her father leave, Mary suddenly felt very alone. The Pearts seemed to be nice enough people, but they were strangers. She hoped she had made the right decision to come and work for them.

'Come on in lass and I'll show you where your room is,' said Mrs Peart, leading the way towards the back door of the house. Mary followed her through the kitchen and into a hallway where a broad staircase led to a dark passage. There were lots of doors on each side and, opening one of them, Mrs Peart said, 'This will be your room while you're with us. It's nothing fancy but you should find everything you need.'

Mary followed her into the room and glanced around. As Mrs Peart turned to leave, she said, 'I know it feels strange, it always does at first, but you'll soon settle in. Most girls get homesick the first time they're away from home, but you're one of the lucky ones. You'll get a full day off every month and you're close enough to go home and visit your family.'

'Thank you,' replied Mary.

'Get yourself freshened up, and then come down and have a bite to eat,' said Mrs Peart as she left. Once she had gone, Mary couldn't stop a tear from falling. She knew Mrs Peart had meant the words kindly, but it was going to be so hard seeing so little of her family when she was used to being with them all the time. She was starting to realise how much she would miss them.

Mary placed her bundle on the bed, wiped her eyes and had a better look around her. The small room was at the back of the house. It had a small window that looked out onto the farmyard and the steep hillside beyond. In the alcove between the door and fireplace was a single bed with a beautiful patchwork quilt in delicate shades of pink, blue and white. A chamber pot peeped out from under the bed. The small fire had been lit before her arrival; it wasn't big enough to warm the room properly, but it did take the chill out of the air. A bucket of coal stood by the hearth, and she added a few pieces to the fire; the smell of the smoke was very different from the peat fire at Fell Top that she was used to. An oak dressing table and chair stood in the other alcove, between the fireplace and the window. The floorboards were polished oak, and there were two clippy mats, one by the bed and the other by the hearth.

Mary thought the room was comfortable rather than cosy and, deciding that it might be nice to sit in front of the fire after work, she carried the chair across the room. There was a brass candlestick, half a candle and some matches on the mantelpiece, and she made a mental note of where they were in case it was dark when she returned to her room.

Opposite the fireplace was a washstand with a jug and bowl and a small towel hanging on the side. The jug was filled with water. Mary dipped her finger in; the water was cold, as she had expected. She poured a small amount into the bowl and quickly washed her face and hands.

As she tidied her hair, Mary thought she would like to have a room to herself. At Fell Top, she had shared the upstairs room with Annie and William, and her parents had slept downstairs in a pull-down bed.

She could only guess how many rooms there were in this house, but she reckoned it must be ten or more. Working here would certainly keep her busy, she thought. She was looking forward to seeing the place and to meeting the family.

Mary went downstairs and entered the kitchen, and she

noticed that the table was set for four people.

Mrs Peart had been waiting for her and said, 'Sit down, lass. The others will be here soon. We're having mutton stew tonight, it's Mr Peart's favourite.'

'Can I do anything to help?' asked Mary.

'No, not tonight. You just sit down there. They shouldn't be long now.'

Mary sat stiffly on the chair that Mrs Peart had indicated and watched the older woman as she flitted around the kitchen. She was small, almost petite, and she had a tiny waist for a woman of her age, which Mary guessed to be somewhere about fifty years old. Her grey hair was pulled up into a bun at the back of her head and was covered with dark blue netting. Mary thought she looked both elegant and delicate at the same time, if that was possible.

Mrs Peart chatted away as she worked, 'Mr Peart's family have owned Springbank Farm for as long as anyone can remember. Farming's in his blood. He's worked here from being a boy and took over the running of it when his father died. His brother's a farmer as well. John's farm is up at St John's Chapel. I came here when we got married, almost thirty years ago. Good Lord! How times flies!'

'You've lived here a long time, then.'

'Yes, I suppose I have. I knew when I came here as a bride that I'd be here for the rest of my days. Mr Peart wouldn't live anywhere else.'

'It's a lovely house, and I'm looking forward to seeing outside as well.'

'Mr Peart would be delighted to show you around the farm. It's his pride and joy. Speak of the devil!' she said to Mary with a smile.

Mr Peart entered the kitchen and sat down at the head of the table. He was a tall, lean man in his fifties. He had white hair and a white beard that was neatly trimmed. Mary noticed that he stood very upright, like an army officer, and took long strides as he walked. Mr Peart looked strong and handsome for his age, and she imagined that he and his wife must have been a beautiful couple in their youth.

He smiled at Mary and said, 'Hello, Mary. Is this your first place?'

'Yes, it's the first time I've worked in service, but I've been helping out at home since I was ten. I can cook, clean, look after children and animals. I've milked goats and cows….'

Mr Peart laughed. 'You'll not be doing any milking here lass, there's plenty of work in the house for you. Mrs Peart will keep you on your toes,' he said as he winked at Mary.

'Now then, Mr Peart, don't you tease the lass,' Mrs Peart scolded.

Their friendly banter was interrupted by a young woman marching into the kitchen. 'And who is this?' she demanded, pointing at Mary.

Mrs Peart answered in a placating tone, 'You know it's our new girl, Mary Watson. We told you yesterday that she was coming. Mary, this is our daughter, Connie.'

Connie flounced into her chair, knocking the table hard enough for some water to spill from the jug.

'Connie, settle yourself,' her father warned.

A little dog had followed Connie into the room. 'Come here, Charlie,' Connie called, patting her knees, and Charlie jumped up and curled up on her lap.

'We will not have a dog at the table,' exclaimed Mr Peart. 'What are you thinking, girl!'

'We have a servant at the table. I'd rather eat with Charlie than a servant.'

'Get up to your room now, young lady, and take that animal with you. If you can't be civil to our guest, you don't deserve any tea!' said her father.

Connie glared at him before storming out of the room.

'I'm so sorry,' said Mrs Peart. 'Connie shouldn't have said that. Don't let her upset you.'

After eating the meal, Mary helped Mrs Peart clear the table and wash the dishes, and when they were finished, she went back to her room. She walked over to the window and looked out onto the dark hillside, and as she closed the curtains, she thought about her father driving home at night. She hoped that he'd get back safely.

Mary sat by the fire and contemplated everything that had happened that day. She thought about the new people she had met - the people she would be living with for the foreseeable future. She had liked Mr and Mrs Peart straight away, they were a lovely couple, but she had never met anyone like Connie before. Connie was a pretty young woman. She was petite like her mother; her hair was blonde, and her large eyes were a bright shade of blue. Mary had been shocked by her behaviour, though, especially at how Connie had spoken to her parents. Nobody she knew would ever have spoken to their parents like that because if they did, they would have got a clout round the lug for it. Mary's instincts told her to be wary of the girl.

Mary changed into her nightdress, extinguished the candle and climbed into bed. As she lay there in the unfamiliar surroundings, her thoughts returned to the handsome, dark-haired farmer she had met on the road to the farm. She imagined his arms around her and his lips kissing her. She closed her eyes and saw his smiling face and couldn't help smiling back into the darkness.

* * *

In a room along the corridor, Connie sat on her bed and stewed. She wasn't happy that her parents had hired another maid, especially after all the bother she'd gone to to get rid of the last one. She hated Mary already, and she knew that it wouldn't be long before her parents would like Mary better than her. It was always the same. They spent more time with their servants than they did with her - and they were nicer to them too.

Charlie was curled up next to her, and she stroked the little dog's head. At least he liked being with her, she thought.

Sally, the last maid, had worked at Springbank Farm for so long that her parents had started to treat her like family. It just wasn't right. She was their only child, and she wanted them to talk to her and be nice to her for a change.

It had taken such a long time to get rid of Sally, and Connie remembered the day that Sally had finally packed her things and left. The final straw had been when Connie had put a dead newt in the teapot. When Sally had poured the tea, the amphibian landed in a teacup with a splash, and Sally had screamed very loudly. She'd been convinced that newts were living in the water pipe between the spring and the house, and she'd said that she couldn't stay there if the farm's water supply was unsanitary.

Her mother had been upset to see Sally go, and she'd actually cried as the maid walked down the track for the last time.

Connie smiled to herself as she remembered that day; it had felt as though she had won.

And now, there was another maid in the house who would no doubt wheedle her way into her parents' affections.

Chapter 2

The following day Mary woke early and went downstairs to prepare breakfast. She was surprised to find that Mrs Peart was already in the kitchen and had lit the range. The older lady showed Mary where everything was kept, in both the kitchen and the pantry, and they made breakfast together.

Mr Peart and Connie appeared at the same time and sat at the table. Connie was quiet during the meal. Mary noticed that she didn't have much appetite for someone who hadn't eaten tea the night before and suspected that she had helped herself to food from the well-stocked pantry during the night.

'Connie, what are you up to today?' asked Mr Peart.

'I'm taking Star out. Phyllis wants to race us with her new mare. We've arranged to meet on Cameron's Flats this morning - it's the best place for a good gallop around here.'

Tapping his fingers on the table, her father said, 'So Sir Thomas has been buying a new horse, has he? He knows his horses, does Sir Thomas. Is it a hunter or a Thoroughbred?'

'I don't know. I haven't seen her yet. Although if Phyllis thinks she stands a chance against Star, I expect she'll be a

Thoroughbred, or maybe an Arabian. I think Henry will come too because he wants to bet on the outcome! That man will bet on anything,' she said with a laugh. 'Anyway, I intend to win - and to take his money!'

'Well, Star can certainly shift so I reckon you stand a good chance. Don't forget to rub him down when you get back this time,' said her father.

After breakfast, Mrs Peart showed Mary around the farmhouse and told her what she would be expected to do. Downstairs, there were five rooms: the drawing-room, dining room, parlour, kitchen and pantry. Upstairs, there were six bedrooms. Mrs Peart had prepared a list of chores for her, which they went through together:

Light the Kitchen Range
Make Breakfast, Dinner and Tea
Make Tea mid-morning and mid-afternoon
Clear the Tables and wash the Dishes
Clean and tidy the House
Make the Beds
Bake Bread, Pies, Scones, Cakes and Biscuits
Make Butter, Cheese, Jam and Chutney
Do the Laundry and Mending
Light and tend the Fires in the Winter Months
Collect the Eggs and take them to Mr Graham's Shop
Collect the Groceries from the Shop

Mrs Peart explained that the list didn't include tending the garden or emptying the ash closet because the men saw to the outside jobs, but she would need to empty the chamber pots when she made the beds every morning.

Even though she would be working indoors, Mr Peart insisted on showing her the farm in the afternoon. As they wandered around with his collie, Tip, at their heels, he explained enthusiastically how the farm worked.

They walked up to the pasture where a herd of shorthorn cows were grazing. Mr Peart said, 'The cows spend most of the day up here but they come down to the byre twice a day for milking. Isaac and Jacob do most of that but I help out now and again.'

He pointed to the meadows down from the farm. 'The grass in these fields will be left to grow for hay soon. We need a good crop to feed the animals in the winter when there's no grass for them.'

Mr Peart was very proud of the place and, although Mary knew quite a bit about hill farming already, she listened intently.

They came across two men repairing a dry stone wall. Mary could see that they were twins. Mr Peart said, 'Mary Watson, I'd like to introduce you to Isaac Rowell and Jacob Rowell. They're identical twins, but we can tell them apart because Jacob has a little mole on his cheek - just here.' He pointed at the left cheek of one of the men. 'That's the only difference between them.'

'Welcome to Springbank,' the twins said in unison, and they all laughed. 'Mr Peart,' said Jacob, 'there's somethin' I need to tell you. One of the ewes is missing from the front field. Her lambs have gone as well. I've checked all the way round and none of the dykes are down and all of the gates are shut. I can't see how they've got out.'

'The ewe might have jumped the wall to get back to the fell, but the lambs are too small. Have a look in the other fields, they can't have gone far.'

'You don't think they could have been taken, do you?'

18

'More likely the bairns from the village have been up again and left a gate open.'

'Aye, you're right,' replied Jacob. 'They'll be around here somewhere. I'll have another look.'

Mr Peart pointed towards the field in front of the farmhouse. 'Those are our Scottish Blackface ewes. Quite a few of them had twins this year - that's good for business when that happens. They're hardy things, but they need to be to live up on these hills in winter.'

His gaze shifted to the high fell above them, the top of which was hidden by cloud.

'The sheep are usually on the fell, but we've brought them down for lambing. When they've finished, they'll go back up. We bring them down again for clipping in the summer and then the lambs are brought down for the autumn sales at St John's Chapel.'

As they walked back towards the farm buildings, Mr Peart pointed out a massive bull grazing in the field beside the barn. 'This here is our Billy. He's a good 'un,' he said. 'He's won every show he's been entered in, and he's thrown some excellent calves, if I do say so myself.'

They stopped and looked over the wall into the pigsties where the sows were feeding their piglets. Mary smiled at the rows of wiggling tails.

A dark-brown hen scratched the earth in the farmyard, showing her chicks how to forage for food.

'Mr Graham buys most of our eggs from us to sell in his shop down in the village,' said Mr Peart. 'There are always a few hens that start clocking at this time of year though. We let them sit on a clutch of eggs and hatch them out because we need the chicks – the pullets are kept for layers and the cockerels for the table. See that cockerel over there - that's Gladstone.'

'Why do you call him Gladstone?'

'He's just like the prime minister - he likes to hear himself!' Mr Peart chuckled, and right on cue, the cockerel stretched to his full height and crowed loudly. They both laughed.

'See what I mean?' said Mr Peart. 'But nobody takes any notice of him.'

Mr Peart showed Mary where the hen houses were so that she'd know where to collect the eggs from.

He then guided her around the outbuildings. They looked in the dairy, the byres, the kennels, the hay barns and the stables. As they entered the stables, a large grey horse whinnied. 'This is my hunter, Thunder,' said Mr Peart as he stopped to stroke the gelding's neck. In the next stall, a pair of black Dales ponies stood nibbling at their hay, and in the last stable stood a beautiful chestnut Thoroughbred with a white star on his forehead. The horse was still saddled, its hair dripped with sweat and steam rose from its back.

'That bloody girl!' shouted Mr Peart. 'Excuse the language, Mary, but she makes me so angry. She has one of the best horses in the dale and she's too lazy to look after him properly. She doesn't deserve to have him!'

He loosened Star's girth and led him over to the trough to drink. Once the horse had had its fill, Mr Peart began to walk it slowly around the yard. 'Go and fetch Isaac, would you?'

Mary returned to where the brothers had been working. She said, 'Isaac, Mr Peart would like you to come down to the yard.'

'What's wrong?'

'Connie left Star saddled in the stable. He's covered in sweat.'

'Not again!' Isaac rushed back with her to the yard. 'It's dangerous for horses to overheat. They've got to be cooled off slowly after they've been ridden hard.'

When they reached the yard, Mr Peart asked Isaac to wipe Star down with a wet cloth and relinquished the horse into his care, and then he went in search of his daughter. A few minutes later, Mary heard raised voices coming from inside the house.

Chapter 3

Springbank Farm, Westgate
April 1872

The next morning, Mrs Peart asked Mary to take the eggs down to Mr Graham's shop and collect a few things for her. Mary took the basket of eggs and a shopping list and set off down the track to Westgate, treading carefully for fear of falling and breaking the eggs. The farm track was uneven, with deep ruts from cartwheels. As she passed the sheep's field, she wondered if the missing ewe had been found yet.

The lower side of the Westgate road was lined with trees, and below them was the River Wear. Mary could hear the sound of running water in the distance, but the cries of young birds demanding food were much louder; their parents darted into the trees with offerings and came straight back out again in search of more.

The first houses Mary passed in the village were small, two-storey, terraced cottages. Their tiny front yards were surrounded by low walls topped with 'bonny bits' that the miners brought out of the mines – white quartz and spar crystals in purple and green sparkled against the brown sandstone walls. Mary found it hard to believe that waste from the mines could be so beautiful.

The public house 'The Half Moon' was closed this early in the day, but the door opened, and a policeman stepped out as she passed by.

'Good morning, lass,' he said. 'I haven't seen you in Westgate before. You must be new here.'

'I'm Mary Watson. I've just started working for Mr Peart at Springbank Farm.'

'Robert Emerson, I'm the constable around these parts.' To Mary's surprise, he held out his hand for her to shake. 'Very pleased to meet you, young lady. You've got a good place up there with the Pearts, you couldn't ask for better. Lovely folks, they are, aye, lovely folks. Anyway, I'd best be on my way. Work to do, aye, there's always plenty work to do.' And then he walked away humming to himself.

On the opposite side of the street, a notice about books in the window of a large building caught Mary's eye. The sign above the door read, 'Westgate Subscription Library AD1788'. She opened the door slowly and peered inside. A small man with an almost entirely bald head sat at a large desk. He removed the reading glass he wore and looked up at her.

'Good morning, and who do we have here?' he asked.

Mary entered the room and gazed in awe at all of the books neatly stacked on shelves. She said, 'I'm Mary Watson and I love reading. I've never seen so many books before!'

'Are you a member of the library, Miss Watson?'

'No sir, I saw the sign outside and I wanted to have a look. I hope you don't mind. I've just started work at Mr Peart's farm, so I'll be living at Westgate for a while. Do you think I could borrow a book, please?'

'If you work for Mr Peart, I can let you borrow a book. Mr

Peart is a member of the library. Let me show you where everything is,' he said as he got up and began to point at the shelves. 'These ones are religious texts – some of them are very old and are a little fragile now; these are science and medical books; over here we have geology and mining; and these ones are novels, plays and poetry. Now, what is it that you're interested in?'

'I don't know really, maybe the novels. I like stories.'

'I'll leave you to have a look. Let me know when you've chosen one.' The librarian returned to his desk and lifted the monocle to his eye.

Mary hadn't read many books; her family only had a bible and a prayer book in the house, but she had read all of the books at school several times and knew them word for word. Mary spent a long time browsing the shelves and eventually selected 'Wuthering Heights' by Emily Bronte. She took it to the desk.

'Ah, Emily Bronte. Did you know that she lived in York-shire?'

'No. That's not far from here, is it?'

'No, it's not. Haworth is in the Pennines as well, but at the southern end.'

The man opened a ledger and carefully entered the book's details, her name, Mr Peart's address, and the date.

'There you go. When you've finished reading it, bring it back and you can borrow another one if you wish.'

'Thank you,' replied Mary.

'I'm Mr Proud. It was nice to meet you, Miss Watson.'

'Thank you, Mr Proud, I'll bring it back soon.'

She left the library and headed to Mr Graham's shop, just a little further up the street. A bell rang as she opened the door, and Mr Graham appeared immediately.

'Hello there, judging by those eggs, I guess you must be the new girl up at Peart's?'

'That's right, Mr Graham, I'm Mary Watson. Mrs Peart sent me down with the eggs and she wants me to pick up a few things while I'm here.' She glanced around the shop and turned a full circle. Every surface of the room was covered in stock. Mary spotted fresh fruit and vegetables, meat and fish, sacks of potatoes and flour, dried rice and barley, dried fruit, butter, sweets, sewing and knitting supplies, cutlery, crockery, vases, small tools and daily newspapers. Yet, the whole room was smaller than the kitchen at Springbank Farm.

'You have everything in here!' she said in amazement.

'We try to stock everything that folks want, so they don't have to go down to Stanhope for them,' Mr Graham said proudly, looking around his shop. 'So, what would Mrs Peart like today?'

Mary passed him the note, and he put the items into a brown paper bag which he handed to her. Then he reached for a book and turned to a page with Mr Peart's name at the top. He carefully entered the date and added all of the items from the list to the Pearts' account. The number of eggs Mr Graham had received was entered into another column in the ledger.

When he had finished, Mary said, 'Thank you, Mr Graham. I'll be back tomorrow with some more.'

'See you tomorrow, lass.'

She left the shop and walked back through the village. As she passed the houses with the bonny yards, she saw a man approaching on horseback, and he pulled up the black stallion by her side.

'Are you the new maid from the Pearts' place?' he asked.

'Yes, I am. I'm Mary Watson.'

'Henry Forster, I'm a friend of Connie's. Please could you give her this note?' He reached into his jacket pocket and brought out a folded piece of paper with a wax seal on one side.

'Yes, of course, I will, Mr Forster.'

He handed the note to her, turned his horse around and urged it to trot.

Mary thought it was odd that he knew who she was and that she would be taking eggs to the shop that morning. As she tucked the letter into her basket with the shopping, she wondered why Henry Forster would be writing to Connie. Perhaps it was something to do with the bet they had on the horse race; maybe it contained Connie's winnings.

Mary enjoyed the walk into Westgate. She liked meeting new people and seeing new places, and it felt so good to be outdoors in the fresh air. The Pearts treated her very well, but it was nice to get away and be alone for a while. It gave her time to think and to dream.

That afternoon, Mary was baking in the kitchen at Springbank Farm. The wonderful smell drifted out into the yard and tempted Isaac and Jacob to come in to see what she was making. Their eyes lit up at the selection of food on offer, and they each chose a pie and went back outside to work.

Mary took a tray of scones from the oven and placed them on the kitchen table. She used an old porcelain teacup to cut more scones from the dough and then arranged them on the baking tray, which she put back into the oven. All the surfaces in the kitchen were covered in cakes, pies and scones.

Mrs Peart fluttered into the kitchen and admired Mary's

work. She lifted a scone to her mouth with both hands and took a small bite. It was still warm, and it tasted delicious. 'These are wonderful, Mary. Is there anything you can't do? I thank the Lord for sending you to us.'

'I love baking,' Mary replied. She spotted Connie standing in the doorway. 'Would you like one, Connie?'

'No! And you should call me Miss Constance or Miss Peart. Only my family call me Connie!' she exclaimed.

Unfazed by the outburst, Mary said, 'Oh, I have a letter for you from Henry Forster.' She went to the basket to retrieve the letter.

Connie snatched it from Mary's hand and marched out of the kitchen.

As Mrs Peart watched her daughter leave, she sighed and shook her head, 'Why can't she be more like you, lass? She's always had everything she ever wanted and still, she's not happy. I don't know what we'll do with her.'

'She's very lucky to have you and Mr Peart for parents,' said Mary sincerely.

'Thank you, Mary, that's very kind of you to say.'

As Mary transferred the bread dough into two bread tins to prove, she thought about how lucky Connie was to have a mother at all. Mary missed her mother so much now that she was gone, but at least she'd appreciated her when she was alive. Why did her mother have to die? Mary put the tins on top of the range and turned towards the window so Mrs Peart couldn't see the tears forming in her eyes.

A couple of days later, Mrs Peart came into the kitchen where Mary was preparing vegetables for dinner. She was dashing about, opening drawers and cupboards, obviously searching for something.

'Is everything alright, Mrs Peart?' asked Mary.

'Have you seen my opal brooch? I'm sure I left it on my dressing table yesterday but it's not there now. I've looked everywhere in my room and I've not been anywhere else but in here since I took it off.'

'It was on the dressing table this morning when I made the bed.'

'It's not there now. I don't know where it could be. I hope I haven't lost it. Mr Peart gave it to me as a Christmas present. Would you help me look for it, please?'

'Of course,' said Mary, following her mistress upstairs.

They scoured Mrs Peart's bedroom. They looked every-where, lifting furniture and mats to check underneath them and opening every drawer and cupboard. They couldn't find the brooch anywhere.

Connie appeared at the door, 'What's going on?'

'I've lost my opal brooch, and Mary's helping me look for it.'

'Oh, is she?' Connie looked smug. She went over to her mother and whispered something in her ear. Mrs Peart looked at Mary and then at her daughter. Without a word, she went to Mary's room and opened the door. Mary followed her inside, wondering what Connie had said to make her go there. Mrs Peart began to search around and, when she lifted Mary's pillow, she uncovered the missing brooch. Curtly, Mrs Peart said, 'Mary, you'd better wait in the parlour.'

'But…but, Mrs Peart, I didn't take it. I wouldn't.'

'Just do as I say and wait in the parlour.'

Connie was standing at the top of the staircase and, as Mary passed, she whispered, 'Do you know what happened to the

Featherstone girl who stole from Sir Thomas?'

'Connie, wipe that smile off your face and come in here,' said Mrs Peart, as she gestured for her daughter to enter the bedroom.

Mary went to the parlour and sat in a chair by the window. Connie's words went around and around in her head, taunting her. Yes, she knew what had happened to Kate Featherstone. Kate was her cousin. But everybody in Weardale knew. The Forster family had accused Kate of stealing from Burnside Hall. They said she'd taken some bed linen, a vase, a pocket watch and some coin but she had denied taking anything. The jury had decided that she was guilty, and the judge had sentenced her to twelve months in Durham prison. While Kate was serving her time, she'd written to her mother and Reverend Richards, the local vicar, professing her innocence and declaring that she had been wrongly imprisoned, but it had done no good. Kate had served her full sentence. She hadn't come back to Weardale after her release, though.

Mary knew that she would be in serious trouble if the Pearts thought she had taken the brooch. The wait was torturous. Her heart beat twice for every tick of the clock. Almost an hour passed before she heard Mr and Mrs Peart's voices outside the door. They sounded vexed, which made Mary fear the worst. Did they think she had stolen the brooch and hidden it under her pillow? Surely, they knew her better than that by now. She would never do such a thing. She wouldn't risk losing her job or going to prison, or bringing disgrace upon her family.

The couple came into the parlour and sat down. Mr Peart began, 'Mary, I'm sorry for what has happened today. Connie can be troublesome at times and it appears she's taken a dislike to you. She admitted that she took the brooch and put it in your room. Her intention was for you to get the blame and to be sent away from here. Now, we want you to stay, lass, you're a good worker, but it's up to you. Please understand that Connie will be punished for this, but we can't promise that she won't do anything like this again. Unfortunately, it's in her nature.' He shook his head. 'I don't know where she gets it from.'

Mary signed audibly. Thank God they had discovered the truth, and she still had her job. She didn't hesitate before saying, 'Thank you. I like working here and I'd like to stay.'

'Good, that's all settled then,' said Mr Peart with a smile, and he left the room.

'I don't know why she does it,' said Mrs Peart. 'You know, it's not the first time she's got girls into trouble with her silly pranks. Now run along, I'm sure you have plenty to do.'

As Mary left the room, she thought, silly prank indeed. Connie's silly prank could have ended in Mary losing her job and her family struggling to put food on their table, or she could have been arrested and sent to prison, like her cousin. Her silly prank could have had dire consequences.

Chapter 4

Springbank Farm, Westgate
May 1872

As Mary was cleaning the upstairs windows, she saw a man walking towards the farm, with a red and white shorthorn cow on a halter, and she was sure it was the handsome farmer she had met on the way to Springbank Farm.

She rushed to finish polishing the windows on the front of the house so she could start on the windows at the back, from where she hoped to catch a glimpse of him in the yard. She wasn't disappointed. There he was, chatting with Mr Peart. After a few minutes, the men took the cow through a gate into the bull's field, but they soon disappeared behind the barn and were hidden from view. Mary continued with her work, hoping to see him again.

She remembered Mr Peart telling her that his shorthorn bull, Billy, had won prizes at all the local agricultural shows. His reputation was so great that farmers from up and down the dale brought their cows to him. The man must have brought his cow to be bulled, she thought.

The silence was pierced by a loud shout, almost a scream. What had happened? Mary waited and waited. It seemed such a long time before she saw two figures emerge from behind the barn, one leaning heavily on the other. Her heart missed a beat when she realised it was her man who was injured. He was limping badly, and blood oozed through the left leg of his trousers. Mr Peart guided him towards the back door of the house, and Mary went downstairs.

Mrs Peart had been in the kitchen when she heard the commotion outside. Realising somebody was hurt, she rushed to open the door. She saw Mr Peart struggling to help the young man across the yard, and she held open the door to let them pass.

'Come on in, Joe,' she said. 'Now, what have you done? Sit him down over here by the window so we can see.'

Mr Peart released the man, and he fell heavily onto a sturdy oak chair. Mrs Peart went over to him and said, 'Now get them trousers off and let's see the damage.'

He took off his trousers, wincing with pain as he undressed.

'Just as well you're wearing short drawers today, lad,' said Mr Peart, trying to lighten the air. 'If you'd been wearing long ones, you'd have had to take them off as well!'

Joe attempted a smile, but it looked more like a grimace. Blood flowed from a gash just above his knee; it ran down his shin and soaked his woollen sock. Mrs Peart turned pale at the sight of the wound. She rushed towards the hall and shouted, 'Mary! Come and see to this, will you?' Mrs Peart remained in the hallway.

Mary passed her mistress and went into the kitchen, where she saw the man sitting in the chair by the window, in nothing but his underwear. She blushed, but on seeing the wound, her thoughts went straight to the matter in hand. She felt the man watching her as she approached, but her eyes purposefully avoided his. Studying the wound, she said calmly, 'He needs the doctor. I'll do what I can to stop the bleeding, but it's deep, it's going to need stitching.'

Mr Peart was standing with his back to the fire, looking very concerned, but he leapt into action at Mary's words, 'I'll send Isaac down to fetch him.'

Mr Peart went outside to find Isaac, leaving Mary alone with the man. There was water in the kettle, and it was still warm. She used this and a small towel to clean the wound, which was bleeding heavily, so she folded another cloth to use as a pad and tied it tightly around his lower thigh.

She couldn't help but notice how strong and toned his leg muscles were, and she wondered if the rest of his body was in such good shape; she imagined it would be.

When Mary had finished dressing the wound, she said, 'There now, all better,' as she had done many times to her siblings when she had patched up their cuts and scrapes. She looked up at the man, and he was watching her with glassy eyes. At that moment, he looked so incredibly vulnerable that she wanted to hold him and comfort him, as she would have done her brother and sister, but she didn't know him well enough.

The colour started to return to his face and, with it, the smile that Mary had seen so many times in her dreams. Their eyes locked again, and he said, 'Thanks, lass.'

Mr Peart returned and realised his blunder at leaving a young woman alone with a partially-dressed man in his house. He cleared his throat, 'Sorry, I should have introduced you two. Joe Milburn, this is Mary Watson, our new help. Doctor Rutherford shouldn't be long now. Mary, please would you make a pot of tea?'

'Of course, Mr Peart,' she replied and went to get some water to fill the kettle. When she returned to the kitchen, Mrs Peart was covering Joe's legs with a blanket, in an attempt at decency. Mary listened to them talk about cattle sales and agricultural shows while she made and served the tea.

Shortly afterwards, they heard the doctor ride into the yard. Mr Peart went out to meet him and, while he tethered his horse, told him briefly what had happened. When the doctor came into the kitchen, he walked directly to Joe, 'I hear you've had an accident, Joe. What happened?'

'I brought a cow over to be bulled. Billy's temperament is usually pretty good - for a bull, anyway - but he must have got out of the wrong side of the bed this morning,' Joe said with a laugh. 'He was eyeing up the cow one minute and then the next he was running straight at me. I had me back against the wall and had nowhere to go. I moved to the side, but not fast enough, he caught me leg with his horn.'

'I see. Well, let's take a look, shall we?'

As the doctor went to remove the blanket from Joe's lap, Mrs Peart said to Mary, 'Perhaps we should leave them to it. The doctor can manage from here.'

Doctor Rutherford looked up and addressed Mary. 'Did you bandage his leg?'

She nodded.

'You've made a good job of it. It may be better if you stay in case I need some help if that's alright with you and Mrs Peart?'

'Of course, I don't mind helping,' she replied.

Mrs Peart nodded her approval and left, with Mr Peart by her side. They preferred not to stay and watch the doctor do his work.

The doctor examined the wound carefully. 'It looks clean, but I'll need some water for cleaning up when I'm done,' he said as he threaded a curved needle.

He noticed that Joe was starting to turn pale. 'Look away, Joe. Think about something else, something nice.' Joe's eyes found Mary, and he watched her moving around the kitchen while the doctor pulled the edges of the wound together and started stitching.

A few minutes later, he had finished.

'All done! That wasn't too bad, was it?'

'No, not too bad,' said Joe. 'Thank you.'

Mr Peart reappeared and said, 'If you're done, Doctor, we'd better get him home. Isaac has the cart ready.'

'Yes, we're finished here.' As the doctor packed his bag, he said, 'Joe, you need to rest. I'll call to take out the stitches on Friday. I don't want you doing much before then.'

'But what about the cow?' asked Joe, standing up and reaching for his trousers.

'Don't worry about the cow,' said Mr Peart. 'We'll keep her here for a few days until Billy's done his job, and Jacob will walk her back over to your place.'

When Joe had managed to pull on his trousers, the doctor and Mr Peart helped him to the door. He turned back to Mary and said, 'Thank you.'

The doctor tipped his hat at Mary, and the men went out to the waiting cart.

Chapter 5

St Andrew's Church, Westgate
July 1872

Since Mary's arrival at Westgate, she discovered there were three places of worship in the village. St Andrew's was the newly-built parish church, but, as Methodism was very popular in Weardale, there were also two Methodist Chapels — one for Primitive Methodists and one for Wesleyan Methodists. All of them were full for the Sunday services, with people walking miles from the surrounding hillsides to congregate in these buildings.

Mary didn't usually attend church with the Pearts. They were Church of England, and Mary was Wesleyan Methodist, so every Sunday, the Pearts went to church, and Mary went to chapel.

However, on this particular day, Mary found herself walking with the Peart family to St Andrew's because they were going to a christening. Ned and Anne Routledge, who farmed at Wellfield on the opposite side of the valley, were having their first baby baptised. Mrs Peart had told her that everyone in the farming community would be there and, as a member of their household, they expected her to go with them.

The church was almost empty when they went in and took their seats in the second row, but it soon started to fill up. Mrs Peart pointed out Sir Thomas Forster and Lady Margaret as they walked up the aisle and entered their family pew, followed by their son Henry and daughter Phyllis. Mary thought they were all very smartly dressed. She saw Lady Margaret look around the church and smile pleasantly at several members of the congregation.

Mary heard people move into the pew behind her and sit down. She recognised Joe's voice immediately. He was chatting with a man and a woman whom he knew well. She couldn't hear what they were saying, but she could tell by the tone of the conversation that these people were comfortable with each other — his family, perhaps?

Mary's thoughts were not on the service or the baptism but the man who sat very close to her. She could feel his presence. Even if she hadn't heard his voice, she thought that she would have sensed he was there.

At the end of the service, Mary felt a hand on her shoulder, and she turned to see Joe's smile.

'Hello, Mary,' he said. 'Just wanted to say thanks again for what you did for me leg. It's healed well, thanks to you.' And then he smiled his lovely smile.

Mary was embarrassed by the public compliment and the effect that his smile and his touch had on her. She said, 'You're welcome. I'm pleased to hear it's better.'

After leaving the church, Mr and Mrs Peart shook the vicar's hand and congratulated him on an excellent service, and then they stopped to speak with Sir Thomas and Lady Margaret. They appeared to be deep in conversation, so Mary stepped away from them to give them some privacy. Nearby, Connie talked with Henry and Phyllis. She was very animated and moved her arms around as she spoke. Mary guessed that they must be discussing horses as it seemed horses were the only thing that could get Connie excited.

Mary watched Joe and a young man approach, and she recognised him as the man who had told her about the job at Springbank Farm.

Joe smiled and said to his companion, 'I'd like you to meet Mary, the new lass at Pearts'. Mary, this is me big brother, Tom.'

'Hello, Tom,' said Mary, with a smile.

'It's nice to see you again, Mary.'

'You two know each other?' Joe said in surprise.

'Yes, we met at Killhope a while back,' replied Tom. 'Mary needed work and I told her that the Pearts wanted someone.'

'So, I've got you to thank for bringing her to Westgate,' said Joe, with a huge smile.

'I'm very grateful that you told me about the job at Springbank Farm. I appreciate it.'

'Pleased I could help.'

Mary was relieved that Tom hadn't explained the full circumstances of their meeting to his brother. She still felt embarrassed thinking about how the master washerman had shown her up that day.

Joe pointed to a plump, middle-aged woman talking to Anne Routledge and cooing over her baby. 'That's our mother over there – Jane Milburn – and we live at High House Farm, the next farm up from Springbank. Our land borders onto Mr Peart's. Since our old fella died, me father that is, there's just been the three of us. Mother and me see to the farm.'

'And what do you do, Tom?' asked Mary.

'I'm a lead miner, up at Grove Rake.'

Mary's father had talked about Grove Rake mine, near Rookhope, and she knew it belonged to WB Lead, the same company that owned Killhope mine. Her father had told her that Grove Rake was one of the deepest mines in Weardale and that an exceptionally rich vein of lead ore had been discovered there.

'My father's a miner as well. He works at Killhope,' said Mary. 'We live at Fell Top.'

'I know the place,' said Tom. 'That's a remote spot. I don't suppose you get to see your folks very often?'

'No, I've been at Springbank since April and I've not been home yet,' she admitted. 'I'm hoping they'll come down for Chapel Show. Mrs Peart said I can have the full day off. I've missed them so much, especially the little ones.'

'You should be visiting now when the days are nice and long. Later in the year, you'll struggle to walk up and back in daylight,' said Tom.

'Yes, you're right.'

Mary would have liked to talk to the brothers longer, but the Pearts were standing at the churchyard gate gesturing for her to go with them.

As she turned to leave, Tom said, 'Wait, will you be going to the dance at Chapel?'

'Yes, I'll be there. Are you going?'

'Yes. See you there.'

'It was nice to see you again, Tom.'

'You too.'

Turning to Joe, she said, 'Bye, Joe.'

'See you, Mary.'

The brothers watched her as she ran to the gate.

Chapter 6

Springbank Farm, Westgate
August 1872

The day of the 'Chapel Dance' finally arrived, and Mary was so excited that she had difficulty concentrating on getting breakfast ready for the family. She had never been to a dance before. She vaguely recalled her mother saying that she'd met her father there, but Mary had never imagined that she would get the chance to go. However, Mr and Mrs Peart had decided that they would go this year, and they'd invited Connie and Mary to go along with them. Mary had been thrilled.

She didn't have many clothes, but there was an old dress that had been her mother's that she thought might be suitable to wear, and she had spent several evenings altering it. When Mrs Peart realised what she had been doing, she'd very kindly given Mary some lace for the dress.

While her thoughts were on the evening ahead, Mrs Peart came into the kitchen. Mary noticed that she was a bit distracted.

'Is everything alright, Mrs Peart?'

'Not really. Mr Peart's not feeling well. He wants to stay in bed for a bit longer. I'll take some breakfast up for him on a tray, but I'll come back down for mine.'

Mary set a tray, and Mrs Peart carried it upstairs. When she returned, she said, 'What a time to be out of fettle! We'll miss the dance tonight, and maybe even the show tomorrow. He's never missed a show.'

'I hope he feels better soon.'

'Yes, me too,' said Mrs Peart, tucking into her breakfast. 'He's hardly ever been ill. It's so unlike him.'

It dawned on Mary that if Mr and Mrs Peart were not going to the dance, she and Connie might not be allowed to go as they would not have a chaperone. Voicing her concern, she asked, 'Can I still go to the dance tonight, if you and Mr Peart don't go?'

'Yes, I suppose so. Connie will be there, so you can look out for each other. I know you don't get on very well with Connie, but please walk home together. It's not safe for girls to walk home alone. Alright?'

'Alright, we will, Mrs Peart.'

Mary would have agreed to anything to go to the dance. She didn't welcome the thought of walking home with Connie, but she would do it. She wanted to go to the dance that much.

When the young women arrived at the town hall in St John's Chapel, Connie walked across to Henry and Phyllis Forster, leaving Mary alone. Mary looked around at all of the people dressed in their best clothes. They were standing at the edges of the room, chatting in small groups, waiting for the band to start playing. The musicians tuned their instruments, took their places and began to play. The caller shouted for people to find a partner and move to the dance floor.

Mary saw Isaac walking towards her. 'Would you like to

41

dance, lass?'

She looked around, 'Yes please, if your wife doesn't mind?'

'She's not here tonight. The baby's due soon and she wanted to put her feet up. Her ankles are swelling up with this one.'

'Sorry to hear that. I should tell you, I've never been to a dance before. I don't know any of the steps.'

'That makes two of us!' Isaac laughed as he led her onto the dance floor, where several other couples stood waiting for the dance to start. The caller shouted out the steps, and, following the instructions, they danced clumsily around the room, laughing at their mistakes.

As the dance came to an end, Mary saw Tom Milburn walking towards them. 'Mind if I have the next dance?' he asked Isaac, but he looked at Mary.

'Go ahead. Me toes have had enough — they're black and blue!'

'You were just as bad as me,' she laughed as Isaac left.

As the music started, Tom took Mary's hand and placed his other arm around her back, holding her closer than Isaac had. She looked up at him in surprise, and he smiled. Tom was light on his feet, and he led her around the dance floor. She soon relaxed and started to enjoy herself. The music ended too quickly. To Mary's surprise, Tom didn't let go of her hand. He stood by her side until the next dance began, and he held her just as close as he had the first time. When this dance ended, the caller announced that the band would take a short break.

'Thank you, Mary,' said Tom. 'Would you like a drink?'

Mary raised her eyebrows. Coming from a Methodist family, she had never had an alcoholic drink before. Seeing the surprise on her face, Tom said, 'There's ginger beer or lemonade.'

'Could I have some ginger beer, please?'

He placed his hand on the small of her back and guided her towards the bar, where he ordered two glasses of ginger beer. They moved to one side.

'Where did you learn to dance?' asked Mary.

'From me mother,' laughed Tom. 'She used to love dancing. When we were little, she used to hum the tunes and teach us the steps. She said it would help us get a lass when we grew up.' His cheeks reddened slightly.

'I wish someone had taught me. I would love to know how to dance properly. Listening to the fella shouting out the steps and then doing what he says, I think I'm always one or two steps behind everyone else!'

'I didn't notice,' said Tom, smiling kindly at her. The band was preparing to start up again. 'Would you like another dance?' he asked.

Joe came into the hall and walked straight over to Mary and Tom. Mary felt his presence behind her before he spoke.

'Mary, I'm pleased to see you're here. Will you dance with me?' He held out his hand, which she took, and he led her onto the dance floor. She glanced back at Tom, but he turned away.

Joe was a good dancer too. His eyes hardly left her face as they performed the steps. Where he touched her, she felt heat. She was aware of nothing but the man in front of her. All thoughts of the steps were gone. She moved in time with the music like she was in a trance. When the music stopped, he said, 'I'd love to stay for another one, but I promised the lads I'd pop over to the King's Head. They're waiting for me. I hope you enjoy the rest of the night.'

As he turned to leave, Mary's face fell, and the hall suddenly felt empty. She looked around to see if there was anyone she recognised. There were a few friends from her school days, but Hughie Jackson, her childhood tormentor, was with them, and he was staring straight at her. Worried that he might ask her to dance, she looked away quickly and spotted Isaac walking across the hall. She felt safe with Isaac.

'Would you like to dance again, Isaac? I think I'm getting better, so your toes should be safe.' He laughed as he led her to the dance floor.

Mary thoroughly enjoyed the evening and had forgotten all about Connie until it was time to leave. She looked around the room but couldn't see her. Come to think of it, she hadn't seen Connie for some time. Mary checked the other rooms and walked around the outside of the building but couldn't find her anywhere. She decided to wait a bit longer just in case Connie turned up, but after half an hour, she concluded that she must have left without her. Mary was disappointed because Connie had known that they'd only been allowed to go to the dance on the condition that they walked back together, but Connie had ignored her parents' wishes.

Mary had to get back to Springbank Farm, though. It was only a couple of miles away, but it was already late. She wondered where Tom and Joe were; they lived near Springbank and would be going home that way. A final glance around the hall confirmed that she knew of nobody who would be going in her direction. She went outside.

The town hall stood in the marketplace at St John Chapel, and there were three public houses across the road. Men stood in the doorways, drinking, shouting, laughing; they appeared to be having a good time. Could she pass those men, enter the pub, and look for Joe and Tom? Women didn't go into pubs, not decent women anyway, and if neither Joe nor Tom were there, she could run into trouble. She resigned herself to walking back alone.

Mary shivered as she left the town hall and pulled her cloak tighter around her body. Walking in the dark was fine when you knew the way, but this area of the dale was still new to her. To avoid the revellers in the marketplace, Mary decided to take the back road home. Cottages lined the Burn Foot road most of the way down to the riverbank. Even though it was dark, she chose to leap across the stepping stones rather than use the footbridge to cross the river. She walked briskly up the road, turning right towards Daddry Shield.

The moon was less than half full and did little to light Mary's way; clouds drifted across the sky, obscuring what little light there was as they passed in front of the moon, leaving Mary in total darkness at times. She jumped as a cow, disturbed by her footsteps, bellowed from behind a wall.

As she approached the village of Daddry Shield, she noticed a few of the cottages had lights in their windows. She heard a horse coming up behind her at a trot but couldn't see it. She moved to the side of the road until her back was pressed against the field wall and waited until it passed, thinking how dangerous it was to walk on these narrow roads at night.

As Mary reached the first cottage, she heard footsteps. Somebody was walking behind her. Mrs Peart's words came back to her, 'It's not safe for girls to walk home alone.' What was she doing? She should have tried harder to find someone to accompany her back to Westgate. Or perhaps she should have asked Isaac if she could stay with him and his family for the night, but Mrs Peart would have been worried if she didn't return to the farm. Mary lengthened her stride, but the footsteps kept pace. Someone was following her. The hairs on the back of her neck stood on end. Mary looked over her shoulder to see who was behind her but couldn't see anyone in the darkness. Should she run? Should she knock at one of the houses for help?

She picked up her skirts and ran.

A voice came out of the darkness, 'Mary, is that you?'

Mary stopped, and her body slumped. Thank God. It was Joe. As he came into view, he said, 'Sorry if I frightened you. Mind if I walk you home?'

Mary smiled with relief. 'I'm so pleased it's you, Joe. I didn't know who it was following me. Aye, I'd like to walk back with you.' She was glad that she was no longer alone.

Joe was clearly in a good mood, and he smiled broadly at her. He had been drinking; she could smell beer on his breath, and he was very talkative. As they strolled towards Westgate, he talked at length about his family and their farm.

'Me and Tom were born at High House, but the farm is just leased – it's rented from the Bishop,' he explained. 'We work it but it's not ours, and it'll never be ours. Now Springbank Farm, that's a different matter. Mr Peart got that from his father and it's been in their family for years. I want a farm that's mine, really mine, so I can pass it on to me son and he can pass it on to his.'

Mary was captivated by his enthusiasm. She hoped beyond hope that she might be part of his dream. Why else would he be walking her home and sharing his thoughts with her? She loved listening to him talk. Mary was so happy; she didn't want the night to end.

'I'll have it one day an' all. A farm and a family. A farm to pass on to your family. What more could a man want?'

As they neared the farmhouse, Joe stopped and took her hand. 'You look beautiful tonight, Mary,' he said, leaning towards her. He kissed her softly on her lips.

'Meet me tomorrow,' he whispered breathlessly into her ear. 'At the river, where the whirlpool is, after the show.' He held her at arm's length and waited for her reply.

Mary hoped he would kiss her again, and when he made no move to, she reached up and kissed him. This time the kiss was much more heated. He stepped back from her. 'You'd better get back. See you tomorrow.'

He turned away, and Mary walked up to the farmhouse.

Mrs Peart was furious when Mary returned home alone. 'Why isn't Connie with you?' she demanded.

'Isn't she back yet?' asked Mary.

Mrs Peart glared at her.

'I looked everywhere for her at the town hall, but she wasn't there. I waited half an hour and she didn't turn up. I didn't have any choice — I couldn't stay there any longer — I had to come back myself. I thought she'd be here when I got back because she must have left before me.'

'Well, she isn't back, and the Lord only knows where she is. If she's not home soon, I'll have to wake Mr Peart and he'll have to go out and find her.'

'I'm sorry, Mrs Peart, but there was nothing else I could do. Please sit down and I'll make you a cup of cocoa. I'm sure she'll be back soon,' Mary said, trying to calm her mistress.

About a quarter of an hour later, while they were sitting at the kitchen table finishing their drinks, they heard hoof beats approaching the house. Mary opened the back door and heard voices outside – Connie and a man. The moonlight silhouetted them, but Mary could see that Henry sat astride the horse, and Connie was sitting in front of him, very close. Henry had his arms around her, and his hands caressed her as he kissed her neck from behind. He pulled back and lifted her gently to the ground. 'You will think about it, won't you?' he asked. Connie replied in a whisper, 'Yes, of course, I will.'

Connie ran across the yard towards Mary and snarled, 'Don't you dare tell my parents about this.' She entered the house, unaware that her mother was waiting in the kitchen and had heard what she'd said.

'Where on earth have you been, girl, at this hour? And who brought you home?'

'I'm old enough to do what I want, Mother. I'm eighteen, for God's sake. I'm old enough to decide who I want to go out with.'

'Don't you blaspheme in this house, young lady! Who were you out with until this time of night?' demanded Mrs Peart.

'If you must know, it was Henry Forster. He's been courting me for quite a while now.'

Mrs Peart moved her hand to her mouth in shock. Mary sat quietly, wondering whether she should leave the room. This was a private matter. She remembered the letter Henry had given to her for Connie and realised that it must have been a love letter.

'I didn't say anything because we didn't want Father or Sir Thomas interfering,' said Connie. 'If we want to see each other, it's our business and not theirs. Anyway, Henry has asked me to marry him!' she declared with a satisfied grin.

'He can't ask you to marry him. He hasn't asked your father for permission. Lord, what is this world coming to? Get yourself to bed and we'll talk about this tomorrow — with your father.'

Lying in bed that night, Mary thought of Joe's kiss and replayed the scene over and over in her mind. She could still feel his kiss on her lips. To her mind, Joe was perfect. He was a farmer, he was handsome, he liked her, and he had kissed her. Mary hugged herself and drifted off to sleep.

* * *

As they left the breakfast table the following day, Mr Peart said, 'Connie, come into the parlour. Your mother says there's something we need to talk about.'

Connie got up from the table and led the way. Once they reached the parlour, they went inside and closed the door.

Mr Peart stood with his back to the unlit fireplace, his hands behind his back. 'Sit down, Connie. I know what happened last night. You left Mary to walk home by herself. That was a stupid thing to do and, what's more, you broke your promise to us, your parents. You were allowed to go to the dance so long as you walked back together. I dread to think what could have happened to Mary. All the lads have a skinful when the dances are on and she's a bonny lass.'

'Well, she got back safely,' said Connie, huffily. 'So, what's all the fuss about?'

'And you came home with Henry Forster, I hear, on his horse. That's not seemly for a young woman unless she's courting — and courting seriously.'

'We are, Father. I've been seeing Henry for months now.'

'Well, that explains why you've been riding out more often. Why didn't you say something? You didn't think I'd object to a union with Henry Forster, did you? The Forsters are a good family and they're good friends of ours. I don't know the boy very well because he spent a lot of time up at that fancy school in Newcastle, but you could do a lot worse than Henry Forster. He'll have a title one day. My daughter — Lady Constance — just imagine that!'

'He still spends a lot of time up at Newcastle. I told him I'd consider his proposal and let him know when I've made a decision.'

'Sensible. Yes, sensible, but don't think about it for too long. Opportunities like this don't come along every day,' her father warned. 'If he comes to ask for your hand, he'll be given it. You have my word.'

Chapter 7

St John's Chapel
August 1872

Mary could remember the first agricultural show at St John's Chapel. Her parents had taken her there when she was just a bairn. She'd been shocked to see crowds of people milling around the show field, more people than she had ever seen before, and by the incredible noise. People talked and laughed, merchants touted their wares, horses' hooves pounded the ground, cows and sheep called to each other, cockerels crowed, and dogs barked. The Weardale Brass Band had played lively tunes, and the sound had been almost deafening near the bandstand. A dancing bear with doleful eyes had been the main attraction, but, as a child, Mary had been mesmerised by it all.

She was pleased that the Pearts had given her the day off to go to the show, and she was very excited about meeting her family there. It seemed such a long time since she'd seen them. She rushed her breakfast and set off far too early and spent over an hour wandering around and watching everyone bring their exhibits to the show. There were classes for animals, poultry, eggs, flowers, vegetables, foods, crafts and minerals.

Some folks took the competition very seriously; others took part just for fun. To pass the time, Mary pretended that she was a judge and chose a winner from each category.

Suddenly, she felt arms hugging her around the waist. It was her brother, William. 'I've missed you, our Mary!' he said as he clung to her.

'I've missed you too.' She hugged him back. 'We have a full day together today. Won't that be fun?'

He nodded and grinned.

Annie's greeting was more subdued, and Mary thought she looked tired. Perhaps looking after Fell Top and the family was taking its toll on her. Annie had carried their baby brother all the way down from Killhope, so they found a seat where she could rest, and they could catch up on the news.

'So, how are you all?' asked Mary.

'Alright, I suppose. Father hasn't given me any money to buy food for ages. I'm struggling to make what we have last,' said Annie. 'And he wants our William to start as a washerboy at Killhope mine. He's only nine, Mary. He's still just a bairn.'

'I'm not a bairn!' said William. 'What do washerboys do, anyway?'

'Well, they work at the mine,' explained Mary. 'They have a very important job. They sort the lead ore from the other minerals. At the end of the day they have a lovely pile of silver-coloured ore that shines in the sun.' She tried to paint a rosy picture of it so he wouldn't worry about having to work there. She didn't mention how physically demanding it was, that his hands would be in cold water for most of the day, or that the pay was pitiful. Mary thought about all the families struggling to feed themselves and had no choice but to send their children out to work. She hoped that William would not become one of those children.

Mary handed her pay to Annie, not keeping a single penny for herself. She had everything she needed at the farm. She'd do everything she could to prevent her brother from having to wash ore.

'Thank you, Mary. That'll keep us going for a bit longer,' said Annie, looking relieved.

As Annie moved John from one arm to the other to get more comfortable, Mary saw a bruise on her left arm and said, 'That looks nasty.'

'The goat kicked me when I was milking her,' Annie replied quickly. 'By the way, our John was bad with fever last week. I hardly slept for three nights. He's fine now though.'

Well, that explained why Annie looked tired, Mary thought. She reached out and took the baby from her sister and felt his brow. He seemed to be well and was sleeping peacefully.

William jumped up and down, tugging at Mary's skirt.

'Why don't you stand over there, by that fence, and watch the horses in the ring?' suggested Mary. The sisters watched him scamper across to the ringside.

'What about you, Mary?' asked Annie. 'What's your new place like?'

Mary told her sister about the farm and her life there and about the people she'd met. She mentioned the Rowell twins who worked there, the Milburns who were neighbours and the library, and finished off by telling Annie about Joe's accident.

Mary realised that her father hadn't turned up. 'Did Father not come down with you?' she asked her sister.

Annie looked away and said, 'He didn't want to come. He wasn't feeling over grand.'

Mary was surprised to hear that because Annie hadn't

mentioned he was ill, but before she had time to ask any more questions, Annie stood up and walked over to join William, who watched the horse classes. Mary followed her sister, wondering why she was being evasive. She hoped their father wasn't seriously ill.

'Annie, what's wrong with him?'

'He's alright really. It's nothing to worry about.'

Mary still wasn't convinced, but she turned to watch the horses with her family. The judge was Sir Thomas Forster, and he stood in the centre of the show ring, turning around on the spot to study the horses' paces as they walked, trotted and cantered about the ring. A young man pulled up his grey mare and rejoined the line. Connie rode out on Star. She looked very elegant in her silk riding habit and top hat, and as she began to canter, the lace flowed behind her and transformed her into an ethereal being. The crowd were spellbound. She was a natural rider, and her round appeared effortless. Mary had to admit that Connie was a beautiful woman – at least on the outside.

As Connie finished her final lap, she returned to the line and smiled at Henry Forster, the last rider in the competition. He looked handsome as he started the round, and his black stallion's coat shone iridescently in the sunlight. When Henry changed from a trot to a canter, the horse reared, but he kept his seat, completed the round and rejoined the line.

It was no surprise to the crowd when Sir Thomas selected Connie as the winner and tied a ribbon onto Star's bridle. Even those who knew nothing about bloodstock had been transfixed watching Connie ride her horse.

As the horses left the ring, several farmers entered with their best cows and walked them around the ring. Annie noticed that Mary was watching one man in particular.

'Do you know him — the dark-haired lad?'

'Yes, that's Joe Milburn, the one I told you about, you know, the accident with the bull.'

'He's handsome, isn't he? Has he got a lass?'

Mary stammered, 'I...I don't think so, not that I know of anyway.'

The farmers stood in line with their cows, and the judge walked up and down, occasionally stopping to examine a cow more closely. As Joe stood there, he noticed the two young women watching him from the ringside and he waved across at them. Mary waved back and blushed furiously when her sister said, 'I think he will have soon. He has his eye on you.'

'Don't be silly,' said Mary, wondering what Annie would say if she knew that she had arranged to meet him after the show. Handing the baby back to Annie, Mary said, 'Come on, you lot, it's time we went to explore — there's loads to see here.'

Mary heard someone say, 'Morning, Mary.' She looked around to see where the words had come from and if they were meant for her. There were lots of Marys in the dale. 'Over here,' said Tom, indicating for her to join him and his mother. 'Enjoying the show?'

'Yes, thank you.'

'Mary, this is me mother, Jane Milburn,' said Tom. 'Mother, this is Mary Watson from Killhope. She works for Mrs Peart.'

'It's nice to meet you, Mary,' said the older woman, with a pleasant smile.

'You too, Mrs Milburn.'

Tom looked up into the cloudless sky. 'It's a beautiful day for the show. It's been a good day all round, hasn't it, Mother? She's just won the best jam, and the best butter in the show!'

he said proudly. 'You'll have to come over for tea sometime. You'll not get a better tea anywhere!'

'Now, now, Tom, there's no need to go on about it. Anyway, you needn't talk. Your shepherd's crook won the sticks category. He likes working with wood, does our Tom.'

'Well done on winning the prizes, Mrs Milburn,' said Mary.

'Call me Jane, lass. We don't stand on ceremony in our house. So, this must be your brother and sister — I can see the resemblance. And the baby?'

'He's my brother, John. Mother died just after she'd had him.'

'I'm sorry to hear that, lass.' Turning to the others, she said, 'By, you lot have had a long walk, haven't you? It must be nice to see your Mary again.'

'Aye, it is,' said Annie. 'We've missed her. All of us have.'

'Ah, here's our Joe comin' now.' When he reached them, she asked, 'How did the heifer do, lad?'

'Second prize, not bad for her first time out. I'm sure she'll win her class next year.' As if to justify his pride, he added, 'I bred her myself. You know, it's a shame I couldn't have brought that ewe today. She would have beaten all the others in the show. She was one of the best I've ever had.'

'We lost two ewes and their lambs,' Tom explained to Mary. 'No sign of them anywhere. They just disappeared. They must have been stolen otherwise we'd have found them — dead or alive.'

'That's odd,' said Mary. 'Mr Peart lost a ewe when I started work there in April. Her lambs went missing as well.'

'Did he now? That's interesting,' replied Joe. Turning to his brother, he said, 'I think we should go and have a word with Mr Peart. Come on.'

'Well, it was nice to meet your family Mary,' said Tom,

nodding at them one by one. 'And to see you again.'

Joe dragged Tom off to begin their search for Mr Peart, and the Watsons continued their stroll around the field.

Mary was aware that Annie had to get William and John back to Fell Top before dark. In the middle of the afternoon, she said to her sister, 'You need to be going soon.'

Annie's face fell. 'I know. I wish we could stay longer. It's been so good to get away for a while, and I've not seen William this happy in a long time.'

'It's been so good to see you all. I missed you,' said Mary sincerely. The sisters hugged.

'Do we have to go now?' asked William. 'Why can't we stay a bit longer?'

'You need to make sure Annie and John get home safely,' said Mary, 'before it gets dark. Can you do that?'

William stood tall and said, 'Yes, of course I can.'

Mary bent down and kissed his brow.

'I'll come up and visit when I can get away. And I hope Father gets better soon.'

As her family walked away, Mary noticed William look questioningly at Annie.

To Mary, the show day had seemed to last forever. After her family left the show field, Mary went straight to Westgate woods. When she reached the waterfall, Joe was already there, leaning against an ash tree. He turned as he heard her approach and moved towards her. He took off his jacket and laid it on the ground, motioning for her to sit on the riverbank. They sat side by side, almost touching. They were so close that she could feel his body heat. Not a word had been spoken.

Joe broke the silence. 'I didn't think you'd come.'

Mary had been thinking about what she'd say to Joe all day, but now that they were alone, she was lost for words.

'I...I wanted to see you again,' she stuttered. 'Last night was...erm...it was nice walking back with you.'

Sensing her discomfort, he took her hands in his and stroked them with his thumbs. 'We're friends now, lass. There's no need to be afraid. I like you and you must like me or you wouldn't be here.'

Before she had a chance to reply, he kissed her. His lips moved gently over hers and his arms wrapped around her. She impulsively moved closer so that their bodies were touching, and this spurred him on. He deepened the kiss, their tongues touching and probing, the heat rising. Mary was surprised by how her body reacted to his and how she felt. This must be love, she thought. She wanted this moment to last forever.

He broke off the kiss, and they looked at each other, seeing their desire reflected in the other's eyes. Mary knew he wanted her, and she had to get away before it was too late.

'Sorry, I must go,' she whispered. They were still holding each other close.

'Will you come back tomorrow, at the same time?' he begged.

'I don't know, Joe,' she said, looking deeply into his eyes. But she did know. She would return the next day and do whatever Joe asked because she wanted him, too.

Mary met Joe almost every night at the same spot by the river for the next two weeks, spending stolen moments in each other's arms. As Mary usually spent her evenings reading in her room, she didn't think anyone had noticed her slipping away from the house. But she was wrong.

* * *

Connie had seen Mary leave one night and, wondering what she was up to, decided to watch the following night to see if she went out again. Connie knew Mary must be meeting someone; why else would she be going out so secretively – and at night? She wanted to find out who it was, and she made sure she was ready to follow Mary when she left the next night.

Mary heard the Pearts retire to the parlour for the evening, as they usually did, and she quietly went downstairs and sneaked out of the kitchen door. She went around the house and walked quickly down the track, utterly unaware that Connie was lurking in the shadows, trailing her at a distance.

Mary went to the small clearing by the waterfall, where Joe was already waiting for her.

From a distance, Connie saw Mary rush into Joe's arms and share a kiss before sitting with him under the warmth of his cloak. They were talking and laughing, but Connie couldn't hear what they said. She watched the couple for a while before walking back to the farm. It was clear to her that Mary and Joe had been meeting in secret and that a romance was blossoming. Connie smirked to herself.

* * *

One evening, when Mary and Joe sat close to each other on the riverbank, their legs dangling over the edge, Joe said, 'I'm going away for a few days. There's a big wrestling tournament on at Gateshead this weekend. Me and Ned Routledge are going. Our Tom should have been coming with us as well, but he's got something on at work. I think we'll probably go on Saturday and get back on Monday. It'll only be a few days.'

Mary's face fell. 'Do you have to go?' she asked.

'Well, I don't have to, but I want to. I like wrestling and it's a chance to win a bit of money. Ned's really good. He usually wins something.'

'Could I come? I have a day off on Sunday.'

'Do you know where Gateshead is? It's miles away. We can't get there and back in a day.'

'Oh, it's just that I hoped we could maybe do something on Sunday. Maybe have a walk somewhere.'

'Sorry, lass. It's all arranged. I'll miss you though.'

Mary was disappointed. She didn't get many days off work, and she had hoped she could spend this one with Joe.

'I'll be here when you get back, waiting for you,' she said. 'I'll miss you too.'

She wondered how many days a few days would be, but it didn't matter. She knew she would wait much longer than that for Joe if she had to.

Chapter 8

Springbank Farm, Westgate
September 1872

The next day was cold and blustery. Mary was polishing the dressing table in Mrs Peart's bedroom when she saw the constable walking up the track towards the farm. He was holding his helmet to stop it from blowing off in the strong gusts of wind. She stopped what she was doing and went downstairs. It wasn't long before she heard a knock at the back door, and she went to open it.

'Hello, Mr Emerson. Come on in and sit down, I'll fetch Mr Peart.'

'Good morning lass, it's nice and warm in here, isn't it?' he said, taking off his coat. 'Aye, it's Mr Peart I'm wanting to see.'

Mary found Mr Peart in the stable, where he was discussing horse feed with Isaac, and they walked back to the house together.

'Good morning, Robert,' said Mr Peart. 'Would you like a drink? Come on through to the parlour.'

'Aye, that would be nice, that would. Thank you.'

As Mary went back upstairs to the room she had been cleaning, she wondered what the constable's visit could be about; she had never known him to call at the farm before. A movement outside caught her eye, and she went to the window to see what it was. Connie and Henry were riding up the track, side by side. Mary quickly finished the room and went downstairs in case they needed her.

The young couple came into the kitchen, and they looked very windswept. Connie's hat had moved to one side, and her hair had come loose in places. Henry's hair was almost standing on end. Mary struggled not to laugh at the sight of them, but what she said was, 'You two look frozen. Sit down and I'll put the kettle on.'

They sat at the kitchen table and whispered to each other so that Mary couldn't hear what they said.

The parlour door opened down the hallway, and men's voices could be heard. The constable came into the kitchen with Mr Peart, and on seeing Henry, he said, 'Good day, Mr Forster. I hope you're in fine fettle?'

'How do you do, Constable? I'm very well indeed.'

'I've just been talking to Mr Peart about the sheep that have gone missing. Have you had any stolen from Burnside Hall?'

'Not that I'm aware of. I'm sure Papa or his farm manager would have told you if they had. Are you any closer to finding out who's taking them?'

'No, sir, I'm afraid not. But I'm surprised anyone around here would dare steal sheep after what happened to that man when I was a lad. You'll remember that, Mr Peart. It was a fella called Thompson. He was hanged for stealing a sheep down at Stanhope — Crawleyside, if I remember right. It was that really bad winter, you know, when the road was blocked for over two weeks. His family were starvin'. He only took one old ewe to feed the poor beggars, but he paid a high price for it. He was hanged at Durham. And you know what? His family ended up in the workhouse anyway,' said the policeman, shaking his head. 'He should have taken them there in the first place — then they'd still have a father. It comes to something when a man would rather steal and risk his life than admit he needs help.'

'Yes, I suppose it does,' said Henry. Standing, he picked up his hat and said, 'Now that you're home safely Connie, I should take my leave. Good day, Mr Peart. Good day, Constable.'

'Aye, I'd better be off an' all. Thanks for that drink Mr Peart. That warmed me insides, it did. Thank you.'

The two of them left together; Henry mounted his horse and trotted down the road, followed by the policeman on foot.

'Father,' said Connie. 'I need to talk to you. Is now a good time?'

'Yes, of course, shall we go into the parlour?'

Mr Peart ushered her into the parlour, where he filled a glass with whisky and sat down. 'I think I know what this is about,' he started. 'You've been out with Henry again. Have you given him an answer?'

'No, not yet. But I have made my decision. I'm going to say no. I'm going to turn him down. Please don't be mad at me – I have my reasons. I don't want to marry someone who spends more time in Newcastle than he does in the dale. Do you know, he's been up at his lodgings on Nun Street almost every weekend since we started riding out together? In fact, all except Chapel Show weekend. He's rarely back before Tuesday and I can still smell drink on him sometimes. I think he drinks a lot – maybe too much? He told me he goes to Taylor's, the club on Clayton Street. He and his so-called friends drink and gamble there. I've heard there are women there as well— you know, those type of women. I don't want to marry someone who lives like that, Father. I couldn't stand it!' said Connie shaking her head vehemently.

'Now, now, hold your horses, girl. He's still young; he has oats to sow and all that. It's normal for a man. He'll settle down in time, you'll see. You shouldn't rush to give him your answer; have a long, hard think about it. Like I said, you could do a lot worse than Henry. And in the meantime, you'd better keep your legs together — and don't look at me like that young lady — a man like that will want a virgin on his wedding night.'

'Oh, Father!' Connie turned and stormed towards the door. She turned back to him, 'I know you were keen to see me married to Henry, but I can't marry him. I'm sorry if you're disappointed in me. I never seem to do anything right, but I can't marry him just to make you happy. I'm going to talk to him tomorrow. I'll tell him that I won't marry him and that I don't want to see him anymore.'

It was a beautiful morning for a ride. Connie didn't hurry to the crossroads. She knew Henry would be waiting for her, but she still hadn't worked out exactly what to say to him. Connie let Star walk at a gentle pace as she went over the words in her head. She knew that Henry wasn't the man for her, and she had to tell him, but she didn't want to hurt his feelings. When she had decided how she would tell him, she urged Star into a canter.

As she approached, Connie saw Henry look at his pocket watch and place it back into his waistcoat pocket, and then he glanced up and saw her. Henry smiled and walked his stallion forwards to meet her. Leaning across, he reached over to kiss her, but she turned her face away, and he caught her cheek instead of her lips.

'What's wrong, Connie?' he asked. 'You don't look very pleased to see me.'

'I have something to tell you.'

He looked at her quizzically, and then his face hardened as he realised what she was about to say.

'Go on,' he said.

Connie launched into her speech which she delivered with sincerity, 'I'm sorry, Henry, but I can't accept your offer of marriage. I like you very much and I don't want to upset you, but you're just not the man for me. I wish you well and I hope you'll find someone who will make you happy.'

Despite her planning, Connie had not expected this reaction. Henry wasn't upset; he was angry.

'How can you turn down a proposal from me?' he asked incredulously. 'You could have been a lady - all you had to do was say, yes. Who else would want to marry a farmer's daughter from the back of beyond?'

'I think I should go.'

As Connie turned to leave, he hissed, 'Yes, you should go. I don't ever want to see you again. And I'll see to it that none of my associates will even look in your direction, Miss Peart.'

Henry tore off at a gallop back towards Burnside Hall.

Connie cantered back in the direction of Springbank Farm with tears in her eyes. It was Henry who should have been upset, not her. She knew she had made the right decision — but his words had stung. "Who else would want to marry a farmer's daughter from the back of beyond?" he had said. Connie wondered if she had just turned down her one and only chance of a society wedding.

* * *

On the following Sunday, Mary set off to walk to Fell Top. As she strolled westwards along the dale road, she listened to the birdsong from the woodland and the distant sound of water flowing over the rocky riverbed. The wild roses on the roadside were laden with red hips; a thrush flew down and pecked at them, seemingly oblivious to Mary walking past. She had heard that a good crop of hips and berries was a sign of a bad winter to come. If the winter was bad, she thought, at least the wildlife would have plenty to eat.

She had only walked about half a mile when she heard a horse coming up behind her. She turned to look. It was a bay horse pulling a flat cart, and Tom Milburn held the reins. He pulled up beside her and tipped his cap. 'Hello Mary, nice morning. Where are you off to so early?'

'I'm going up to Fell Top, to see me family.'

'I'm going as far as Newhouse if you'd like a lift? You've a long way to go and it would save you an hour or so. Sorry, I can't take you all the way up, the agent's expecting me. I need to see him about work.'

Mary considered his offer. It was a long way to Fell Top, and Tom was going almost halfway. She wondered why she was hesitating. Was it because if they were seen together, people would assume they were courting? If she accepted his offer of a ride, though, she would get home quicker and would have more time to spend with her family. That settled it.

'Thank you, Tom. That's very kind of you.' She climbed up and sat next to him. The seat was small; she sat so close to him that their arms touched when the cart swayed on the uneven road.

'It was good to meet your family at the show, although I didn't see your father there,' said Tom.

'No, he didn't go. Annie said he wasn't well.'

'Sorry to hear that. I hope he's better now.'

'Thank you, I'm sure he will be.'

'So, what was it like, living right at the top end of the dale?'

'Quiet, I suppose. There's not many people up there. And it was a long walk to school!'

'Aye, it must have been. What do you think of Westgate?'

'I prefer living at Westgate, but I do miss Killhope.'

'Has your father always worked at Killhope mine?'

'Yes, for as long as I remember anyway. He likes mining, but he's had a few bad bargains lately so he's not earning much. They're struggling up there. That's why I came to work for the Pearts. My wages go back home to help out.'

'I like mining as well. It is a bit of a gamble though. Some bargains work out well and others don't. We've been lucky lately. We've got a decent bit of ground to work in and there's plenty of ore. Best we've ever had.' He paused briefly before asking, 'So when you're not working, what do you like to do?'

'I like reading. I've been borrowing books from the library. There are so many in there, I don't think I could read them all in a lifetime! I like learning about new things and I used to like teaching the younger children at school. I wanted to stay on and train to be a teacher, but I suppose the best I can hope for now is a houseful of bairns to teach.'

'Women teachers can only teach until they get married anyway. Once they have a husband, they have to give up work.'

'I'd not really thought about that. What do you like doing then, apart from mining?'

'I make all kinds of things out of wood. It's lovely to work with and, with the right piece and the right tools, you can work magic.'

'What was the last thing you made? Was it the crook that was at the show?'

'No, it was a sculpture of a dog. A collie. I modelled it on our Floss.'

'I love animals. All kinds of animals, except snakes. I've always been a bit frightened of snakes.'

'Most are harmless. Just watch for the ones with a diamond pattern on their backs — give them a wide berth. They're adders and they're the only poisonous ones around here.'

They talked like old friends. Time passed so quickly that Mary was surprised when Tom pulled up the horse next to a narrow bridge and said, 'I'm sorry but this is as far as I'm going. I've got to head up this way now, they're expecting me.'

'Oh, are we at Ireshopeburn already? I'd better get down. Thank you for the ride, it was very good of you.'

'My pleasure. I enjoyed the company.'

Tom jumped off the cart and went around to the other side to help Mary down. He took hold of her hand, and they smiled at each other, then he tipped his cap and climbed back up. She straightened her skirts and walked away. As he watched her, she looked back at him over her shoulder and, when she saw him watching, she waved at him. He waved back and then continued on his way to the agent's office at Newhouse.

Mary arrived at Fell Top late in the morning and on opening the door, she found Annie sitting by the fireplace feeding John. Annie turned instinctively towards the door at the sound of the latch. Mary's eyes widened when she saw a large bruise on her sister's face; the purple mark covered Annie's left eye and cheek.

'What happened?' asked Mary.

Annie turned her face back to the fire to hide the mark.

Mary went to her sister and knelt on the proddy mat in front of her chair. She put her arms around Annie's waist and waited for her to speak.

'It's father,' said Annie. 'He's been drinking ever since you left.'

'Drinking! I don't believe it,' said Mary, but the evidence was staring her in the face. 'Where is he?'

'Where he's always at when he's not at work - 'The Travellers' Rest'.'

'Tell me what's been going on, please — everything.'

William, startled by Annie's outburst, watched his sisters from the corner of the room where he was playing with two lead soldiers. He went back to his battle game.

Annie sat John down on the mat next to William and gave him a spoon to play with. Then she began to tell Mary what life had been like at Fell Top since her sister had left.

'After he dropped you off that day, he didn't come straight home. He should've been back that night, but he didn't show up until early the next day. He stumbled through the door and he pulled his bed down. I'd just got the lads up and we were all having our breakfasts. You'll never guess what he did? He got undressed, right in front of us all. Everything, there wasn't a stitch left on him.'

'My God!' said Mary. 'What did he do then?'

'He fell, face down, onto the mattress and within minutes he started snoring. I don't think he even knew we were there. He never said a word.'

'Why didn't he come home? Where had he been?' asked

Mary.

'I can guess. 'The Travellers' Rest', most likely. Since then, he's been drinking nearly every night. I don't know where he gets the money from.'

'No wonder you're struggling to pay the bills. And what happened to your face? Did he hit you?'

'Aye, he did. Yesterday,' Annie said, lifting her hand to her bruised face. 'But don't get me wrong, he's not often violent with it — just a couple of times. I keep the bairns out of his way, just in case. But last night John was unsettled — he's teething — so I brought him down to change his nappy and get him a drink. Father came in and started cursing under his breath because the baby was crying. He got undressed, muttering to himself, and then suddenly he turned around and punched me in the face. I was so shocked. I never expected him to do that. He shouted at me to shut the "bloody bairn" up, and do you know what he said after that? He said that I was useless, and that mother could have shut him up.'

Tears started to run down Annie's cheeks. 'He's right an' all, isn't he? She could have, because she was his mother. Oh, I wish she was still here.'

Annie started to sob, and Mary put her arm around her sister's shoulder and held her until she stopped.

It was hard to believe what Annie had said, but Mary had seen the evidence for herself. She could never have imagined her father turning to drink, not ever. He was a Methodist and always had been, and he'd taken a vow not to drink alcohol.

Then, she thought about how much she was missing Joe. He had only been away for a few days, and she hadn't known him long.

Her mother and father had loved each other and had been

together for nearly twenty years. She couldn't imagine the pain her father must have felt when his wife died or how much he must miss her.

But he hadn't started drinking when she'd died; he'd started drinking when Mary left home. Did that mean it was her fault for leaving? Her father knew how bad the money situation was and that she had needed to go out to work. As there was nothing suitable for her near home, she'd had to move away. There had been no choice.

Anyway, whatever the reason for his drinking, there was no excuse for hitting Annie. Mary remembered the bruise she had seen on her sister's arm when they had met at the show. She had suspected the goat story was a fib at the time, but she hadn't realised the awful truth that Annie had been hiding.

Annie, William and John — and perhaps her father — needed her here.

Mary didn't know what she should do. If she stayed at Fell Top to look after her family, she could protect the bairns from their father, and she might even be able to stop him drinking, but they wouldn't have enough money coming in to manage on. Her wages from Springbank Farm were small, but they were essential to put food on the table at Fell Top. There was no way the family could manage unless she went back to work. She had to go back to Westgate and continue to send her earnings home. Her family needed her money more than they needed her there. Annie could look after the children.

'I'd really like to stay and help you, Annie, but I must go back. You need my wages here. You do understand, don't you?'

'I know, we depend on your pay. We'll manage, don't worry. I'll keep the bairns away from him as much as I can. I wish

71

there was some way to stop him drinking, though. I asked the minister to have a word with him, but father's stopped going to chapel and, when the minister came here to visit, he wouldn't let him in the house.'

'He never used to miss chapel. Listen, if things get any worse — if he gets worse — go to Aunt Lizzie's. You remember, up at The Moss? It's only a few miles away, near Lanehead. I think you'll remember the way. We walked there a few times with Mother but, if you've forgotten, just ask anyone where Lizzie Featherstone lives and they'll point you in the right direction. I'm sure she'd take you in, but if not, come down to me at Westgate. Now, take care and I'll be back up to check on things as soon as I can.'

* * *

Mr Peart paced up and down in the kitchen. He'd spent the last two days in Newcastle-upon-Tyne on business, and there was nobody to greet him when he got home. Where was everybody?

Ordinarily, he wouldn't have been concerned about the house being empty, but what he had heard in Newcastle was preying on his mind. He needed to speak with his wife and daughter. Oh, poor Connie. How could he tell her what he had heard? She would be distraught.

Mrs Peart and Connie came into the house with smiles on their faces.

'Oh! You're home early, dear,' said Mrs Peart. 'We weren't expecting you back until tomorrow.'

'Yes, I had to come back sooner than I'd planned. Where have you been?'

'Just up to the pasture. Jacob delivered a new calf up there this morning. She's a bonny one and feeding well. You should have a walk up to see her.'

'That's good,' he said distractedly, but his mind was not on the newborn calf. 'Can I see you in the parlour for a moment?'

'Is something the matter?'

'Please, come into the parlour.'

Mr Peart ushered his wife into the parlour and closed the door behind them. 'You'd better sit down,' he said.

Mrs Peart sat down and asked, 'What's wrong?'

'It's about our Connie. When I was in Newcastle, I heard something quite shocking. I have it on good authority that a rumour is being spread about her….'

Mr Peart cleared his throat and continued, '…about her reputation. It is being said that her…hmm…virtue is no longer intact.'

'But that's not true! Our Connie wouldn't have.'

'I hope you're right — and I'm sure you are — but people hear rumours and they believe them.'

'But who would say such a thing?' asked Mrs Peart.

'I can only think of one person, and that's Henry Forster. His pride must have been hurt when she refused to marry him. That's got to be hard for any man, but for a young, handsome gentleman of his standing…well….'

'Oh, no,' said Mrs Peart, wringing her hands together.

'Connie told me that he spends a lot of time socialising in Newcastle. He could easily have said something to start a rumour in that quarter.' Mr Peart walked across to the window. 'Bloody hell!' he cursed, banging his fist down on the table. Turning back to his wife, he said, 'I hoped for a good match for our Connie. But who will want her if they believe what's being said about her. She'll be lucky to find someone who will take her on. Guilty or not, her reputation is ruined.'

'What should we do? Should we tell her?'

'Yes, I think she needs to know.'

'Will you speak with her? Or shall I?'

'I will,' he said as he poured himself a glass of whisky. 'Tell her to come through, will you?'

Mrs Peart found Connie sitting at her dressing table, brushing her hair. She went up to her and took the brush from her daughter's hand.

'Connie, your father would like a word. He's waiting for you in the parlour.'

'He looked upset when we came in. What's wrong?' asked Connie.

'He'll tell you all about it when you get downstairs.'

Mrs Peart put down the hairbrush and watched her daughter walk out of the door. She listened to her footsteps going down the stairs, heard her husband's voice in the distance and then the parlour door click shut. She wandered aimlessly around her daughter's room.

Downstairs, Mr Peart asked Connie to take a seat and offered her a glass of sherry.

'It must be bad news if you're offering me a drink at this time of day. Please, Father, just tell me what's going on.'

'As you know, I've just got back from Newcastle. While I was there, I heard something that was quite disturbing, something that affects you.'

Connie looked perplexed.

'It appears that there's a rumour going around about you. It is being said that you are not a virgin.'

'What! That's a lie. I've never been with a man. Why are

people saying that I have? Who told you?'

As the implications of the rumour began to sink in, tears formed in Connie's eyes.

'I really don't know, dear.' He put his hand on his daughter's shoulder. 'An old friend of mine took me to one side and told me that he thought I should know what was being said about you. That's all I know.'

'It was Henry, wasn't it?' she asked. 'He was angry with me when I turned down his proposal. He's done this to get revenge. Thank God I didn't agree to marry him!'

'Yes, with hindsight, I believe you made the right decision.'

* * *

Mary had waited every night in the woods since Joe left, in case he had decided not to go, or had returned early from his trip to Gateshead. It was four days before he came to meet her. She was so pleased to see him that she ran into his arms, and they clung to each other.

'I've missed you, lass.'

'I've missed you, too. I came every night in case you were back early.'

'I just got back a few hours ago.'

He lowered his lips to hers and kissed her passionately. He whispered in her ear, 'Do you know what I've been thinking about while I was away?'

'Wrestling?' she laughed.

'Wrong.'

He kissed her neck. 'That.'

He kissed her lips. 'That.'

He moved his hands to her breasts. 'These.'

And then he lowered his hand and placed it between her thighs. 'And this,' he said. His hand rubbed against her, and it felt so good that she leaned forward to get more contact.

'Oh, Mary.'

He removed his hand and replaced it with his body. He moved against her, so Mary could feel how much he wanted her. They stood together for a while, enjoying the feel of each other's bodies.

Mary whispered into his ear, 'I love you, Joe.'

Joe unfastened his cloak and laid it flat on the grass. He took Mary's hand and invited her to sit down. His eyes were dark, and his intentions were clear.

Mary sat down and pulled him down towards her. She gave herself to him fully.

Chapter 9

Springbank Farm, Westgate
Autumn 1872

October had been a wet month and it had passed slowly. The weather looked set in for November too. The Peart household was busy preparing for winter. Isaac and Jacob spent days on end chopping logs to fill the wood sheds. They brought in all the potatoes and root vegetables they had grown in the garden, and Mary packed them in barrels full of straw to keep them dry and fresh.

Mr Peart helped the men kill and butcher the young pigs. Mrs Peart salted the meat to preserve it before hanging it in the larder. Mary hung onions on strings and put herbs that they had cut and dried earlier in the year into jars. Mrs Peart wrapped apples in newspaper and carefully placed them in baskets, so they didn't bruise. Jams, chutneys and pickles that Mary had made in the summer months filled a long shelf. The pantry at Springbank Farm was full.

The rain ran down the window panes in streams, and a flash of lightning lit up the house. Mary counted to herself, 'One, two, three....'

Thunder rumbled loudly overhead.

'That was close!' said Mrs Peart.

'I feel sorry for those poor animals outside,' said Mary, looking out of the window as she ironed the laundry. 'The horses and cows are alright inside, but the sheep must be drenched, poor things.'

'Their wool helps to keep them dry. It's got oil in it,' said Mr Peart, who was sat by the fire smoking his pipe, with Tip by his feet. 'But still, we lost another ewe this morning. They're just fed up of it.'

'I can't believe the weather's still so bad,' said Mrs Peart. 'It's been like this for ages.'

'It's the worst autumn I can remember, and I've seen some bad ones. The whole country's been affected. I read in the paper this morning that there's been another shipwreck, off the coast of Devon this time. No survivors.'

Isaac and Jacob came into the kitchen, water dripping from them. Mrs Peart saw pools forming at their feet and said, 'Take them wet things off and get warmed through.'

'We're not stopping, Mrs Peart,' replied Isaac. 'We've just come to let Mr Peart know that we've buried that ewe. Everything's done that needs doing for the day, so we'll get away home, if that's alright?'

'Aye, lads, thank you. See you tomorrow.'

As they left, Connie came in. 'This weather is so annoying! I wish I could go out riding. Star is so restless stuck in his stable. And all the trees that have fallen would make excellent jumps, but the ground's too sodden to ride on. What a waste! I bet they'll all have been cut up for firewood by the time the rain stops.' She ran upstairs to change out of her wet clothing.

Mary was fretting because she had been unable to meet Joe very often since that night that he had returned from the wrestling tournament — the first night she had lain with him.

On the few occasions when it wasn't raining, they had met in the woods, but the ground had been too wet for them to sit down. When she had suggested meeting somewhere else, somewhere it would be dry — like a hay barn or stable — Joe had said it was too risky, that they were more likely to be found together if they met in the farm buildings. She missed Joe, and she missed his touch.

What made it even worse was that she had been feeling unwell for a few weeks now. One night she had woken very early when it was still dark outside. She had heard a young tawny owl squeak like a gate swinging on a rusty hinge. She realised that she was going to vomit and rushed to the bowl on the washstand. After she had finished emptying her stomach, she opened the bedroom window. The cold breeze cut through her nightdress, and the fresh air made her feel better.

After a few minutes, she moved away from the window and got dressed. She didn't want Mrs Peart to know she was ill, or she would expect Mary to stay in her room all day. Furtively, she took the bowl outside, tipped the contents into the ash privy and rinsed it thoroughly before taking it back to her room. Nobody else was up yet, so Mary wasn't seen.

A few hours later, Mary cooked breakfast for the family. They liked bacon, eggs and freshly baked bread with lashings of butter. When the food was almost ready to serve, and the family had gathered in the kitchen and sat down at the table, she felt queasy and thought she might be sick again. She really did feel unwell. She made the excuse that she needed more water and went out into the yard. Before long, her head cleared and her stomach settled, and she returned to the kitchen to serve breakfast but ate little herself.

The same thing had happened nearly every morning since. Mary always felt worse at breakfast time, but her stomach seemed to improve as the day went on. She was worried that she might need to see the doctor, but she didn't have any money to pay him because her wages went to her family.

That morning, after they had finished eating breakfast and the family had left the kitchen, Mrs Peart said, 'You're looking a bit peaky today, Mary. Are you feeling alright?'

'I'm fine, thank you,' replied Mary. She didn't want Mrs Peart to know that she had been ill for a while because she might send her home.

'Sorry, lass, it's probably just your time of the month. I know what it's like.' She nodded to herself as she left Mary alone in the room.

'Time of the month' echoed in Mary's head. She sat down. When had her last 'time of the month' been? She couldn't remember. And slowly, it dawned on her. All the pieces fell into place, and she knew — she was with child.

Her mother had been sick a lot when she was pregnant with John, especially on a morning, and she had often asked Mary to cook breakfast and sometimes dinner because the smell of food had made her feel ill. It all added up; she was carrying Joe's baby.

Mary realised that what she and Joe had been doing was wrong because they weren't married yet. She was a country girl and knew that it could result in her having a baby, but she didn't think that would happen so soon, especially when they hadn't been together many times. But it was alright because they both wanted to marry and have a family and a farm. Joe had said as much on the way back from the dance. He had said he wanted a farm and a family, in that order, but she was sure he would be happy whichever came first. She was thrilled that they were going to have a baby.

She had to see Joe; she had to tell him.

The evening was dry, so she set off to the woods, hoping that Joe would do the same. On her way there, Mary thought about the life that was growing inside her. It was hard to imagine that there was a baby in there, her and Joe's baby. She was so excited about telling Joe the news that she ran most of the way to the woods to meet him. It was the first evening for over a week that it hadn't rained, and she hoped he would be there.

She came into the clearing and saw him standing near the ash tree. The ground was wet and muddy, and she went over to him and stood in front of him. Looking up, she said, 'Joe, I've got something to tell you.'

'What is it, Mary? What's happened?'

She smiled up at him and said, 'I'm going to have a baby. Our baby.'

'What?' exclaimed Joe as he took a step back. 'A baby?'

'Yes, Joe, a baby.'

He looked shocked. He turned away and wiped his brow with the back of his hand.

'Aren't you happy that you're going to be a father?' asked Mary. Her shoulders slumped.

Joe shook his head from side to side, 'I don't know. I hadn't given it any thought. No thought at all.'

'Well, you should have. It's what happens when lads and lasses lie together. I thought you'd be pleased. You told me that you wanted to have a family and a farm. We can get married and we can have them both. Just think, Joe,' she said as she touched her tummy, 'Our baby's in here. A little boy or a little girl. A part of you and a part of me. Don't you think that's wonderful?'

'Mary, I don't know what to say. I'm sorry, I've got to go.'

Mary watched him walk away through the trees and into the night. She stood there alone, wondering what had just happened.

Chapter 10

Springbank Farm, Westgate
January 1873

Christmas and the New Year came and went. Joe was leaving
the farmhouse through the front door, and he was so deep
in thought that he didn't see Mary watching him. She was
polishing the walnut breakfast table that stood by the parlour
window, and her eyes followed him until he was out of sight.

Joe hoped he had done the right thing. It had always been
his dream to own a farm, and he had to take this opportunity
before someone else did. If he missed out on this chance to get
Springbank Farm, he knew that he would regret it for the rest
of his life. He had wanted it for as long as he could remember.
As a boy, he'd played there and helped out whenever Mr Peart
had needed an extra pair of hands. It was as familiar to him
as his mother's farm, which he could never own. High House
Farm belonged to the Bishop of Durham's estate, and it would
never be for sale, but even if it was, there was no way that Joe
could afford to buy it. He had to find another way — and this
was it.

To own land was a step up. The villagers would look up to
him as they did Mr Peart. He would even be able to vote in

elections. Yes, he was sure that he had done the right thing. He wanted Springbank Farm more than anything.

Joe had heard the rumour about Connie and knew that no gentleman would consider marriage to her in case there was truth in it. He didn't mind if it was true or not; Connie's virginity was not a major concern to him. She was his ticket to securing Springbank Farm and, as her options were limited now, it meant that she was more likely to give his proposal serious consideration.

His thoughts turned to Mary. She had reminded him of what he wanted when they'd met in the woods that night. He grimaced. He thought of her standing there telling him she was going to have his baby and that they could get married. Where had she got that idea from? Aye, she was a bonny lass, and he liked her well enough, and he might have considered marrying her if it wasn't for the farm. He thought that it was a pity her family were only miners and that she hadn't anything to bring to a marriage.

Anyway, Mary wasn't his problem. She could take care of herself. She was a strong lass, and she had a family who would look out for her. Families always did. He knew in his mind that he had made the right choice. If Connie agreed to be his wife, he would inherit the farm when Mr Peart died.

* * *

Connie had been summoned to the parlour; her father wanted to see her. When she entered the room, he was sitting in an armchair and he held a glass of whisky in his hand.

'Come in, Connie. Have a seat. There's something I need to talk to you about.'

'What is it?' She asked as she sat down.

'I know it's not long since you broke up with Henry.'

'Please don't even mention his name to me,' said Connie, rolling her eyes.

'It's not about him. I just hope that experience hasn't put you off marrying anybody else.'

'No, why would it?'

'It's just that I've had a gentleman here this morning and he asked me for your hand in marriage.'

'What!' she said in surprise. 'Who was it?'

'Joe Milburn.'

'Joe!' she laughed. 'You said a gentleman.'

'Joe Milburn is a decent young man. You've known each other since you were children. He's a hard worker. He knows this farm better than anyone. Why not Joe?'

'I don't know. It's just I've never thought of him in that way. I had no idea that he even liked me.'

'Well, perhaps you should have a think about it. He's coming back tomorrow for an answer. Let me know what you decide in the morning.'

Connie went back to her room and sat by the window, staring out across the sodden fields. So, Joe Milburn wanted to marry her. Her father had asked, 'Why not Joe?' and she asked herself the same question. She had to admit that he was handsome, with his dark hair and dark eyes. He was a bit rough around the edges, perhaps, but she could help him with that. He was young and strong, and he would be capable of running the farm when the time came.

She knew it bothered her father that he didn't have a son to inherit the farm. The man she married would eventually own it and, if she chose someone who had no interest in farming, he could sell off Springbank Farm to the highest bidder. She wouldn't like to see that happen.

If she chose Joe, she thought, the farm's future would be secure, and it would stay in the family. Surely, that would make her father like her more. She knew he had always been disappointed that she'd been born a girl and that her mother had been unable to bear him a son.

Joe Milburn had played at the farm as a boy. He had worked there regularly at clipping time and at hay time and whenever necessary. He was one of the most frequent visitors at the farmhouse. Her parents had grown close to Joe over the years. When she thought about it, she was surprised that she wasn't jealous of their friendship. Joe had always been there for as long as she could remember.

Connie knew that it must have been Henry who had started that rumour about her, and she would never forgive him for that. Since then, nobody had shown any interest in her, and she hadn't received any invitations to society parties or events. Would that change in future? Would anyone else want to marry her? Or would she end up an old spinster living alone?

And then there was Mary. She had seen for herself that Mary was interested in Joe. If she accepted Joe's offer and married him, Mary wouldn't be able to have him, and that thought pleased her.

Marriage was a big step, a lifelong commitment. Connie decided to sleep on it, and in the morning, she would know the answer.

Chapter 11

Springbank Farm, Westgate
January 1873

The next day, Mrs Peart was in a state of excitement as she bustled around the house looking for Mary. She found her in the kitchen, preparing vegetables for dinner. 'Mary, come and sit in the parlour, we have a lot to talk about.'

Mary's stomach lurched as she followed the older woman along the corridor and towards the parlour. How could Mrs Peart have found out about the baby? Mary had been so careful to hide her pregnancy. Surely, Joe wouldn't have said anything. Is that why he had been to the house yesterday? The Pearts would throw her out if they knew she was expecting, and she would have to go home to Fell Top — if her father would take her in.

'Mary, are you listening?' asked Mrs Peart. 'Please sit down.'

Mary sat obediently in the comfortable armchair facing her employer, but she felt far from comfortable. She couldn't understand why Mrs Peart was smiling; it didn't make any sense. What was that she said? 'So, the wedding will take place as soon as the banns can be read, in about a month. Just one month! That's all the time we have to prepare and there's so much to do. I'm going to need your help, Mary. We want our Connie and Joe to have the best wedding Westgate has ever seen.'

Mary's heart missed a beat. Had she heard correctly? Connie and Joe were to be married. How could he marry Connie? He was supposed to marry her. She was having his baby, and she loved him. Didn't he love her? Obviously not, she thought. There was no way that he would consider marrying Connie if he loved her.

Mrs Peart paused and looked directly at Mary. She reached out and touched her brow. 'Are you not feeling very well? I don't think you've heard a word I've been saying. Go and make a cup of tea for now. We'll start making the arrangements in the morning.'

Mary's mind drifted. When she had first realised she was going to have Joe's baby, she assumed that he would be pleased, that they would get married and then get a farm together and have more children. That is what he had wanted; he had said so on the way back from the dance. Why had he changed his mind?

It slowly dawned on Mary that he hadn't changed his mind. She wasn't part of Joe's plan, and she had never been. He didn't want to settle down with her. Springbank Farm had been what he had wanted all along. He couldn't buy it, so the only way he could get it was by marrying Connie. Connie would inherit the farm when her father died and, as married women couldn't own property, it would belong to her husband. If Joe married Connie, he would become the next owner of Springbank Farm. Oh Joe, how could you? She couldn't imagine her Joe married to such a selfish woman. Mary felt sick. She had thought that Joe loved her, really loved her. How could she have been so stupid? And now Mary would have a baby, but she would never have its father. Mary remembered her father's words of warning, 'There's plenty that'll take advantage of a bonny young lass like you.' She had been such a fool.

'I'm not feeling well, Mrs Peart. Will you manage if I go and lie down for a bit?' Mary didn't wait for an answer. She ran upstairs to her room, flopped down on her bed and sobbed into the bedspread. She cried and cried until there were no more tears left to fall.

During the next four weeks, wedding preparations kept everyone in the Peart household busy. Mrs Peart and Connie made several trips to Newcastle to buy everything they needed for the celebrations. They met with a distinguished dressmaker, and they were both very excited about Connie's wedding dress.

The house was cleaned from top to bottom, and this was left almost entirely to Mary, although Mrs Peart did help a little.

Mrs Peart discussed food for the wedding feast with Mary and told her what food would be ordered, what animals would be slaughtered and what Mary would need to prepare. They planned what she would make in the days preceding the wedding and what would be made on the day.

Reverend Richards was a frequent visitor during this time. He met with Joe and Connie to discuss the institution of marriage and met with the family to discuss the wedding service, and sometimes, it seemed to Mary, he just came for tea.

Everything for Connie's big day was managed down to the finest detail.

Mrs Peart wrote the wedding invitations in her neat hand-writing, and she gave Mary a large pile of them to post. On the way to the village, Mary had been so tempted to tear them up, drop them in the mud and stamp on them or float them down the river. But she didn't.

* * *

Joe and Connie didn't start courting until the time of their engagement. Although they had known each other since child-hood, they felt like strangers when they walked together and chatted. Connie showed little interest in Joe's conversation about the farm and livestock and his plans for the future, so he let her do most of the talking. He thought she prattled on about the daftest things — hairstyles, clothes, Star and her pet dog, Charlie.

Charlie was a little red and white dog with a flat nose, and he was just a pet. Connie insisted on taking Charlie on their walks, and, much to Joe's astonishment, she talked to the dog as if he was a child. She petted him, and sometimes she even picked him up and carried him when the path was rough or muddy. Joe didn't know anyone else who kept a dog as a pet. Dogs were meant to work. They herded sheep, guarded property, killed rats or retrieved game. What use was a pet?

Joe held Connie's hand when she wasn't carrying the dog. He had tried to kiss her several times, but Charlie started to bark at him and nipped at his heels whenever he moved towards her. Joe had laughed at the time, but it was very frustrating. He thought that perhaps he had discovered Charlie's job — guardian of his mistress's innocence. The dog needed discipline and training.

Once Connie was living with him at High House Farm, he would put a stop to all her daftness.

Chapter 12

St Andrew's Church, Westgate
February 1873

Connie looked beautiful on her wedding day. Her parents had made sure of that. She had an outfit fit for a princess. The white silk wedding dress had been copied from a design by Worth of Paris. The bodice fitted perfectly and showed off her tiny waist to perfection. The skirt had a huge bustle and long train; both the height of fashion. A long, delicate lace veil covered her face, and around her neck, she wore a pearl pendant on a gold chain, a wedding gift from her father.

As Connie walked down the aisle towards Joe, he was utterly dazzled by her. She looked stunning. He realised he was standing with his mouth open and promptly closed it. He couldn't believe his luck — he had a beautiful bride and, in time, he would also have the farm that he had always wanted. Dreams really could come true.

His brother stood by his side. After Tom's initial surprise at the news of the marriage, he had agreed to be Joe's best man. Tom had questioned Joe about his relationship with Connie because everything seemed to have happened very quickly. He'd never seen Joe and Connie together; he didn't even know that Joe was interested in her. During the conversation, Tom had reminded Joe about when the three of them were young. As children, they had played tricks on each other. Connie had loved playing pranks on the boys but had hated it when the joke was on her. She'd had such a temper back then. Her face would go bright red, and then she would yell at the top of her voice and then she would storm off to tell her father. They had laughed at the memory. Joe marvelled at how different the woman walking down the aisle towards him was from the girl he remembered.

Mr Peart kissed his daughter's cheek and sat down next to his wife on the front pew. Reverend Richards performed the ceremony without a hitch, and it didn't seem long before he said, 'You may now kiss the bride.' Joe put his arms around Connie and kissed her on the lips, and he was pleasantly surprised when she kissed him back, somewhat passionately considering they were in company. Some of the congregation cheered, and others smiled knowingly at their partners.

* * *

Mary watched the ceremony from the back of the church, and she felt utterly miserable. She had just witnessed the man she loved marry a woman she didn't even like. After that ridiculously long kiss, Mary had seen Connie looking at her and, when their eyes met, Connie had smiled triumphantly, making Mary feel angry and bitter. She didn't know how she would endure the rest of the day.

The guests returned to the farmhouse for the wedding reception, which was a grand affair. All the relatives and villagers who had been to the service were invited. The wedding cake was the largest Mary had ever seen; it had a large round cake at the bottom and a medium-sized round cake sitting on top of it, and it was all covered in fancy white icing. Connie took a knife from Mrs Peart, and she and Joe cut the cake to a round of applause. Then, she passed the knife back to Mrs Peart so that she could cut it into small portions for the guests, most of whom were drinking sherry and chatting loudly.

* * *

Mr Peart tapped the table with a spoon, stood up and waited for the noise to die down before he said, 'Congratulations to my beautiful daughter, Connie, and my new son-in-law, Joe, on their wedding day. I hope they'll have a long and happy life together, and give us lots of grandchildren.' He smiled at his wife, then shouted, 'To Joe and Connie!' He raised his glass, and everyone in the room followed his lead, 'To Joe and Connie!'

Isaac waited until the cheers had subsided and normal conversations had resumed before he approached Mr Peart and whispered, 'There's two gentlemen at the door. They're askin' if Mr Henry Forster is here.' Mr Peart glanced across at Sir Thomas and Lady Margaret, who were offering their congratulations to the newly married couple. Phyllis was with them, but where was Henry? Mr Peart hadn't noticed Henry's absence, but, as Henry had been a former suitor of Connie's, perhaps it wasn't surprising that he would prefer not to attend her wedding to another man. Feeling annoyed at the interruption, he said, 'Alright, I'll come and see what they want.'

The men were standing outside the back door. One was tall and the other of average height, but both were well-built like wrestlers. They looked like gentlemen — their clothes were well cut — but there was something about them, something that Mr Peart couldn't quite put his finger on, that made him uncomfortable. In a no-nonsense voice, he said, 'Gentlemen, I'm Mr Peart. This is my house and it's my daughter's wedding day. Who are you and what's your business here?'

The tall man replied, 'I'm sorry to interrupt the nuptials. I'm William Price and this is my associate, James Benton. We're friends of Henry Forster and we believe he is here. We would like to see him on urgent business.'

'The guests at my daughter's wedding are none of your concern.'

'Guests?' the taller of the two said, raising an eyebrow. 'Isn't Henry the groom?'

Mr Peart's patience was wearing thin. 'No, he is not.'

'But your daughter, she is Constance Peart, isn't she?'

'Well, she was until this morning. Now, she's Mrs Joseph Milburn.'

'Oh, I see. So, she didn't marry Henry, then?'

'No, she didn't. Henry is not here, so I'll ask you to leave.' He closed the door and sighed. It had been months since Connie declined Henry's proposal. If they were Henry's friends, as they claimed to be, they would have known that. As Mr Peart rejoined the party, he decided not to tell Sir Thomas and Lady Margaret about the visitors; he didn't want to worry them.

'Mary, would you help Connie change out of her dress? They'll be leaving for High House soon.'

'But...'

'Never mind the guests, I'll see everyone has full glasses,' said Mrs Peart, as she picked up a sherry bottle from the table.

'Yes, Mrs Peart.'

Connie waited at the bottom of the stairs and led the way to her room. When they were alone, she said, 'Well Mary, I'm Mrs Joseph Milburn now. What have you got to say about that?'

'Congratulations.' Mary's voice faltered.

'You don't sound too sure,' Connie smirked as she removed her necklace. 'Are you jealous?'

Mary was seething inside. The whole day had been like a nightmare from which she couldn't wake up. By rights, Joe should have been hers; she should have been Mrs Joseph Milburn. The last thing she needed was Connie rubbing salt into the wound. Trying her hardest to stay calm, she said, 'Why would I be jealous?'

'I know you liked him,' Connie gloated. 'You used to meet him by the river. I saw you together, kissing and cuddling, all lovey-dovey.'

'So what! He was a single man and I was a single woman. It didn't mean anything to either of us.' That was at least half true, Mary thought, trying very hard not to show that she was upset.

'I don't believe you, you little liar. You wanted him and now you can't have him. He's mine. He's my husband, to have and to hold, to love and to….'

'But it's me that's having his baby!' shouted Mary in retaliation. She stepped back and covered her mouth with her hands as she realised what she had said.

Connie's face changed from pink to white to red.

Glaring at Mary, Connie yelled, 'How dare you stand here, in my bedroom, and tell me that you're having my husband's baby. I knew you had your eye on him, but it never crossed my mind that you were lovers! Meeting him in secret like that. I should have guessed that you'd bedded him, that you were his whore. How disgusting! I would never have married him if I'd known he'd been with you.'

Connie lowered her voice and hissed, 'From the day you came here, I hated you. Everyone else loved you. I heard them, 'Mary can do this,' and 'Mary can do that,' and 'Why can't you be more like Mary?' They liked you more than me, their own daughter!' Connie sniggered, 'But who'll have the last laugh now? I will! Because Miss Goody-Two-Shoes has disgraced herself! You're nothing but a whore, with a bastard in your belly. It'll never have a father because Joe … is … mine!'

Connie sat back on her bed and laughed hysterically. She was still in her wedding dress.

Mary had to get away. She left Connie and ran to her room, where she paced up and down. After watching her lover marry Connie that morning, Connie's taunts had been too much for Mary to take. Seeing Joe marry somebody else had been one of the hardest things Mary had ever done, but she should have kept her mouth shut, and she was cursing herself for saying what she had. Just another hour and Connie would have left, and it would all have been over.

But now that Connie knew she was pregnant, it wouldn't be long before her secret became the dale's latest gossip, and everyone would know. She had to go. She had to get away from Springbank Farm and from Connie and Joe. She picked up the few things in her room that belonged to her and bundled them together. Quietly, without being seen, she left by the back door.

Chapter 13

High House Farm, Westgate
February 1873

After carrying Connie over the threshold at High House Farm, Joe led her into the parlour, where he poured two glasses of sherry. He handed one to his new bride, and she took it eagerly and drank it straight down. Joe would rather have had another whisky, but he downed the sherry anyway. Connie was fidgeting with her bracelet and was unusually quiet for Connie. Thinking that she was nervous about what would happen next, Joe decided not to delay any longer. He took her hand and led her upstairs to their bedroom.

He undressed her slowly, and because she seemed anxious, he spent a long time stroking and kissing her before touching her intimately. She showed little reaction to his advances, neither returning his kisses nor touching him. She just lay there silently. He was so taken aback by her behaviour that he didn't know what to do. But he needed to consummate the marriage; that's all that stood between him and Springbank Farm.

'What's wrong, Connie?' he asked.

'I'm your wife and I'll do my duty. Please, just get on with it.'

Joe wasn't proud of himself for taking her under those circumstances, but she didn't offer any resistance. He wasn't inexperienced when it came to women, but he had never known anyone act like that before. He found it hard to believe that his worst sexual experience ever was with his bride on his wedding day.

As this was going through his mind, he pictured a scantily clad Mary on a large bed, and he couldn't help thinking about how much fun it would have been to spend the night with her.

Joe was up early the following day. He sat at the kitchen table to eat the breakfast his mother had made for him. He looked tired. His mother left the kitchen with a smile on her face. He knew that she thought his new bride had kept him up half the night, but that wasn't the reason he hadn't slept. He had lain awake, wondering what was wrong with Connie.

He mulled over the events of the previous day, trying to work out why she had behaved the way she had. The wedding had gone well. When they had said their vows to each other, Connie looked sincere and smiled at him — and there had been promise in that kiss. He had been looking forward to getting her into bed.

At the reception, Connie had taken his hand as they stood together to welcome the guests. She looked happy and talked to everyone who was there. The atmosphere had been jovial — as a wedding should be. It was when she came downstairs to leave for High House that she had become distant. Didn't she want to leave her home? Or her family? Was she having second thoughts about marrying him?

Connie had been fine until she went to change out of her wedding dress. She had been upstairs ages. Then, he remembered that Mary had gone to help her. Surely, Mary wouldn't have said anything about them or the baby. If she had, wouldn't Connie have confronted him? But it might explain her behaviour the previous night. He had to sort this out now. Connie would be his wife for a very long time, and they hadn't gotten off to a good start. He had to try and make it work.

He went back to the bedroom. Connie woke as he opened the door. She looked around at the unfamiliar surroundings, and it took a moment before she remembered where she was. She saw Joe standing in the doorway; her large blue eyes watched him approach the bed.

'Good morning, Mrs Milburn,' he said as he sat on the edge of the bed and kissed her on the lips. She was an attractive woman and, despite the disappointment of the previous night, he wanted her.

'About last night, it shouldn't be like that. I'm sorry,' he said. 'You should enjoy it just as much as me.'

She looked away. 'I know you enjoy it, Joe. I found that out yesterday, and you're not too fussy who you enjoy it with.'

He had guessed right. Mary had said something. Feigning ignorance, he asked, 'What do you mean?'

'Mary told me, on my wedding day, that you fathered the bastard she's carrying.'

Taking her hands and looking her in the eye, he said, 'I'm so sorry, Connie. I should have been the one to tell you. What I did was wrong, I know that, and I'm sorry. What happened between Mary and me is over now. I chose you. I married you. We're man and wife and that's....'

'I'm well aware of all that. For better or worse, et cetera, et cetera.'

'I know you're upset Connie, and you have every right to be. But it's you I want to be with. It's you I want.'

'I knew you and Mary were meeting by the river. I saw you. I didn't think you were lovers though. I don't know why the thought had never crossed my mind. I didn't want her to have you.'

'Don't say that Connie, you're upset. I understand that. But we're man and wife now and nothing else matters; nothing that happened before matters anymore.'

Connie's face softened a little at his words.

'And about last night,' he said. 'It will get better. I promise.' Joe winked at her before he left the room.

Chapter 14

Upper Weardale
March 1873

Without being seen, Mary ran across several fields to escape from Springbank Farm. The afternoon sky was dark, and snowflakes began to fall softly to the ground. Mary came to a halt. Should she take the road, go across the fields, or go up onto the fell? All of the routes would take her to Fell Top, but she decided she was less likely to be seen if she went the fell way. She climbed up the hill and through the gate. There were many tracks on the fell: miners' tracks from home to work, carriers' tracks from mines to ports, and sheep tracks from grazing to shelter. The snow was coming down heavier on the hills and blanketed the ground. She stayed close to the fell wall so she wouldn't lose her way.

After walking for over an hour, the snow was getting deeper underfoot. Mary was cold and tired, and she looked around for somewhere to rest for a while. There was a natural hollow in the hillside which had less snow than the hills around it, but it would offer little shelter. Up ahead was a mine entrance leading into the hillside, the opening black against the snow-covered grass. Her father used to say that it was warmer inside the mines than outside in winter, so she went to the opening and looked in. It was small but, if she stooped, she could just about walk in it. She didn't have a candle, so she felt her way carefully, using her hands and her feet to guide her, one foot at a time. When she could no longer feel the draught from outside, she sat down on the stone floor. Her father had been right — it was warmer than outside. Her cloak was wet, so she took it off. Apart from the hem of her dress, the rest of her clothes were dry.

Mary sat in complete darkness, and her other senses sharpened. She had expected it to be silent underground, but she heard water dripping and some strange noises that she couldn't identify. There was a bad smell. Her father had talked about 'bad air' in the mines, where a candle wouldn't burn, and men couldn't breathe. She listened to her own steady breathing and knew the air must be good. Perhaps it was damp or mould, she thought. In this alien environment, her body was resting, but her mind remained alert. After a while, she grew used to her surroundings and relaxed, and eventually, she slipped into sleep.

She woke with a start, covered in sweat. Her troubled dreams had been of Connie and Joe, and of Springbank Farm and the workhouse, and of running forever and ever with no end to her journey. How could she bear the shame of having a bastard child? Or of being jilted by its father? How could she have been so wrong about Joe? Connie's words had cut her deeply, and they were etched into her mind. Perhaps she should just curl up and die here. It would be easier than carrying on.

But she had to carry on for her baby.

* * *

Mrs Peart was up early the next morning and was surprised to find that Mary hadn't returned. She hadn't seen her since the wedding reception. Last night, Mrs Peart had cleared up after the guests by herself, and she'd been very cross with Mary for leaving her with so much work to do, but she hadn't been worried about her. She thought that Mary must have gone out walking with a lad. Girls got fanciful notions in their heads sometimes, and a wedding could bring that sort of thing on.

But Mary hadn't come back, and her bed hadn't been slept in. She would have to tell Mr Peart; he would know what to do.

She found her husband at the kitchen table waiting for his breakfast. 'Where's Mary? It's not her day off again, is it?' he asked.

'No. Now, don't get alarmed. I haven't seen Mary since yesterday afternoon. I thought she'd gone off with a lad, but she's been out all night and she's not back yet.'

'You mean to say that Mary's missing?'

'Yes, since yesterday.'

'Good God, woman! She's our responsibility while she's living under our roof. We'll have to find her. Did you see her with a lad at the wedding?'

'No.'

'Any idea where she might have gone?'

'Her home at Killhope is the only place she's mentioned going to in all the time she's been here.'

'I can't imagine why a sensible lass like Mary would leave without telling us, especially in such bad weather. Something must be wrong.'

Mr Peart looked out of the window and across the fields. It had snowed heavily overnight, and it had been freezing.

'Jacob will have to see to the stock on his own today. I'll ask Isaac and Joe to go and look for her,' he said.

'You can't ask Joe. Not on the day after his wedding,' replied Mrs Peart.

'You're right. I'll ask Tom.'

Mr Peart sent Isaac to High House Farm to ask Tom for his help. Tom was happy to oblige and returned to Springbank Farm with Isaac. Mr Peart invited them into the kitchen and said soberly, 'Mary hasn't been seen since yesterday afternoon. She has never spent a night away from the farm since she's been here. We have no idea where she is and obviously we're concerned for her safety.'

Nobody said it, but they all knew that there was little chance of finding her alive if Mary had been out overnight in the snow.

'We'll do our best to find her,' said Tom. 'It's probably worth trying Fell Top first. She might have gone home.'

'Good idea,' replied Mr Peart.

Isaac and Tom wrapped themselves up well and set off on horseback for Killhope. They decided that would be the best place to start their search, and they could ask anyone they met on the way if they had seen Mary.

* * *

It took a few moments for Mary to realise where she was. She had opened her eyes, but it was still dark. She stretched; she was stiff with lying on cold rocks all night. Her stomach rumbled; she had left in such a hurry that she hadn't taken any food with her. She made her way to the mine opening. More snow had fallen overnight, and it sparkled on the ground. She looked down the valley of Weardale and wondered at its beauty as she set off for home.

Mary trudged up the steep bank to Fell Top, the home she had left almost a year ago. The winding path was hidden, but Mary knew the way between the tufts of reeds sticking out through the covering of snow. She paused for breath and, as she looked across the barren landscape, she saw the familiar scattered houses nestled into the hillsides; she had forgotten how few houses there were up here. Mary's eyes were drawn to the valley bottom; there was no movement at Killhope mine. The water must be frozen, she thought. Mary turned to continue her climb, wishing that her mother would be there to greet her when she got home.

Hannah Watson had been a typical Weardale woman — stocky, hardworking and straight-talking. Her outward appearance was tough but friendly. She rarely showed affection for her children, being quick to chastise, but that was how children were brought up in the harsh Durham dales. Her family and her home had been her life. Yes, her mother would have disapproved of the baby, but she would have helped her. Her father was a different matter altogether. Mary didn't know what kind of reception she would get from him and, now that he was drinking, she couldn't predict how he would react to her news.

She reached for the door and opened it slowly. Her father was sitting on a cracket by a roaring fire when Mary entered the house. He turned to her and asked, 'What the hell are you doin' here? It's not yer day off, is it? Or have them bastards down there sacked you?'

Mary was shocked to hear George swear. He hardly ever swore at home and never when he thought the children could hear. She looked around and saw that she was alone with him. Annie must have taken the children out to play in the snow.

Mary spotted a bottle on the table; it was almost empty. He had been drinking. Well, that explained his language. Now was probably not a good time to tell him why she had come home, but how could she explain why she was there?

She wasn't sure how long she had been standing behind the closed door wondering what to say when her father's glazed eyes looked at her, and he said, 'Well, I'm waiting!'

'I...I need to tell you something. Please don't be angry.'

'Well, what is it? Out with it!' he said impatiently.

She looked down at her wet boots and said, 'I'm going to have a baby.'

Mary saw a movement in the corner of her eye as her father leapt up, upsetting the little stool so that it rolled across the flagstone floor.

Mary stepped back just in time and missed the blow her father had meant for her. 'You dirty whore! Who's the bastard that did this to you? I'll kill him,' George ranted.

He didn't wait for an answer. 'You've brought shame on this house. Your mother will be turnin' in her grave. Get out! I don't ever want to see you again.' In a low voice, he said, 'You're no daughter of mine. You're nothin' but a dirty, filthy whore. Now get out!'

He picked up the bottle from the table, drank what was left, and then threw the bottle against the fireplace, where it shattered into smithereens. He went over to where the cracket lay, placed it by the fire and sat down in silence. He stared

107

into the flames.

Mary opened the door and left just as quietly. She stifled her sobs until she was far enough away from the house so that her father couldn't hear her. Then, she sat down in the snow and cried.

She hadn't expected him to welcome her back with open arms, but she hadn't thought that he would throw her out either — his own daughter. What would happen to her now? Where would she go? She had heard of girls in her condition being put in the workhouse.

Everybody feared the workhouse. Poor people who could not care for themselves or support themselves ended up there — orphans, the elderly, the sick and the unemployed. Some were lucky enough to get out again if they were offered a job or had relatives who would take them in.

She couldn't allow her child to be born in the workhouse. There was no way she would let that happen. But what could she do?

Mary remembered telling Annie to go to Aunt Lizzie's if she needed help, and she wondered about going there. It was only a couple of miles away. Would she get a better reception there, or would she be thrown out again in disgrace? She didn't have any better ideas, so she dried her face on her sleeve, stood up and set off for The Moss.

* * *

Tom and Isaac reached Fell Top about midday. There were footprints in the snow, so they knew someone had walked up to the cottage that morning. Tom hoped he would find Mary there. He dismounted and knocked at the door.

'I told you not to come back, lass. You're not welcome here.'

'Mr Watson,' shouted Tom. 'Are you there?'

The door opened slightly; the smell of alcohol on George's breath was unmistakable.

'Who's that out there pesterin' me? Why can't ya just piss off and leave us alone?'

'Sorry to bother you, Mr Watson, we're looking for Mary. Is she here?'

'No, and I don't ever want to set eyes on her again.'

'Have you seen her today?' asked Tom, hopefully.

'Who are you? The father. If you're the father, I'll kick you from here all the way back down that bloody dale.'

George's words made no sense to Tom. He looked at Isaac, who shrugged back at him.

'Mr Watson, I believe that you're Mary's father. Has Mary been here this morning?'

'Aye, she was here, and I told the bloody whore never to come back.'

Tom remembered Mary talking about her father. She had never said that he was a drunk, but then again, who would admit to something like that. Perhaps that was what she meant when she'd told him that her father was ill.

From what George had said, they could assume the footprints to the house were Mary's and that she had been there that morning. There were three sets of prints going on up the hill; Annie, William and John going out for a walk in the snow, they decided, as one was the footprint of a young child. They followed Mary's footprints back to the road, but it wasn't possible to see which direction she had taken as several horses, and people had used it.

Chapter 15

The Moss, Lanehead
February 1873

Mary hadn't been to The Moss in years, but she still remembered how to get there. As she approached the smallholding, she thought it looked like so many others in Weardale. The brown, stone-built house was set into the hillside, a smoking chimney rose from its stone-flagged roof, and a small barn was attached to one side. There was a distinctive smell of peat smoke in the air. An almost circular wall surrounded the house, and the land inside was divided up: a large area for grazing a cow, a few sheep and a small flock of geese; a hen run for chickens and a garden for growing fruit and vegetables.

Mary saw a lad chopping firewood in front of the barn, and she said, 'Hello. Is Aunt Lizzie at home?'

Putting on a man's deep voice, he asked, 'Who are you and what do you want?'

'I'm Mary Watson. You must be Ben. You were just a bairn the last time I was here.'

In his normal voice, he shouted, 'Mother! Mary Watson's here to see you.'

The door opened, and a thin, red-haired lady came out

of the house. 'Mary, what are you doing here? Is everyone alright?'

'We're all fine, Aunt Lizzie.'

'Well, you'd better come in, lass.'

Once inside, Aunt Lizzie noticed Mary's wet clothes. 'Take off them wet things and dry them by the fire before you catch your death. Come on, sit here and get warmed through. You're dotherin', lass.'

While Mary took off her top layers and hung them up, Aunt Lizzie made a pot of tea and placed some ginger biscuits on a plate.

'I've not seen you since your mother's funeral. How's your father getting on?'

'He's not doing very well to be honest. He's been drinking.'

'Well, I never! George taken to drink! He's about as Methodist as they come, he is. He's never touched a drop in his life. My God, he must miss her for him to turn to drink. So, that's why you've come to see me, lass. You want me to talk some sense into him. You know, it's been nearly two years since your Uncle Ben was killed at the mine, and I still miss him every day, but drink doesn't solve anything, it won't bring him back.'

Mary warmed her hands on the teacup and reached out for a biscuit, and she wolfed it down and got another. 'By, you're hungry. Do they not feed you at your new place?'

'I've not had anything today.'

Aunt Lizzie cut a slice of bread, spread some butter and jam on it and handed it to Mary on a plate.

'You look a bit peaky. Are you alright?'

'I'm just cold.' Mary was still shivering.

'It's the Peart's place you're at, isn't it? How's it going?'

'I…I left. I had to leave.'

'Why's that, then?'

'Oh, Aunt Lizzie, I don't know how to tell you.'

'Straight out's always the best, I've found.'

After her experience telling her father, Mary wasn't sure about that, but she took her aunt's advice.

'I met a lad down there, and I liked him, and I thought he felt the same way about me. I thought he would marry me, but he's married someone else now. And…and I'm going to have his bairn.'

Aunt Lizzie showed no surprise at Mary's words, so Mary continued. 'I couldn't stay there, so I went home but…but Father threw me out. He shouted at me, called me names and he would have hit me an' all, if I hadn't moved in time. He's disowned me — he says he never wants to see me again.' Mary's voice trailed off as tears returned to her eyes.

'Well, well, that's more like the George Watson I know. Not that he was ever violent, but self-righteous, yes, that's what he was, wanting everyone around him to do everything right. Life's not like that lass, as you're finding out. Things happen, not always of our own doing, but we just have to pick ourselves up and get on with it,' said Lizzie, obviously reflecting on her own life's ups and downs. 'So, you need somewhere to stay then, that's why you've come?'

'Aye, if that's alright?'

'Course it is, lass. That's what families are for — for helping out when it's needed.'

'Thank you,' said Mary, looking relieved. 'I was worried I'd end up in the workhouse! I'll help here. I'll do anything that needs doing.'

'I'm sure you will, lass. Don't worry, it'll all work out. Things have a way of working out. You can stay here for as long as you need to.'

* * *

Ben came in as his mother finished speaking. 'Is Mary staying?'

'Aye, lad, she'll be here for a while. Now that you're going out to work, I could do with a hand seeing to the house and the stock.'

Thinking his mother was having a go at him for leaving her to manage the place on her own, he said, 'But I had to go to work, Mother. We'd have lost the house if I didn't. When Father died, the agent was going to throw us out, remember? He would have an' all if you hadn't told him that we could manage to pay the rent between us, with me job down there and you selling stuff from the farm. I s'pose we did expect our Kate to come back and help you, though.'

'I know, I know,' said Lizzie, thinking her son worried far too much for a boy of his age. She didn't know where Kate was, but she hoped that her daughter was well and happy with her life wherever it was. She hoped she might have gone to Australia to start a new life as her brother had twenty years ago. He'd gone to find gold, and he had done well for himself. His letters had encouraged the rest of the family to follow him, but none of them had gone. They'd all stayed in the dale.

'Could you be a good lad and take them taties down for Ted, please?' she asked her son. 'They're by the back door.'

Ben picked up the sack of potatoes and said, 'Aye, I'll take Fly out with me. Come on, boy!' A lurcher sprang up from the corner of the room and followed him out of the house.

Aunt Lizzie picked up the dishes and carried them to the sink. She turned and watched her niece, who looked so much like her sister, Hannah, had at that age. Mary was chewing her bottom lip and seemed far away in her thoughts.

Chapter 16

Springbank Farm, Westgate
February 1873

Mr Peart saw the riders coming back up the road to the farm and went to tell his wife that Tom and Isaac were back. When the men reached the yard, the couple had already come out to hear their news.

Tom shook his head and jumped down from his horse.

'Come inside,' said Mr Peart. 'Get warmed up and you can tell us what's going on.'

The men followed the couple into the kitchen.

'Sit yourselves down,' said Mrs Peart. 'You must be hungry. I'll pour you some broth.' She ladled broth from a large pan into two bowls and carried them to the table. 'There now, tuck in.'

Mr Peart asked the question that Mrs Peart was avoided. 'Well lads, any sign of her?'

'Not really,' replied Isaac. 'Well, we know she went home to her father's place this morning, but she'd left by the time we got there. Mr Watson was drunk and spouting a load of rubbish. He didn't know where she'd gone.'

'The silly thing, going out in this weather.' Mrs Peart sighed.

'The Lord only knows why the lass didn't stay there. Or here, for that matter.'

'We didn't know where else to look,' said Tom. 'Nobody we met on the road had seen her.'

'Maybe you should let Robert know what's going on,' said Mr Peart. 'She's not exactly missing if she went home, but we don't know where she is.'

The men finished their meal, thanked Mrs Peart, and then rode down to the village to find the constable, who they discovered sitting in 'The Half Moon' drinking ale.

'Good evening, lads. Too cold to wander the streets tonight, isn't it? What are you drinking?'

'We've just come to talk to you,' said Isaac. 'There's something you should know. But I suppose we could have a small one while we're here.'

The innkeeper brought over their drinks and put them down on the table.

The two men sat down next to the policeman, and Tom said, 'Mary Watson, the girl who works for Mr Peart, is missing. She left the house yesterday afternoon. We know she went home to Fell Top at Killhope sometime this morning, but her father doesn't know where she went after that. He didn't say very much really — not that made sense anyway. The Pearts are obviously worried. They don't know why she left and they don't know where she is.'

'I see. So, we have a missing person. It's been a long time since we had a missing person enquiry. If I remember right, the last one had gone off to Canada. Wrote a letter home and told his family where he was. There was another one, long time ago, that was found floating down the river. Dunno if he did himself in or if he'd fallen in and drowned, accidental, like.'

'That's enough,' said Isaac. 'We all care for the lass and want to know she's safe. Will you keep an eye out for her? And let us know if you find out where she is?'

'Aye, of course I will. I wouldn't like to see her come to any harm. I think there's some relations of her mother live near Fell Top. Now, what did they call them? Featherstone. The fella got killed in the mine. You must have known him, Tom.'

'You mean Ben Featherstone?'

'Aye, that's him. His widow and Mary's mother were sisters. So, that makes Lizzie Featherstone Mary's aunt. Maybe she went there. That's where I'd try.'

Impressed by the policeman's local knowledge, Tom said, 'The Featherstones live up at The Moss. I'll ride up there in the morning.'

'I'll come with you,' said Isaac. 'I want to know that the lass is alright.'

They finished their drinks and went their separate ways.

Isaac and Tom met in Westgate early the following day, their breaths visible in the cold air. Yesterday's slush had frozen overnight, making the roads treacherous. They walked their horses in single file on the grassy verge, and it took much longer to reach The Moss than Tom had expected.

When they reached the smallholding, the door opened slightly, and Ben peered through the gap.

'Hello?' he said.

'Hello, I'm Tom Milburn, from Westgate. I've come to ask if you've seen Mary Watson? Or if she's been here?'

'Yes, she's been here. She's staying with us. Do you want to see her?'

A voice from inside the house said, 'Who's that asking about Mary?' A woman pulled the door open so that she could see the visitors.

'Hello, Mrs Featherstone. I'm Tom Milburn, from the farm next to the Pearts, and this is Isaac Rowell who works for them. We're just checking that Mary's alright. Everyone's worried about her.'

'Ben, go and check on the cow.'

'I've already done ....'

'Just go!'

The boy ran off to the barn, followed by his dog.

'You've got a nerve coming here. Which one of you was it?' Lizzie looked at them in turn but could see that neither of them knew what she was talking about.

'So, she didn't tell you that she was having a bairn?'

Tom was shocked, and he could see that Isaac was too. That explained why Mary had left, he thought, but who on earth was the father?

Isaac asked the question that was on Tom's mind. 'Who's the father?'

'You mean it's not one of you?'

They looked at each other, and both said, 'No.'

'Oh, I'm sorry. I thought when you'd come looking for her that....'

Tom interrupted her, 'I suppose that's a natural assumption. So, you don't know who the father is, then?'

'No, she hasn't said anything, apart from that she met him when she was working at Westgate and that he's married.'

'Can we see her?' asked Tom. 'Just to check she's alright.'

'I don't think that's a good idea,' said Lizzie. 'She's asleep and she needs the rest. It's lucky she made it here at all after being out all night. Her clothes were drenched, and she was frozen. You can tell Mr and Mrs Peart that she'll be alright though. She can stay with us for as long as she likes.'

Looking at Tom, Lizzie said, 'I've seen you before, haven't I? I can't remember where.'

'I worked with Ben at Greensike mine.'

'You used to work with my Ben? Why didn't you say so? Come on in and get warmed up for a bit. You must be frozen out there today. Be quiet, though. We don't want to wake the lass, do we?'

Once again, the Pearts went out to the yard when they saw the men ride up the track.

'Well?' asked Mrs Peart.

'Better news than yesterday, I think,' said Isaac.

'You'd better come in and tell us.'

In the kitchen, Mr Peart stood by the stove and Mrs Peart by the window. The men sat at the table where Mrs Peart had laid out some sandwiches for them.

'The lass is safe,' said Isaac. 'She's staying at her aunt's place, near Lanehead.'

'That's good!' exclaimed Mrs Peart. 'When is she coming back?'

'She won't be coming back,' replied Tom. 'We've been told she's going to have a baby.' He watched for their reactions.

Mr Peart was pulling at his shirt collar, and Mrs Peart was standing with her mouth open. She sat down and slumped in the chair, the colour draining from her face. She looked at her husband and said, 'Mr Peart?'

'What?' When he saw her accusatory stare directed at him, he said firmly, 'This has nothing to do with me. I've never

119

touched the girl.'

'You're the only man in this house. Who else could it have been?'

Mr Peart bent over his wife and looked into her eyes. 'I may be the only man in this house, but I'm not the only man around here. This is not my doing. How dare you accuse me? And in front of guests!' He marched to the door and slammed it behind him.

Tom wondered whether Mr Peart could be the father. As well as being under the same roof, he was married. If he had suggested anything to Mary, would she have dared to refuse him and risk losing her job? He knew Mary's family depended on her wages. But Mr Peart's denial had seemed genuine enough.

Isaac and Jacob Rowell were both married men, and they worked at the farm so they had regular contact with Mary. After spending the best part of two days with Isaac, he was sure it wasn't him, but could his twin brother be the father?

Mary took eggs down to the shop in Westgate nearly every day, and she must have met quite a few men from the village. The father could be any one of them — and that is if she had been willing. God forbid, if someone had taken her against her will, the father could be absolutely anybody. If someone had hurt Mary, Tom swore that he would kill them himself.

'We'd better be getting on, Mrs Peart,' said Isaac. They left her staring out of the window.

Chapter 17

Westgate Village
April 1873

Mr Peart and Joe climbed the steps and went into 'The Half Moon'. The smell of stale beer and tobacco hit them as they entered the bar. The members of the 'Weardale Association for the Prosecution of Felons and other Offenders' gathered at one end of the room to discuss the spate of sheep rustling that threatened their livelihoods.

Ned Routledge had called the meeting because he had lost a substantial part of his small flock. Five of his twenty sheep had been taken, which put his business at serious risk of failure. All of the farmers could sympathise, even those with large concerns, because they had all been young once, and they could remember how tough it was when they had first started farming.

When everyone had arrived, they sat around a table and, as chairman, Mr Peart addressed the group.

'You all know why we're here tonight. A few weeks ago, Ned lost five ewes that were in lamb. That's a huge loss for him. And we're all here because we've lost sheep this past year as well. This stealing has been going on for far too long. We can't let it continue. Robert Emerson, the constable, knows all about it, yet he's never seen anyone about, nor caught anyone for it. It's time we did something about it — ourselves.'

The men were nodding and saying aye, so Mr Peart continued, 'As you know, the Felons was founded well before there was a police constable here. Weardale men have always protected their own. I propose that we should go out at night and wait for the thieves. One night, we'll get lucky and catch them. We'll make sure they go before the magistrates for this. Justice will be done.'

'Right! So, when do we start?' asked Ned.

'After talking to you all, it seems that most of the sheep went missing during the week, so why don't we start next Wednesday?'

'It'll be dark by half eight,' said Joe, 'but they'll not be out that early. Should we meet in the village at about ten o'clock?'

'We'll be here,' said Isaac, for himself and his brother.

'I'll be here an' all,' said Ned. 'I'd like to get me hands on them buggers.'

'Good, good,' said Mr Peart. 'I'll tell Sir Thomas about the plan. He likes a bit of hunting, so I'm sure he'll join us.'

The men laughed.

'What about Robert?' asked Jacob.

'Aye, we should probably tell him as well,' said Mr Peart. 'He's propping up the bar over there. I'll go and have a word.' He got up from his seat and went to speak with the policeman.

Now that there was a plan in place, the men relaxed and continued drinking well into the night.

Wednesday evening was clear and dry. The men met outside 'The Half Moon' as planned and spoke in hushed voices as they discussed where they would go that night. The farms where thefts had occurred covered both sides of the valley and stretched for several miles in both directions from Westgate. They decided to go over the ford, up the southern hillside and onto the fell. From there, they could watch Ned's farm and a couple of his neighbours' farms too. As they set off, Robert came down the steps from the pub to join them, taking their number up to seven.

The men spent a long night on their watch but saw nothing and heard nothing out of the ordinary. There were no thieves out that night. They arranged to meet the following Tuesday and agreed to make this a regular event until the thieves were caught.

Chapter 18

The Moss, Lanehead
April 1873

Mary liked staying at The Moss with her aunt and her cousin. It was quiet and peaceful, and she didn't have to hide anything from them. Even though she helped with the house and the garden, Mary had plenty of time to reflect on what had happened at Springbank Farm, and she'd come to realise how stupid she had been.

When she and Joe had been walking back from the dance that night, she had heard what she had wanted to hear and not what Joe had said. If she had listened, she would have known that she wasn't part of his plan. He had made it clear that it was Springbank Farm he wanted, and there was only one way he could get that. Why had she not worked that out at the time? She knew the answer — she'd been taken in by his good looks and flattered that he had wanted to spend time with her.

But Joe had been wrong to lead her on and ask her to meet him when he had no intention of courting her. She had liked him from the day she had first met him on her way to Springbank Farm, and she thought he had been interested in her too. Well, he had been, but not in the way that she wanted.

When the weather was too bad for them to meet in the woods, she had wondered why he hadn't wanted to meet her in the farm buildings where it was dry. He'd said it was because they were more likely to be found together, and at the time, she couldn't see why that mattered. Now, she realised it was because he didn't want anyone to find out that they were seeing each other.

Mary was sorry that she had fled from Westgate without saying anything; Mr and Mrs Peart must have been so worried about her. But as much as she missed them, she couldn't have stayed there much longer anyway. While working there, she'd been frightened that somebody would notice the changes to her body, but luckily her thick winter skirt and pinny had hidden her condition well. Her pregnancy was evident now; her tummy was growing, and she could feel the baby moving inside her.

Even though Mary disliked Connie, she wished she could take back what she had said to her that day. Connie was mean and spiteful, and she shouldn't have been taunting her about her marriage to Joe, but even Connie didn't deserve to find out about her husband fathering a child in that way on her special day. That was the trouble with words, thought Mary; there was no way to take them back once they were out.

During the month that Mary had stayed at The Moss, Lizzie had never mentioned the baby or asked about its father, and Mary was grateful for that. She felt as though her aunt deserved an explanation and, now that she had come to terms with what had happened, she was ready to talk about it. She waited until they were alone one evening, sitting by the fire after dinner. Ben had gone out hunting with Fly.

'Is now a good time to talk?' asked Mary.

'As good as any, and better than most,' replied her aunt with a smile.

'I just wanted to tell you what happened when I was staying at Westgate.' She waited for her aunt's approval, and when Lizzie nodded kindly, Mary continued, 'I fell for the lad from the next farm. Joe Milburn. I don't know if you know him?'

'No, I don't. Is he any relation to Tom Milburn?'

'They're brothers.'

'Hmm. Tom came here looking for you the day after you got here. He had one of the Rowell twins with him. I think the Pearts had sent them to search for you. He told me he didn't know who the father was.'

'You told them I was having a baby?' Mary raised her eyebrows.

'Yes. They wanted to take you back to the farm and obviously you couldn't go. I thought, with them being the ones out looking for you, that one of them might be the man who was responsible, but I could tell from their faces that they had no idea what I was talking about.'

Mary realised that everyone at Springbank Farm and High House Farm and quite a few people in Westgate would know by now about her being with child, and she and her unborn baby would be the subject of gossip.

Mary continued telling her story and, by the time she had finished, she felt much better for having shared it. She had been concerned that Aunt Lizzie might hear rumours, and she wanted her aunt to know the truth about the baby's father and why he had abandoned them.

Chapter 19

Newcastle-upon-Tyne
April 1873

Tom, Joe and Ned set off with Joe's horse and cart and enough bait and ale to last them for several days. They were heading to Newcastle to take part in the annual Easter Wrestling competition.

'You stand a good chance this year, Ned,' said Joe. 'If you hadn't been drawn against George Steadman in the third round, you could've made it to the final.' He added with a laugh, 'But even the fourth round wasn't bad — twenty shillings just for messing around!'

'You wouldn't call it messing around if you'd been up against him. He's strong, and cunning. It's like he can read your mind. It's no wonder he wins so many matches — he's a legend!'

'You did much better than Tom and me. I was out in the first round and Tom in the second. I wonder who we'll be up against this year?'.

'Well, I hope I'm up against you Joe — because then I'm sure to get through!' said Tom in jest.

'Are you entering any of the other events?' asked Ned.

'No, not me,' replied Tom.

'Dunno, I might have a go at the sack race.' said Joe. 'It cannot be that hard — and you get a pound for winning! I don't mind making a fool of myself for a chance of winning some cash.'

'Remember the first time the three of us went to the Easter Wresting?' asked Tom.

'You mean when we were young and daft,' laughed Ned.

'Aye, we were that,' said Tom. 'We'd drank so much ale that none of us could remember how we got home. Good job that horse knew where he was going, 'cos we were all passed out in the cart!'

They all laughed.

It was dark when the men reached Forth Banks at Newcastle, and a sizeable crowd had gathered already. Joe unharnessed the horse, tethered it next to his cart, and then filled a bucket with water. When he returned, they ate some of the food and drank a little ale that they'd brought with them and settled down for the night in the back of the cart.

The next day dawned fine and clear. Tiered seating was in place for the spectators, and multicoloured banners had been raised around the field. Excitement was in the air. The first competition was for men weighing less than eleven stones, and there were sixty-four entries when Tom and Joe went to put their names down. It was the largest class, scheduled to last most of the day.

Tom and Joe both won their first rounds with ease. While they waited for the second-round names to be drawn, they saw Henry Forster walking towards them, 'Nicely done, gentlemen. I had money on both of you to win. Good luck in the next round!'

'Thank you, Mr Forster,' said Tom.

The second-round names were announced soon after; Tom and Joe were drawn against each other. They had practised together many times and were closely matched in both weight and skill.

'Well, you've got what you wanted, Tom,' said Ned. 'Let's see if you can beat your brother — or if you're all talk.'

'I'll beat him,' replied Tom.

The two brothers got into position and took hold of each other. On the command, they started to wrestle. They tried various moves, but neither of them released their grip or fell. Both were determined to win. In the first hold, it looked like Joe would tip Tom over, but Tom pulled him round, and they landed on the ground, shoulder to shoulder. The referee shouted, 'Dog fall.' He leaned towards the brothers, 'That one isn't counted, so we'll start again — best of three. Alright?' Tom and Joe nodded and heard him say, 'En guarde — Wrestle!' The crowd cheered as the brothers started to kick and shove and twist without letting go of the other, each trying to land the other onto the grass. This time Joe tripped and fell backwards, and Tom landed heavily on top of him. That was one to Tom.

Joe and Tom got to their feet and took hold of each other again. They grappled for some time before Joe lifted Tom off his feet, swung him round to the side and dropped him to the ground. That was one to each of them.

The tiered seats were full of spectators, and there was a huge crowd around the wrestlers when they got into position for the final time. Brother versus brother. They heard a shout, 'May the best man win!' This hold lasted longer than the previous ones, and the men battled on without losing their grip, trying to trip and trick each other into falling. The crowd were shouting their support and cheering wildly. Tom felt Joe's grip loosen and immediately took advantage by tripping him so that he lost his balance. Joe tried to reach out and grab Tom to pull him down as he fell, but he missed and landed on the ground alone. The crowd roared. Tom had won.

Ned ran over to them. He shook Tom's hand and helped Joe up from the grass. 'That was an epic bout, lads. Listen to the crowd!' Tom took his brother's hand and raised their arms into the air, and the crowd cheered even louder.

'I could do with a drink,' said Joe, and the three friends walked off in search of a bar. It would be a while before Tom's next tournament, so they had plenty of time. The field was crowded, and people slapped them on their backs in congratulations as they passed.

They found a small public house on the edge of the wrestling ground and went inside. The room was dark, and the ceilings low. Tobacco smoke filled the air, and masked other fouler smells. Tom bought a round of drinks, and they found a corner to sit and sup their ale. The discussion was dominated by wrestling — the matches that had taken place and those yet to come.

The conversation was interrupted by a commotion beside the bar. Two broad men had their backs to them, and from the raised voices, they appeared to be threatening a man hidden from their sight. One of them punched the man, and he groaned. As he bent double and held his stomach, Tom caught a glimpse of his face.

'That's Henry Forster!' he said, standing up and moving towards the bar. The others followed.

'Get off him, he's with us.' Tom said to the thugs.

They turned and looked at Tom, sized him up, and smiled,

but then they noticed Joe and Ned standing behind Tom. Turning back to Henry, one of the men said, 'We'll be seeing you again, you can bet on that!' and they hurriedly left the pub.

'Are you alright, Mr Forster?' asked Tom.

'I…I'm fine now, thanks to you. They tried to rob me. Can you believe that? In broad daylight! Thank God you were here.'

'Just as long as you're alright.'

Henry was visibly shaking, but he said, 'I'm fine, really. I'll be off now. Thank you for coming to my rescue.'

The men returned to their drinks.

'He was lying about them being thieves, wasn't he?' asked Joe.

'I didn't believe him,' said Ned. 'Thieves around here pick your pockets and you don't feel a thing; they don't beat you up in broad daylight!'

'I got the impression he knew those men,' said Tom. 'He was hiding something. Anyway, it's about time we got back. The next round will be starting soon.'

Tom lost in the third round, but he didn't mind. Getting to the third round had earned him nine shillings, and it had been fun. He had enjoyed a good day out with his mates, and they still had Ned's contest to look forward to tomorrow.

That evening was warm and dry. Tom and Ned sat on the grass by the cart, discussing the day's events and enjoying their ale.

'You did well today,' said Ned. 'Have you thought about taking up wrestling seriously? You can earn quite a bit if you travel around the shows.'

'No, I don't think it's for me. It was fun today, but going away every weekend doesn't appeal, and it would mean leaving the lads in the mine to manage without me sometimes. It wouldn't be fair on them.'

'With a bit of training, you could be really good. You mightn't need to work in the mine anymore.'

'Aye, that's easy to say, but earning a living from wrestling can't be easy.'

'No, mebbe not. The likes of George Steadman do, but most of them have another job as well.'

'Did you see where Joe went?' asked Tom.

'No.'

'He's been away a while. I think I'll go and look for him.'

Tom left Ned by the cart and wandered off in the direction his brother had taken an hour or so earlier. In the distance, he could see the gas lights on the surrounding streets. On the open land by the riverbank, lanterns were glowing at many of the makeshift camps. He walked between the horses and carts, being careful not to fall over people sleeping on the ground. When he reached the river, Tom looked out over the dark expanse of water which flowed down towards the bridge that linked Newcastle on the north bank of the Tyne to Gateshead on the south. As he glanced downstream, he spotted Joe sitting on the river bank, looking as though he was deep in thought.

'So that's where you've got to,' Tom called out to let Joe know he was there. When he got closer, he could see Joe was upset. 'What's wrong?' he asked.

'I've made such a mess of everything, Tom.'

Tom thought it was very unlike Joe to admit that he had done anything wrong. He went over to his brother and sat down next to him. 'What do you mean?'

Joe put his head in his hands and rubbed his face before replying, 'I shouldn't have married Connie. She's not the one for me.'

Tom was confused. 'You mean you've found someone else already? You've only been married five bloody minutes.'

'No, it's not someone else. Well, I suppose it is, because it's not Connie. I knew her before I got married and I really liked her an' all. I should have married her, not Connie.' A few seconds later, he said, 'She said she loved me as well. Can you believe that? Connie would never say that, she can hardly bring herself to lie with me, for God's sake.'

'I'm sorry Joe,' said Tom sincerely. 'I didn't know things were that bad between you. Who's the other lass?'

Without thinking, Joe said, 'Mary, of course, who else would it be?'

'Mary Watson?' asked Tom, trying not to let Joe see how upset he was by this revelation. 'And she said she loves you?'

'Aye, she did.'

Tom was silent for a second while he took stock of this. Lizzie Featherstone had said that the father of Mary's baby was married. How had he not thought of Joe? Mary had left on his wedding day!

'Right, let's get this straight. Are you the father of Mary's baby?

'Aye.'

'And Mary was in love with you but you split up with her so you could marry Connie Peart?'

'Aye, that's about it.'

'What on earth were you thinking? You're stupider than I thought, Joe Milburn.'

Joe nodded silently.

'You didn't?' Tom shook his head in disbelief and then looked Joe in the eye. 'You did, didn't you? You married Connie just so you could get your hands on that damned farm?'

Joe gave a slight nod before holding his head in his hands once more.

Tom was dumbfounded. After a while, he cleared his throat and said, 'Mary was a decent lass until you got your hands on her. How could you do that to her?'

Joe didn't respond. He stood up and wiped the grass from his trousers.

'Has she had the bairn yet?' asked Tom.

'No, I think it'll be a few months yet. I've not seen her since she left.'

Tom could hardly control the rage that was building up inside him. Joe had always been selfish, but this was unbelievable, even for him. He had taken advantage of a beautiful, young woman — for pleasure. He had ruined her and then left her alone to have a child. A woman who loved him. What a fool! And then he had married a spoilt brat — for greed. And he had only just realised his mistake. It was no wonder that he'd been sat there with his head in his hands. He deserved far worse. How could he be feeling sorry for himself?

'You've made a hell of a mess of things. How could you?' Tom said through clenched teeth. He wanted to turn around and walk away, turn the other cheek, but instead, he turned towards Joe and shouted at the top of his voice, 'You stupid, selfish bastard!' He punched him hard in the face, and then he walked away.

The following day, Joe had a black eye, and the two brothers had hardly spoken a word to each other since dawn. The atmosphere between them was very tense. Ned asked Tom, 'What happened last night?'

'Nothing.'

He asked Joe the same question and got the same response.

'Whatever it is that's going on between you two, I hope you'll both be there to support me today.'

'Aye, we will be, Ned,' said Tom, and Joe nodded. They followed their friend to the competition area.

An even larger crowd had come to watch the heavyweight tournament that Ned had entered. There were fewer entrants, and there would only be five rounds. Tom and Joe stood several feet apart but cheered Ned on as they had promised. He got through his first two rounds without much effort, but the contestant in the third round was much harder to beat. Ned scraped through to the semi-final.

He waited with the other semi-finalists to find out who he would be drawn against, and he hoped it wouldn't be George Steadman again, or there would be very little chance of him making it to the final. When the draw was announced, he was pleased to hear that he would be wrestling against Billy Coulthard. Billy was a big man, but he could be beaten.

The first hold went to Coulthard. For such a large man, he was remarkably quick on his feet. Ned picked himself up off the ground and prepared for the second hold. This one went in Ned's favour. The third hold would decide which of them would get a place in the final. Unfortunately, Ned lost his balance first and fell to the ground. Coulthard had won.

Ned was smiling as Tom and Joe went over to help him up. He had won three pounds in the competition and was very pleased with himself.

The men stayed to watch the final, where Steadman beat Coulthard and took the top prize. Then, they began their journey back to Weardale.

Chapter 20

The Moss, Lanehead
June 1873

The sun shone, and the hills beckoned Mary to go out onto them. Her baby was restless, and she thought that a walk might settle him. She had no idea if she was carrying a boy or a girl, but she had always thought of her baby as him. She would find out soon; he was due in a few weeks.

The familiar track leading to the fell was edged with long grass and dandelions, with an occasional clump of purple clover. It was so pretty at this time of year. A young blackbird landed on the stone wall and watched Mary inquisitively. It still had a few fluffy feathers, so it had recently flown the nest. Its mother flew over Mary's head in warning, protecting her youngster, and the fledgling took off again and landed clumsily further along the wall. A crow swooped down towards it, but the mother bolted and attacked the larger bird in mid-air. The crow flew off, and the blackbird chick remained unaware of the danger that its mother had averted.

Mary wondered what kind of mother she would make. She knew that she would love her baby; she already did. She would teach him and protect him, just like the blackbird had protected her chick. She would make his life as happy as she could and tell him that not having a father didn't matter. He would be a bastard. What a cruel word spoken by cruel people, she thought. Mary remembered children at school being bullied for being bastards. Still, children could always find a reason for bullying others — being tall, short, red-haired, cross-eyed, an incomer, in fact, for being different in any way.

In a small valley like Weardale, where everybody knows everybody, Mary knew that word of her condition would have spread quickly and that the dale's people would be gossiping about why she had left the farm. Girls in service didn't leave a job for no reason; they either left because they were marrying, they were needed at home, or they were expecting a bairn.

Mary thought it strange that the minister often quoted the verse from John, Chapter 8 in his sermons, 'He that is without sin among you, let him first cast a stone at her.' Well, it just went to show that the people either didn't listen or didn't want to hear. There were plenty of them eager to cast their stones in the dale and very few of them without sin.

As far as these people were concerned, Mary knew that falling pregnant before marriage was one of the most sinful things that could happen to a young woman, but it happened with surprising frequency. Some folk, especially the older women, shunned fallen girls and never let their transgressions be forgotten. Getting married before the birth would lessen the sin, at least in their eyes, but there would still be speculation about whether or not the new husband was the child's father. Mary was pleased that she was staying at The Moss and was well away from the gossips.

A gruff voice broke through her thoughts.

'Tena, lena, catra, horna, dic.'

Mary was walking along the top side of the fell wall when she heard the strange chant coming from the pasture on the other side. The dry stone wall had a row of tie stones sticking out about a foot from the ground. With difficulty, because of her huge belly, she pulled herself up onto the ledge and peered over the wall. A wizened old man looked to be counting sheep in a pen, but she didn't understand what he was saying. Her interest piqued, she climbed down and walked along to a small gate into the pasture and approached the shepherd.

'Hello,' she said.

'Whee's that?' he said, peering at her with rheumy eyes and pointing his crook at her. 'Is that thoo, Hannah?'

'I'm Mary, Hannah's daughter. I'm staying at Aunt Lizzie's, over at The Moss.'

'Ah, you look just like tha' mother. She used to walk ower here an' bother me an' all,' he said with a croaky laugh. 'We're neighbours. Ted Curry's me name, but they call me 'Owd Ted', 'cos I'm getting on a bit thoo knows. I'm eighty-nine!'

'You don't look that old,' said Mary tactfully.

'I put that down to plenty of fresh air — and a drop of firewater every night afore I gan to bed.'

Mary smiled. 'I heard you talking before. Were you counting the sheep?'

'Aye, I was. There's a few lambs missin'. I've been all ower t'fell and cannot find them anywhere.'

'A lot of sheep have gone missing lately. The constable at Westgate thinks they've been stolen.'

'Well, I never did. Stolen yer say? I've never heared tell of any bein' stolen — not since that man from Stanhope was hanged.' He shook his head in disbelief.

'Before, when you were counting, it sounded strange.'

'That's the way we've always counted sheep hereabouts. It's just numbers. I learnt them from me father and they were passed down from his.'

'Would you say the words again, please? I'd like to hear them.'

'Aye lass, if yer want. It's yan, tan, tether, mether, pip — that's one to five. Then, it's tena, lena, catra, horna, dic — and that takes yer to ten.'

Mary recited the ancient numbers back to him. 'It sounds like a rhyme,' she said.

'Aye, s'pose it does,' he said thoughtfully. When he refocused on Mary, he said, 'Are you alright, you look a bit upset, like?'

'I was just thinking about how much I miss reading. I used to borrow books from the library at Westgate when I was staying there — mainly novels, but sometimes medical books and poetry.'

'Don't think I've read a book since I left school — never had an inclination.' He pointed his crook at Mary's belly. 'It looks like yer time's gettin' near.'

Mary lowered her eyes at the reference to her pregnancy.

'Sorry, lass. Me an' me big mouth.' He shifted uncomfortably. 'Now, I see why you're stayin' at Lizzie's. She'll take good care of yer when yer time comes.'

Mary smiled at Ted. 'I'd better be getting back to help with dinner. She'll wonder where I've got to. It was nice to meet you, Mr Curry, and I hope I see you next time I'm walking this way.'

It was just a week later, the first week of July when Mary woke in the middle of the night. Her bed was wet. She wondered if she had wet herself. No, she would have woken if her bladder had been full. She needed to get up, dry herself and change her bedding. As she sat up, a pain gripped her around her middle. It was so strong that it took her by surprise. She couldn't shout for help. It lasted a few seconds and then subsided. When it had gone, she stood up and went to Aunt Lizzie's bedroom door. She knocked and shouted, 'I think the baby's coming!'

Aunt Lizzie's sleepy voice came through the door, 'Baby's don't come that quick. Just give us a minute.'

It felt like ages before Aunt Lizzie came to her room. Another pain came, and Aunt Lizzie held her hand until it stopped, and she said, 'It'll be here before the day's out, lass.'

Aunt Lizzie bustled around the house, getting everything in place for the birth. Mary stayed in her bedroom. The pains were coming more frequently, and she had vomited on the floor. Aunt Lizzie cleaned up after her. Mary found she was most comfortable standing up, and looking out the window gave her something to concentrate on between the pains.

'It's taking ages, shouldn't it be here by now?' she asked her aunt between contractions.

'Bairns come when they're ready. You can't rush them,' said Aunt Lizzie. 'You're doing well. Ben can fetch the doctor if you need him later on, but you're a long way off that.'

Mary was pleased to have her aunt with her for reassurance. Her mother had died after giving birth to John, which had been preying on her mind recently. Mary hoped that she and her baby would get through this birth safely; she knew she was in good hands.

It was late afternoon when the baby made an appearance. Mary felt exhausted by the time her daughter took her first breath. Lizzie cleaned her up, wrapped her in a clean sheet and placed her in her mother's arms.

The new mother touched the wrinkled little face, the sparse downy hair on her baby's head, and the small fingers with tiny fingernails. She opened the sheet so that she could see her little feet with teeny toes. She wondered how she could have made something so perfect — how she and Joe could have made something so perfect. She wept silent tears— of joy or sadness; she didn't know.

Lizzie brought Mary a glass of milk and sat on the edge of the bed. 'It's a privilege to be a mother. You think their yours and that you've got them forever once they're here but remember you only have them on loan. They go their own way once they're grown — if they're lucky. Enjoy every day you have with her.'

A week later, Mary was ready to get up. She felt well and was bored lying in bed. She also felt guilty watching Lizzie do everything for her and the baby, on top of the usual work. Mary knew women were supposed to lie up for a month after having a bairn, but she couldn't stand being in bed any longer. When she first got out of bed, she was surprised at how weak her legs were, but they soon began to feel better as she walked around the room.

Lizzie had heard Mary moving upstairs and was pouring tea by the time she came down. 'It's nice to see you up and about, lass.'

'Thank you. I couldn't stay in bed, knowing how much you have to do.'

'Don't worry about that yet, it'll take a while for you to get your strength back. Anyway, I was thinking. Isn't it about time that little one had a name? We'll have to get her registered.'

Mary looked down at the little bundle wrapped in a woollen

shawl. Her baby looked back at her, pulling faces as she tried to focus on her mother. Mary knew what her name would be. She had already been calling her by it in private, testing it out, and it suited her. Josephine. Her daughter couldn't have her father's surname, and Joe's name wouldn't appear on her birth certificate — it would say 'Father unknown' — but she could give her his first name, albeit the female version. Her little Josie.

Mary took the cup of tea that Aunt Lizzie handed her and said, 'I've already decided on a name. I'm calling her Josephine'.

Immediately realising the connection, Lizzie asked, 'Is that wise? Not many people know who gave you this bairn, but with a name like that, one that's not common around here, people might put two and two together, you know, with you leaving the farm the day Joe Milburn got married.'

'I don't care,' said Mary softly. 'I want her to know who her father is — when the time's right.' She wondered if Joe knew that she had given birth to their baby yet, or if he even cared.

Lizzie's voice interrupted her thoughts, 'What about Hannah for your mother, or Margaret for Lady Margaret, or a more common name that won't stand out? There's nothing wrong with Ann or Jane — or Elizabeth, like me.'

'No, I've made up my mind,' said Mary. 'She's Josephine, and I'm going to call her Josie for short.'

'Alright, alright, Josephine it is. She's your bairn so it's your choice. I'll walk down to the registrar's on Friday, if it's a nice day. You'll not be fit enough to walk that far for a while yet. It takes it out of you, having a bairn.'

Mary was recovering well from the birth, but she tired quickly, more from the sleepless nights than from the birth itself. Josie had woken at least twice for feeding every night since she'd been born.

Mary was walking high on the fells with Josie strapped to her chest in a makeshift sling. She'd been cooped up in the cottage for such a long time that she'd had to escape for a while. It was so tranquil up on the fell, and the view was beautiful. She could hear peewits calling and the rasping noise of a grasshopper. The air was fresh, and she breathed deeply, simply enjoying being there with her baby.

But thoughts of Joe were never far away, disrupting her peace and happiness. Josie looked so much like her Joe. No, not her Joe anymore; he was Connie's Joe now. She kept wondering why Joe had chosen Connie, but the answer was obvious. He wanted the farm. It was as simple as that. He had given up Mary and their baby for Connie and her farm. Well, Joe and Connie were married now. She would have to get used to that, and she and Josie would have to find their own way in the world.

Mary noticed that the temperature had dropped and dark clouds were gathering in the sky, so she turned towards The Moss before the rain came.

Lizzie had gone down to the registrar's office at St John's Chapel to register Josie's birth. Ben had gone to work early that morning, and he wouldn't be home for hours. Mary and Josie had the house to themselves. Mary placed Josie carefully in her makeshift crib and settled down to rest in the chair by the window. It wasn't long before she drifted off to sleep.

Mary woke with a start. Rain was pelting the window, but that wasn't what had woken her. Someone was knocking at the door. Visitors to The Moss were few and far between, and they weren't expecting anybody. She got up and lifted the sneck on the heavy wooden door. As she pulled it open, she saw Joe Milburn standing there in the rain, twisting his cap in his hands. Their eyes met, and Mary felt the attraction they had shared pulling her towards him, but she stopped. He didn't want her anymore.

'I saw Mrs Featherstone in town, and I thought you might be on your own up here,' he said.

'Have you come to see the baby?'

Joe was looking deeply into her eyes. 'Aye, I'd like that very much. I'd like to talk to you as well.'

Mary led him to where Josie slept.

'You've got her in a drawer. That's no place for a baby!'

'What do you expect? A new crib! Are you going to make us one? I don't have any money, everything I earned went back home, and I can't work now with a bairn to look after. Aunt Lizzie doesn't have much money coming in, but she still took us in after you left us for — for Connie.' Mary's voice broke, 'Why did it have to be Connie? Of all people, why her? How could you, Joe?'

'I'm sorry I hurt you, Mary. I never wanted to do that. Please believe me.'

Joe bent over the drawer to look at his baby daughter. He reached in and stroked Josie's hand; tiny fingers gripped his little finger. Mary's heart melted as she watched them, and she found herself smiling. Lowering her voice, she said, 'I named her after you. She's called Josie, short for Josephine.'

Josie woke with a gurgle and stretched. Joe was mesmerised and sat staring at his daughter.

'Would you like to hold her while I put the kettle on? I'll make a pot of tea,' said Mary, aware that he'd said he wanted to talk with her and that he'd hardly said a word yet.

Joe carefully tucked the baby into the crook of his arm and started pulling faces at her. Josie stared back at her father. Then, he began to make baby noises at her, and Mary laughed.

By the time the tea was ready, Josie had become restless and turned her head towards her father's chest, wanting another feed. 'You'll not get anything from me, lass. I'd better give you back to your mother.'

Mary took their daughter from Joe and, as they sat down, she loosened her top and held her baby to her breast. She wasn't embarrassed about feeding her baby in front of its father.

Joe watched them in wonder, happiness shining in his eyes.

After Josie had finished her feed, Mary fastened her bodice, put Josie back in her bed, and sat back down.

Joe approached Mary and knelt on the mat in front of her chair. He took her hand and held it against his chest. Looking longingly into her eyes, he said, 'Mary, I'm so sorry. I made the wrong choice. I shouldn't have married Connie, I should have married you. I can't undo what I've done. God knows I wish I could, you've no idea what my life is like with her. I would much rather be with you and — I still want to be with you.'

Mary heard the words but didn't understand what he meant. 'How can you be with me? You're married to Connie.'

Joe leaned forward and took Mary into his arms. 'I want to spend time with you, you know, like we used to — last year. What I'm saying is that I want you, Mary. I've never stopped wanting you.'

His meaning slowly dawned on her, and she pushed him away.

'Like we used to!' she exclaimed. 'Last year was different. Last year I thought I loved you, and that you loved me. Now, I know that you don't love me, you never did, or you wouldn't have married her. Aye, I know you wanted me — to lie with me — but you never wanted me enough to make me your wife. I won't lie with you again, Joe — not ever. I can't believe what you're asking. You want me to be your whore! You're a married man now. You should be ashamed of yourself!'

Joe moved back, surprised by her outburst. He was about to speak, but Mary cut him off. 'I want you to go. Get out!' she said firmly.

Joe looked into her eyes, and she could see that, for a split second, he was unsure whether or not he should try to change her mind. Then, just as quickly, the indecision was replaced by defeat, and he left without saying another word.

Mary watched him wander down the path until he was out of sight. How could he think she would be his mistress after what he'd done? Yes, she still had feelings for him, although she wasn't really sure what they were anymore. The attraction was real; that was undoubtedly true. But he must have been courting Connie at the same time that he'd been seeing her, and it had been serious with Connie because they were married soon after. Not just that, he had walked away from her when she'd needed him the most, abandoned her and their baby. Her father had thrown her out and disowned her for disgracing her family. And Josie would have been born in the workhouse if it hadn't been for Aunt Lizzie taking them in. What Joe had done to her and Josie was unforgivable.

Chapter 21

The Moss, Lanehead
August 1873

'Mother, I want to go Westgate tonight, to help the 'The Felons', said Ben, between spoonfuls of porridge. 'I know I'm not old enough to join them yet, officially, but I can still help them to find the thieves. Ted had some of his sheep stolen and he'd like to go, but he says he's too old. I should go in his place. Father would have if he was here. And if we catch them, it means they can't come here and steal our sheep.'

Lizzie turned to look at her son, who was quickly becoming a man. His sense of duty impressed her, but she was worried that he didn't know the people in Westgate and didn't know the hills around there very well either.

'Do you know who'll be there?' she asked.

'Yes, there will be loads of people there. Mary knows most of them. Ted said Mr Peart and the men that work for him will be there, and Tom and Joe Milburn. I think Sir Thomas and a few others as well.'

Mary was sitting by the fire, knitting clothes for Josie. Her needles fell silent when she heard Joe's name, and she put them down on her knee.

'Mary, is that right? Do you know them?'

'Yes, I know all of them. They're good men and they'll keep an eye on Ben.'

'Alright, if that's what you want to do. Take Fly with you — and be careful.'

'I will,' Ben smiled as he left the table and called for Fly. The dog followed him out of the house as he went to begin his chores.

* * *

That evening, the men gathered outside 'The Half Moon' as usual. They were surprised to see a young lad with a dog walking towards them.

'Hello there, what can we do for you?' asked Mr Peart. The other men stopped talking and listened to the boy's reply.

'I've come to help you catch the thieves.'

'Have you, now? What's your name, lad?'

'Ben Featherstone. I live up at The Moss.'

'You've come a long way to help us. Why would you do that?'

'Because our neighbour, Ted Curry, had some sheep stolen. He would've come if he could, but he said he's too old to go out chasing thieves. I don't want them to come and steal ours either. Me mother cannot afford to lose any.'

'Alright lad, you're welcome to join us. Just listen carefully and do what you're told.'

'Aye, I will.'

'Right men, everyone is here now, let's make a start.' Mr Peart led the way, and the men followed without question.

The night was dark and misty. The crescent moon, when

it could be seen, did little to light the farmers' way. It was a hard, steep climb up to Westgate Fell in the dark. The path was uneven at the best of times, but the cows in the pasture had walked that route when the ground was muddy and, now that it was dry, small craters were left where their hooves had been. Mr Peart and Sir Thomas led the way with lamps, and Tom and Ned brought up the rear. They walked in silence, dogs weaving in and out between them. When the procession had reached the final gate that opened out onto the fell, Mr Peart said, 'Right men, here we are. We'll split up and sit along this dyke back. If anyone sees anything, give the signal — one long, low whistle.'

The lack of sightings had disheartened the men. They'd met on the fells every week since April, and they'd seen nothing. There were no new reports of sheep going missing either, and they wondered if perhaps the thieves had heard about their vigils.

Despite that, they murmured their agreement and went off in both directions, followed by their dogs, and they sat in the darkness with their backs to the wall. If anyone came onto this fell that night, someone would see them or hear them. They extinguished the lamps and waited patiently.

As their eyes adjusted, they could see small mounds dotted over the rugged landscape — silent, sleeping sheep. Occasional sounds could be heard from the men, the odd cough and a short burst of snoring when Sir Thomas fell asleep against the dry stone wall.

An hour or two later, there was a creaking noise as the gate swung open. All eyes turned towards it. A figure could be seen coming through the gate and, rather than turning to close it, it continued onward up the fell with a dog at heel. The farmers watched and waited, all wondering what would happen next. Was this someone simply passing through, or was it one of the sheep rustlers?

The figure let out a high-pitched whistle, and the dog left its owner's side. It began to nip at a few of the sheep to wake them up. Another more prolonged, lower whistle and the dog went around them and started to drive them towards the open gateway.

There was no doubt this was the thief; nobody gathered sheep at night. Mr Peart gave the signal, and all the farmers stood up and moved towards the culprit, as quickly as the coarse, tufted grass would allow. The figure froze for a second and then put his hand into his coat and brought out a pistol. Some farmers saw what he held and stopped in their tracks; others didn't and continued moving forward. A shot rang out, followed by a groan. Had somebody been shot?

The thief was running away. Sir Thomas signalled for his dog to follow, and the keen hound gladly gave chase. Sir Thomas wished he had been on horseback as he would have been able to catch the blackguard, but he knew he was too slow on foot. He saw Ben run past with his lurcher, following the path of the gunman. Ned and Isaac followed them.

The farmers regrouped at the gate. Joe asked, 'Who got shot?' but there was no reply. 'Right, who's missing then?'

Sir Thomas replied, 'The young lad's alright. He ran down the field after the blasted thief.'

'I'm fine,' said Jacob, 'and so are Isaac and Ned. They followed the boy.'

'I'm alright,' said Tom.

'So that leaves...Mr Peart! Where's Mr Peart?' implored Joe. Silence. 'Mr Peart!' he shouted at the top of his voice, and the words echoed into the night, but there was no reply. Joe turned around in a circle in a vain attempt to see into the darkness. 'Where's Mr Peart? Does anyone know?'

'He was just across from me,' replied Sir Thomas. 'After the whistle sounded, I saw him advance. Find the lamps lads, and bring them over this way. We'll find him.'

Somewhere close by, a dog whined. 'Tip, where are you lad?' said Joe. Mr Peart's dog ran up to Joe and looked up at him; his eyes pleaded with Joe to follow him. Jacob picked up a lamp. The dog turned and led the men to his master. Mr Peart was lying on the ground when they found him. He was not moving; he was not conscious; he was not breathing. There was a dark patch on the front of his coat where a bullet had entered his chest. He was dead.

The men stood and looked down at the body of their friend in disbelief. Mr Peart had been shot and killed by the thief.

'He can't be dead!' Joe fell onto his knees beside the body, placed his head on Mr Peart's shoulder and cried. The others looked on helplessly.

Jacob wandered away, cursing to himself about the injustice of it all. Mr Peart, his employer, had been killed by a common thief.

His voice breaking with emotion, Joe said, 'He's been like a father to me since me own father died. He's…he was such a good man.'

'One of the best,' said Sir Thomas. The others nodded in agreement.

'So, what happens now?' asked Jacob, his voice still tinged with anger.

'We need to get him down from here,' said Sir Thomas. 'We need to tell his family what has happened, and then we need to bring the man who did this to justice!'

'Let's hope the others have managed to catch him,' said Tom.

'Aye, I hope our Isaac has him by the neck,' said Jacob. 'The bastard will hang for this!'

'Sir Thomas is right.' said Tom. 'We need to get him down from here. There are four of us. Do you think we should carry him or would it be better to fetch a horse up?' Tom looked at Sir Thomas as he was the oldest man present.

'I think we should carry him down,' replied Sir Thomas. 'It'll be quicker. Mrs Peart should know what's happened before word spreads — you know what it's like around here. Joe and Jacob hold him under his arms. Tom and I will take his legs.' When everyone was in place, he said, 'Alright, everyone — lift!'

They slowly carried Mr Peart down through the pasture and into a meadow belonging to Springbank Farm, one or another of them stumbling several times on the way.

The unmistakable sound of a gunshot reverberated through the valley.

'Where did that come from?' asked Jacob.

They stopped and lowered the body to the ground. In the distance, the men could hear a dog whining and scratching at what sounded like wood. There was a barn a couple of fields down from them.

'I'll stay with Mr Peart,' said Joe. 'I can't leave him here, it's not right. You go and see what's going on.'

The three men walked quickly down the fields, and when they got closer, they saw Ben kneeling on the ground sobbing. Tom walked over to the boy and put his hand on his shoulder. Ben was leaning over Fly, and when he looked up, tears were streaming down his face. He cried, 'He shot Fly. Fly grabbed his leg and the bastard shot him!' The dog was dead.

Sir Thomas's hound scratched at the wooden door. He wagged his tail as his master approached and sat down, looking proud that he had found the thief. 'He must be hiding in the barn,' said Sir Thomas.

The three men approached the barn quietly. 'Good boy,' whispered Sir Thomas as he went to look through the gap between the doors. He could see that the door at the back of the barn was wide open.

'We'd better catch him,' said Tom. 'It's not just stealing sheep that he's wanted for now — it's murder! He shot Mr Peart and he's dead.'

Isaac and Ned turned to Tom in disbelief and swore to themselves as the news began to sink in.

Sir Thomas opened the barn door and took his dog through the barn and followed him out of the back door. All eyes were on the hound as he sniffed the ground in search of a scent to follow. He went around in circles.

'Maybe he just opened the door to make us think he'd gone that way,' suggested Tom. 'He might still be hiding in the barn.'

The men carried out a thorough search of the barn but to no avail. The gunman had disappeared. They gathered together beside Ben and his dog.

'Did anyone get a look at him?' asked Sir Thomas. 'Did anyone recognise him?'

There was no answer.

'I know it was dark and everything happened so quickly, but anything at all might help.'

'He was tall and thin,' said Isaac. 'That's all I can say.'

'And a good runner,' added Jacob.

'That's a start, I suppose,' said Sir Thomas. 'Ned, could

you go and ask the constable to come to Springbank Farm? Tell him it's urgent and to come straightaway. I'll tell him what's happened when he gets there. And then go to Doctor Rutherford's. Tell him to go to the farm too. Tell him that Mr Peart is dead. Isaac, could you help the lad bury his dog? The rest of us had better get Mr Peart home.'

* * *

While the men had been hunting for sheep rustlers, Connie had gone over to Springbank Farm to keep her mother company. When Joe returned, he found them sitting in the kitchen together. They were sewing in the lamplight. Connie passed a needle that she had just threaded back to Mrs Peart while Mrs Peart held the cloth as far away from her as she could reach and strained her eyes to see the stitching that she had already done. This was probably the most peaceful scene that Joe had ever witnessed between the two ladies in all the time he had known them. He moved forward into the room, and they looked up from their work.

'You're back early, Joe. I'll put the kettle on,' said Mrs Peart, as she put her sewing down on the table and stood up. 'Any luck tonight?'

'Please, Mrs Peart, you'd better sit down.'

The tone of his voice, rather than his words, made the women realise that something bad had happened. Mrs Peart took Connie's hand and held it tightly.

'I'm afraid I've got some bad news — very bad news.'

'What's wrong, Joe?' Connie asked impatiently. 'What's happened?'

Joe cleared his throat. 'It's Mr Peart. He was shot on the fell.

155

I'm sorry, but he's dead.' He waited for the words to sink in before adding, 'He didn't suffer.'

Connie cried, 'Father, oh no, not my father.' She burst into tears and ran upstairs to her old room.

Mrs Peart stood up clumsily, knocking her sewing off the table, and asked, 'But — but who shot him?'

'We don't know. It was the sheep rustler — but he got away.'

'Where is he?'

By the look of despair on her face, he realised she meant her husband and not the killer. 'They've carried him down. He's outside.'

'No, he can't stay outside. Bring him in,' ordered Mrs Peart. 'He should be in here.'

Joe went to the door and motioned for the men to bring the body inside. They carried him into the parlour and laid him down on the sofa. Mrs Peart sat beside her husband and took hold of his lifeless hand. She wept quietly. Joe put his hand on her shoulder and, after a few words of condolence, the men left her to grieve.

Doctor Rutherford called at the farmhouse that evening. After listening to Sir Thomas's account of events, he confirmed the death, signed the paperwork and gave Connie a sedative to help her sleep. As he left, he said he would ask the undertaker to visit first thing in the morning.

* * *

It was dawn by the time Ben returned to The Moss. Over breakfast, Ben told Lizzie and Mary the story. They were horrified to learn that the thief had killed Mr Peart and Ben's dog.

As Lizzie fussed over Ben, who was upset at losing Fly, Mary could tell that her aunt was just relieved that Ben had returned home safely. He could have been shot too.

Mary's thoughts were on Mr Peart, who had been a good man and a decent employer. She had liked and respected him. Poor Mrs Peart— she would be lost without him. Mary felt sorry that she couldn't go and help her, but she wouldn't be welcome after the way she had run away. She couldn't even go to the funeral because Joe and Connie would be there.

St Andrew's church didn't have enough seating for everyone who turned out for Mr Peart's funeral. The women and the elderly sat in the pews. Men stood in the aisle, at the back and even in the porch. Mr Peart had been a farmer, a landowner, a gentleman and a dale's man born and bred. He was well-known and well-respected by all. The service was long and very moving.

Mary stood behind a tree in the churchyard, watching from a distance. She knew she couldn't attend the funeral, but she wanted to pay her respects to Mr Peart, a man who she had greatly admired.

Mr Jeremiah Peart was laid to rest in a burial plot near the church door, with his family and friends around the graveside. After the committal, the vicar invited everyone back to Springbank Farm on behalf of the family, and most of them went back to the farmhouse for refreshments, as was the custom.

Mary saw the family leading the way down the path to the gates, followed by well over a hundred people. Their voices were subdued out of respect. She clutched Josie to her chest and began walking back to The Moss before anyone saw her.

* * *

Back at Springbank Farm, food and drinks were served in both the drawing room and dining room, but people overflowed into the kitchen and hallway. Mrs Peart couldn't remember a time when there had been so many visitors at Springbank Farm, and she was humbled by how many people had come to pay their respects to her husband. She thanked every single one of them.

When most of them had left, Mr Bainbridge, the family solicitor, gathered together Mrs Peart, Connie and Joe and asked them if there was somewhere he could speak with them privately. Mrs Peart led the way to the parlour, and she closed the door behind them, and they all took a seat.

Mr Bainbridge began, 'As you may know, Mr Peart left a will and it is customary for the will to be read to the family after the funeral has taken place. There's no need to be alarmed, I'm sure there will be no surprises in it. It's just something that must be done.'

Mrs Peart nodded her consent, and he began to read the will:

'This is the Last Will and Testament of me Jeremiah Peart of Springbank Farm in the parish of Stanhope in the County of Durham, Farmer. I give to my dear wife, Anne Peart, an annuity of fifty pounds payable half-yearly for the term of her natural life. I also give to my said wife all the household furniture, ready money and my other personal estates. It is my mind that my said wife shall live at my house for the term of her natural life without paying any rent for the same.

I give to my daughter Constance my real estate, the mes-suage house garden with all the appurtenances known as

Springbank Farm situate near Westgate in the parish of Stanhope. In the event of her marriage, my real estate will pass to her husband, for as long as he is her husband or widower, and shall be enjoyed forever by their heirs.

And I do hereby nominate and appoint my said wife sole Executrix of this my will. In witness hereof I Jeremiah Peart set and subscribe my hand and seal this third day of February in the year of our Lord One Thousand Eight Hundred and Sixty Two.

Witnesses: Joseph Bainbridge, Solicitor, Stanhope, and John Peart, Farmer, St John's Chapel.'

Mrs Peart thanked the solicitor, and they all returned to the dining room to mingle with the remaining guests.

* * *

The will was just as everyone had expected. Joe was the new owner of Springbank Farm, and it would pass to his children after him. He had been devastated by the death of Mr Peart but couldn't help smiling to himself as he topped up his glass. He had achieved his dream. Joe Milburn was now a landowner.

Chapter 22

The Moss, Lanehead
September 1873

Weeks and months had passed peacefully at The Moss, and Mary kept herself to herself. She didn't go anywhere, not even to chapel on Sundays. Mary couldn't face the disapproving looks that she knew would be directed at her. Her aunt, her cousin and her baby were all the company she wanted for now.

Since the birth, Mary had gradually started doing more and more to help out, and now she did the weekly bake and prepared meals as well as looking after Josie. Even these few tasks were difficult because Josie was a hungry baby and Mary had to feed her often. Aunt Lizzie said it was because she was small and that she had some catching up to do. If Josie cried because she was hungry, Mary fed her regardless of the time since the last feed. Listening to her baby cry made her milk flow and stain her clothes. She didn't have many clothes, and she didn't want her aunt to complain about the noise of a crying baby.

Lizzie thought babies should be swaddled at all times. In her mind, babies that were not swaddled would get all manner of conditions and ailments. Mary disagreed with her aunt; she loved to watch her baby wave her arms and legs in the air. Night-time was different, though; swaddling seemed to have a calming effect and helped Josie to sleep.

Mary thought Aunt Lizzie's ideas about childcare were old-fashioned, but she bit her tongue and kept her opinions to herself. She was so grateful to her aunt for taking her in that the last thing she wanted was to be troublesome after her aunt had been so kind.

When Mary had arrived at The Moss, Lizzie had said that she was welcome to stay for as long as she needed to, but Mary wondered if she was outstaying her welcome. Not that she had ever felt unwelcome at The Moss. Lizzie seemed to enjoy her company and appreciate her help around the place, and it was evident that she liked having a baby in the house again, but she needed to be sure that her aunt didn't mind that they were still there.

One morning, she broached the subject when they were collecting brambles, from bushes laden with fruit, on the path leading to the smallholding.

'I was thinking,' said Mary. 'Maybe I should look for another place, you know, somewhere I could work and take Josie with me.'

'Don't you like it here?' asked her aunt.

'I love it here, and you've been so good to us. It's just that I don't want to be a burden.'

'A burden? You're not a burden, lass. It's nice having you and the bairn here. It feels more like a home again. The place was so quiet with just me and Ben. When you came here, I said you're welcome to stay as long as you want, and I meant it. If you want to go, I won't stop you. If you want to stay, you're welcome to. I can't afford to pay you, but I can give you bed and board in return, and to be honest, I could do with a hand here with Ben working at the mine.'

'If you're sure, then I'm more than happy to stay. Thank you.' Mary smiled at her aunt.

The Featherstone household was not totally self-sufficient, but the smallholding provided enough food to ensure they could eat well even when money was short. The Moss was tiny compared to Springbank Farm, but it was clear that Lizzie was proud of her three acres. Every single piece of it was used for something. Potatoes, turnips, onions, carrots, cabbages, gooseberries, currants, rhubarb and herbs grew in neat rows. She had one cow that grazed alongside a few sheep and a flock of geese in a small garth. Her dozen hens were supposed to stay in the hen run, but they ranged absolutely everywhere, led by a bad-tempered cockerel called Jack. The vegetable plot was their favourite spot, and they were forever being chased out of there. Indeed, there was plenty of work to keep both Lizzie and Mary busy.

One warm, sunny Sunday in September, a surprise visitor called. There was a loud knock at the door. Mary opened it and couldn't believe her eyes. Standing there, with his cap in his hands, was Tom Milburn.

'Tom, what a surprise!'

He thought Mary looked tired and a little thinner than she had been. 'How are you, Mary?' he asked with genuine concern.

'I'm well, thank you.'

'Would you like to take a walk with me?'

Aunt Lizzie heard the question and almost shoved Mary

out of the door before she had time to reply. 'Don't worry about Josie, I'll see to her,' she called after them.

'Looks like she wants rid of me,' Mary joked. 'Where do you want to go?'

'I don't know this area very well,' said Tom. 'Where do you like to go?'

'My favourite walk is up this way. It's a steep climb but the view from the top is well worth it.' Mary led the way along the old path up to the fell. She didn't know what to say to Tom. She didn't know why he'd come to see her, and she didn't know how much he knew about her, Joe, and Josie. It was the first time that she'd felt awkward with him.

As they reached the higher ground, beautiful purple heather surrounded them. Tom talked about what they saw and heard during the walk: the weather, black grouse, roe deer and the landscape. Mary was sure he hadn't come all this way just to chat, and she was surprised that he hadn't mentioned anything to do with Westgate.

They reached a natural limestone outcrop on the hillside. The giant grey boulder protruded from the hillside and looked invitingly like a seat. 'Please sit with me, Mary. There's something we need to talk about.'

This was it. She knew Tom had a reason for coming, but she still hadn't worked out what it was. Had Joe sent him? Did Mrs Peart want her back? That was unlikely after she had left there in disgrace, she thought. Well, she was about to find out why he was here. Mary sat down nervously.

Tom took off his cap and sat beside her on the warm rock. Small, white clouds moved slowly across the blue sky. The valley below was peaceful, and there was not a soul in sight.

'This may come as a surprise, Mary, but a good one, I hope.'

Tom turned so he could look directly at her and gently took hold of her hands.

'I want to marry you,' he said with conviction and watched for her reaction. When there was none, he said, 'I want you to be my wife.'

Mary was shocked. This was totally unexpected. She hardly knew Tom. Yet, it felt like he had always been there. When she had been at Westgate, she'd only had eyes for Joe. She had never really noticed Tom — he was simply Joe's brother. She had never considered him as a husband. They were just acquaintances. No, that wasn't true. They had been friends.

She looked at him now through new eyes. His fair hair shone in the sunlight and his deep blue eyes looked back at her with understanding — and longing. He was almost as tall as his brother, and he was fit and strong.

She realised that she was staring at him. 'I'm sorry,' she said.

'You're sorry? What have you got to be sorry for?'

Before she could reply, he said, 'I can't believe what our Joe did to you. I'm so sorry for what he's put you through. I don't know what he was thinking of, marrying Connie, when he should have married you. He's a selfish fool, that's what he is.'

'I don't want anyone feeling sorry for me. I can look after myself,' Mary said, holding her head up high. 'If that's why you're here, then you're wasting your time.'

'I feel sorry for what's happened, but that's in the past now, and it's not the reason I'm here. I've always liked you, Mary — more than liked. You must have known that. I want you to be my wife. Please say yes.'

Those beautiful blue eyes were searching her face for an answer, any clue as to what she might say. Mary was speechless. She had been caught completely off guard, and her thoughts were somersaulting. She didn't know if she wanted to marry Tom. She'd only talked to him a few times before. What did she know about him? He was well-respected, he went to church, and he didn't drink to excess. He was a lead miner, he was kind, he was a good dancer and he liked to make things from wood — and he was Joe's brother. That could make life difficult. If she married Tom, Joe would be her brother-in-law.

Mary didn't feel the attraction to Tom that she had felt when she was around Joe, but she couldn't have Joe. She thought she had found her dream man when she had met him, but he had broken her heart. Would she ever be able to give her heart to someone else?

There were few men that she would seriously consider marrying. Some were cruel, and some were drunks. Some were too old, or ugly, or smelly, or foolish. Tom was none of these things. She didn't find him repulsive in any way, and now that she had actually noticed him, as a man and not just as Joe's brother, she was surprised that she thought him attractive.

But marrying Tom would mean settling for a marriage of convenience, and she had always dreamed of marrying for love. She liked Tom, but she didn't love him. He didn't love her either, he just felt sorry for her, and he wanted to make up for what his brother had done. That was why he had asked her to marry him.

Since Joe's betrayal, she had never considered marriage, but thinking about it seriously, who else would take on a fallen woman with a bastard child? She had Josie's future to think about too. It would be much easier for Josie to grow up with a father — and this might be their only chance. Tom was a decent man who wanted a wife; she needed a husband, and Josie needed a father. It made perfect sense — it was a convenient solution for them all.

She had made her decision.

Still holding her hands, Tom stood up and faced her. 'I take it your silence means you're thinking about it, at least?'

'Tom, I don't know you very well, but I do know that you're a good man and I want you to know that I appreciate your offer.'

Tom lifted her hands to his mouth and kissed them. He looked into her eyes. 'Please, Mary, don't say no. You don't need to give me an answer now. I can come back next Sunday?'

'There's no need for that. I've made up my mind.'

Tom's face fell.

Mary quickly added, 'Yes, Tom, I'll marry you.'

Tom smiled broadly and leaned forward, wrapping Mary in his arms. He kissed her firmly on the lips and then stayed there, holding her, enjoying the feel of her body pressed against his.

'I'll be a good husband to you,' he said, 'and a good father to Josie, I promise. We'll be happy together.'

When they returned to The Moss, Mary invited Tom into the house. He followed her through the low door and into a pleasant kitchen, where she gestured for him to sit down.

A whimper came from a room at the back of the house.

'Aren't you going to introduce us?' Tom said kindly.

Mary went to fetch her daughter. She carried Josie out and leaned over Tom's chair so that he could see her. 'Josie Watson, this is your Uncle Tom.'

'Uncle Tom? Don't you mean Dada?' he asked.

'Soon-to-be-Dada,' she said and smiled at him.

'And when we're married, I'd like her to have my name — she'll be Josie Milburn.'

'Thank you, I'd like that,' said Mary. She was very touched that Tom had even thought of it.

She placed Josie in Tom's arms, and he held her for the remainder of his visit, talking to her and cooing. Mary wished that everyone would accept her and her baby as quickly as Tom had.

Chapter 23

Tom came to visit Mary every Sunday. Leaving Josie in Lizzie's care, they walked together and talked for hours. On the last Sunday before their wedding day, Tom came to the door as usual, but he was hiding something under his jacket.

'Hello Mary,' he said as he kissed her on the cheek. 'I'd like to see Ben, if he's around?'

'Yes, he's cleaning out the hen house.' Wondering what this was about, she said, 'I'll come with you.'

Ben saw Tom and Mary walking towards him and stopped shovelling. 'Hello, Tom,' he said.

'Morning, Ben,' said Tom, smiling broadly. 'I have a surprise for you.'

'Oh! What is it?'

Then, they all heard a slight whine coming from inside Tom's jacket. Ben's eyes lit up.

'A pup?' Ben asked expectantly.

Tom removed his hand from under his jacket and in it was a small black and white collie pup. He held it out to Ben.

'Is it for me?'

'Yes, she's yours. Our Floss had a litter and I've been waiting until they were old enough to leave her.'

Ben took the pup into his hands and looked into her face. The puppy stuck out her tongue, and Ben laughed. The puppy got excited and tried to wriggle towards him to lick his face.

'I think she likes me.' Ben grinned. 'Thanks, Tom, she's great!'

'You're welcome, lad.'

Mary and Tom watched Ben carry the puppy around the smallholding, introducing her to the animals, the hen house cleaning forgotten.

'That was a lovely thing to do, Tom. He's been so sad since he lost Fly.'

'It's the least I could do after what happened. Are you ready to go?'

Tom held out his hand, and Mary took it. They set off on their walk hand in hand. Mary realised they had wandered onto the track that she'd taken when she'd fled from Springbank Farm. That felt like such a long time ago, and she thought about how much her life had changed since then. She was a mother now and soon to become a married woman. In just a few days, she and Tom would say their marriage vows and be man and wife.

Mary spotted a hole in the hillside, the entrance to the mine where she had sheltered on that snowy night.

'This is where I stayed that night after I left the farm,' she told Tom. 'I know I shouldn't have. Father used to say that it was bad luck for women to go in the mines. I don't know if he really believed that or if he just wanted to scare us from going in them because they can be dangerous.'

'Aye, you have to be careful in old mines,' said Tom. 'Even experienced miners are wary about going into the old man's workings.'

'I remembered Father saying that it was warmer underground in the mines than outside in the winter. And I was so cold by the time I got here that I didn't care about his warnings — I went in anyway.'

'Your father was right about the temperature. It doesn't change much underground all year round, so in summer it feels colder than outside and in winter it feels warmer. I'm pleased you remembered what he said and that you weren't too scared to go in because if you'd stayed outside in the snow that night, I dread to think what would have happened. You could have died up here. You definitely did the right thing.'

'I didn't have a light,' said Mary, remembering how scared she'd been. 'I had to feel my way in by touching the walls and feeling the ground with my feet, step by step.'

Tom looked closely at the mine entrance. 'That's a really old tunnel. I think it must be heading towards Pearson's vein.' Taking a candle from his pocket, he lit it with a match and walked towards the adit. 'You're lucky it was an old mine, really. The more recent ones sometimes have shafts going down to the lower levels. They're death traps.'

'I was careful, and thankfully I was alright. But if the shafts are so dangerous, why don't the miners fall down them?'

'It has happened,' said Tom. 'Most are covered over with timber when they're not being used, but wooden planks rot away pretty quickly when there's water running over them.'

Tom led the way into the tunnel. Ferns were growing from the stone archway, as far as light could penetrate the mine. Spiders sat waiting for prey at the centre of their webs. Mary was pleased that she hadn't seen them when she had been there alone; it didn't seem anywhere near as scary with Tom by her side. She followed close behind him so that she could see the light from his candle. The flame flickered as he moved onward, deeper into the mine.

'I've never been in this one before,' he said. 'A lot of these old levels cave in at the entrances, where the timber supports or stone arching would have been, but once you get inside them, into the solid rock, they're very well built. Amazing what they could do with just hand tools. They didn't have powder for blasting the rock, back then. Look, you can see the chisel marks on the walls.' Tom held the candle next to the wall, and Mary reached out and ran her fingers along the wall, feeling the grooves left by ancient chisels on the cold, damp stone.

Referring to the past miners of the dale, Tom continued, 'I've got a lot of respect for the old man. He knew what he was doing — where the veins were and everything. They didn't have the advancements that we have, for pumping water and blasting rock, but they used their brains. You know, some miners won't set foot in the old man's workings, won't go anywhere near them. I don't know why. I think they're interesting. Mind your head in here. There's not much height to these old tunnels and they're narrow. Did you know that they're called coffin levels?'

'Why? Because men died in them?' asked Mary.

'No. Well, I suppose they might have, but that's not the reason. It's because they're shaped like a coffin stood on end: narrow at the top, widest at the shoulders and narrow at the bottom. They were made just big enough for a man to walk through.'

After they had walked about thirty feet into the tunnel, there were no longer any signs of life; underground was an inhospitable place.

'What's that smell?' asked Mary. 'I noticed it the last time I was in here. Is it mould?'

'That's a dead smell, maybe a ewe that came in here to die. They look for places to shelter when they're on their last legs.'

She heard water dripping somewhere ahead and looked forward. There was something small and white on the ground up ahead. When they reached it, Tom bent down and picked it up. It was a handkerchief.

'That's mine,' said Mary. 'This must be where I slept.'

'You chose a good spot. It's nice and dry here. There's water further on, but it must have found a way down into the limestone further back. This would have been a drainage level when it was dug, and the water would have run along here.'

Tom moved the candle around the small space and saw something else just a little further up the level. He stepped forward, hoping he was wrong. But he wasn't. 'Mary, you'd better go back now. I'll be out soon.'

Before he had time to stop her, Mary leaned past him to see what was there. She couldn't believe her eyes. The body of a woman was lying on the floor of the tunnel. Her clothes were old and tattered, and blonde curls covered a skeletal face.

Had she been in the mine when Mary had spent the night there? Oh no, the smell! She had spent the night in an abandoned mine with a corpse. Tom took her in his arms and comforted her.

When she could speak, Mary said, 'Thank God I didn't walk any further. If I'd come across her that night, I would have died of fright. I wonder if she came in here to shelter, like I did.'

'Who knows? If her clothes were wet, the cold could have killed her.'

Mary was pleased she had taken off her wet cloak that night, or she could have been rotting in here too.

'The poor woman, whoever she is,' said Tom. 'Nobody deserves to die in a place like this, all alone.'

'It's very sad. What should we do? We can't leave her in here.'

'We have to, for now. I'll walk you home and when I get back to Westgate, I'll let the constable know . He might be able to find out who she is and, at the very least, he'll make sure she's taken out of here and given a decent burial.'

Chapter 24

The following day, Tom met Robert Emerson. He had a stretcher and sheet ready to take with them to the mine. When they arrived at the entrance, Robert was surprised at how small the opening to the level was. He was a large man, and he struggled to get into the tunnel, frequently bumping his head and cursing as he followed Tom to where the body lay. He wondered how miners could work in these places almost every day of their lives and was thankful he didn't have to spend much time underground.

Robert held a candle by the head of the corpse.

'She's been here a while. You wouldn't recognise her even if she was your wife. Let's get her onto the stretcher and get her out of here.'

They lifted her carefully by her clothes onto a stretcher and began the journey back through the tunnel. They walked awkwardly in the restricted space.

'They say it's unlucky for women to go in the mines,' said Robert. 'It certainly was for this one.'

'Aye,' agreed Tom.

It wasn't long before Robert said, 'I can't wait to get out of here. I need some fresh air. I don't know how you miners stand working underground.'

'You get used to it. And it's interesting when you know about the veins and the minerals.'

'I'll take your word for that, lad.'

When they reached the surface, the policeman covered the stretcher with a sheet, and he and Tom carried it down to Westgate.

Robert's first job was to determine what had happened to this woman and then attempt to identify her. He presumed that she had got lost and died of exposure, but he had to look for evidence. He asked Doctor Rutherford to come over and help him examine the body and look for any signs of how she might have died or who she was. He made notes as they did so.

Body found in old mine above The Shieling.

Unknown female.

Bones — very little flesh.

Height approximately 5ft 4in

No distinguishing marks.

Blonde curly hair.

No grey hairs, so probably young — under 35 years?

Her clothes were basic, and they were well-worn and dirty. From the poorer end of working-class, Robert thought. During his examination of the body, he felt something in her skirt. He noticed that a small pocket had been sewn into the hem and in it was a locket. Robert thought it might be gold, and on closer inspection, he was sure it was. The initials

CF were engraved on the front, and there were hallmarks on the back. He was sure he hadn't seen it before, and the doctor didn't recognise it either.

Robert opened the locket and found a small piece of purple heather inside. His instinct told him that there was something amiss here. Why would a poor, young woman be hiding a gold locket in her skirt? He picked up his notebook and wrote a few more notes.

Fully dressed.

Clothes old and torn. Repaired in places.

Gold locket hidden in skirt. Engraved with the initials C.F.

No other items found.

Doctor Rutherford checked for broken bones and didn't find any to the torso, arms or legs. He noticed an old fracture to the lower left arm that had healed, and it had left the arm slightly bent out of shape. He felt the skull, under the full head of hair, and it moved slightly. On parting the hair, he found that the skull was fractured. She had been hit on the head with something hard, something that would have killed her outright. The woman had been murdered.

There was no way they could tell exactly how long the woman had been dead, and he guessed that it could be anywhere between six months and two years. Her clothes were similar to those worn by women in the dale now; they wouldn't be considered old-fashioned.

An old injury to lower left arm.

Left side of skull smashed in with heavy object.

Victim of Murder!

Death estimated at between 6 months and 2 years.

Robert always thought it particularly sad when he dealt with the bodies of young people. What a waste of a life! He wanted to find out who this woman was, he wanted to find out who had killed her, and why.

Chapter 25

High House Chapel, Ireshopeburn
November 1873

Mary walked from The Moss to Ireshopeburn, carrying Josie in her arms. She wore a blue dress Lizzie had made for her, with a woollen shawl over it to keep her warm until she reached the chapel. Her hair was tied up in a braided bun that shone in the autumnal sunlight.

She thought about the day ahead as she walked and was pleased that the marriage would be a private affair. She didn't want everyone in the dale talking about her and Tom. When news of the wedding got out, they would think that Tom was Josie's father, with her being just a few months old, but there would be some speculation as to why he hadn't married her before the baby had been born. Well, they could talk, thought Mary. She would rather they wondered than know the truth.

To Mary, it seemed such a long time since Tom had first come to visit her at The Moss and asked her to marry him, but it was only two months ago. During his weekly visits, Mary had got to know him better and looked forward to seeing him. She enjoyed his company, and she liked feeling loved again, but she had to remind herself that he wasn't marrying her for love. He didn't love her, he was just marrying her to put things right. It was a marriage of convenience, that's all, and after today, they would be together forever — for better or worse.

Tom and Mary had discussed their wedding day and they both agreed that they would like a quiet service at the chapel with just a few family and friends there. Tom had obtained a marriage licence so that the banns wouldn't have to be read out in chapel three times prior to the wedding. They arranged a private ceremony with the minister and only those they wanted to be there were invited by word of mouth.

Jane Milburn and George Watson were asked to be witnesses. Mary would rather her father hadn't been invited but, as she was under the age of twenty-one, she needed her father's consent to marry — so he had to be there. Lizzie had promised to make sure he turned up and she and Ben had left early that morning to go to Fell Top so that they could accompany him to the chapel.

Joe wouldn't be coming; Tom had told his brother, in no uncertain terms, that it would be better if he stayed away.

When Mary arrived, the guests greeted her with smiles. She handed Josie to Ben, who kindly offered to hold her during the service. Tom had arrived early and was waiting inside the chapel with his best man, Watson Heslop, and Reverend Hodgson. Lizzie took the shawl from Mary's shoulders and went inside with the others, leaving Mary alone with her father, whom she hadn't seen since the day she had gone to him for help — the day he had disowned her.

'Mary, I'm sorry about the way I spoke to you,' he said. 'It was the drink talkin'. I was upset, aye, but that's no excuse for what I said. I've given up drinkin'. I've not touched a drop for over two months.'

Mary wasn't sure she could forgive him for how he had treated her or her sister, but she said, 'I'm pleased to hear you've stopped drinking.'

Standing back to admire his daughter, he said, 'You look beautiful, lass. Tom's a lucky fella.'

'Thank you.'

With their truce of sorts, George took Mary's arm and led her down the aisle. They took their places, and the Reverend began the service, 'Dearly beloved, we are gathered here today in the sight of God to join this man and this woman in holy matrimony. Not to be entered into lightly, holy matrimony should be entered into solemnly and with reverence and honour. Into this holy agreement these two persons come together to be joined. If any person here can show just cause why these two people should not be joined in holy matrimony, speak now or forever hold your peace.'

Mary's heart beat faster. She was worried that someone would say that she had lain with another man and had his child out of wedlock, or that she didn't deserve to be married to a good man like Tom, or that they didn't love one another.

The room remained silent, and Reverend Hodgson continued. Mary was conscious of the friendly faces in the room. She looked at Tom, and his smile was reassuring. She felt as though she was dreaming and that she wasn't really present.

'Thomas Milburn, do you take Mary Watson to be your wedded wife, to live together in marriage? Do you promise to love her, comfort her, honour her and keep her for better or worse, for richer or poorer, in sickness and in health, and forsaking all others, be faithful only to her, for as long as you both shall live?'

Tom's voice rang out clearly, 'I do.'

'Mary Watson, do you take Thomas Milburn to be your wedded husband, to live together in marriage? Do you promise to love him, comfort him, honour him, obey him and keep him for better or worse, for richer or poorer, in sickness and in health, and forsaking all others, be faithful only to him, for as long as you both shall live?'

'I do.'

That was it; they were married. Mary sighed with relief and smiled.

Watson handed the ring to the minister, who blessed it, and then Tom reached for her hand, and he gently placed a narrow gold band on her wedding finger.

The minister took their hands and declared, 'Now that Mary and Tom have given themselves to each other by solemn vows, with the joining of hands and the giving and receiving of a ring, I pronounce that they are husband and wife, in the name of the Father, and the Son, and the Holy Spirit. Those whom God has joined together, let no man put asunder.'

Tom was smiling at her, and he looked so happy. Not waiting for the minister's words, he took a step towards her and held her firmly as he kissed her.

Everyone came up to them and offered their congratulations. Tom thanked Reverend Hodgson before leaving the chapel. When the minister opened the outer door, they were all shocked to see that a small crowd had gathered outside.

Tom and Mary hadn't wanted a big fuss because they didn't want to draw attention to the marriage. They knew it would fuel the gossip about Josie. Neither of them wanted that for their families' sake or hers. But word must have got out that the wedding was taking place and people had left what they were doing to see the wedding party at the chapel.

Tom saw Connie among the people, and it dawned on him who was responsible for drawing the crowd to the chapel. She was one of the few people who had known about the wedding and where they would be that day. He heard someone say, '… not content with one brother, she had to have them both.' At that moment, Tom realised what a vindictive person Joe had married. Connie hadn't only told everyone when the wedding would take place but she'd also named the father of Mary's baby — even though he was her husband!

Tom pointed out his horse and cart standing at the roadside. 'Lizzie, please take Mary and Josie over to the cart. Get them away from here.'

Mary started to object, but Lizzie led her away, telling her to let Tom take care of things. Ben followed them with Josie in his arms. They stood by the cart, watching and waiting. Bobby pawed at the ground, eager to be on his way.

Connie's voice could be heard above the rest. 'Tom, why did you marry your brother's whore?'

Tom walked over to her, with his new father-in-law on his heels.

'How can you do this, Connie?' asked Tom. 'We've known each other all of our lives and we're related now. You're married to me brother, for God's sake.'

'That bitch ruined my wedding day, so I'm going to ruin hers!' spat Connie.

George butted in, and said, 'There's only one bitch around here and it's not my daughter.'

The crowd cheered as he turned his back on Connie, but she leapt forward and began to hit him as hard as she could.

A large grey horse edged its way between the people in

the crowd. Joe directed Thunder towards the centre of the commotion. He reached down and grabbed Connie, pulling her up in front of him and holding her firmly as she squirmed to get free. Joe uttered words of apology to both Tom and George, and he nodded in Mary's direction before he took his wife home.

Knowing the show was over, the onlookers started to disperse. That display would undoubtedly provide them with plenty to talk about for a while, thought Mary. The bairns were still hanging around, waiting for the groom to throw some money. Tom reached into his pocket and threw a handful of change onto the road behind them and smiled as he watched the children scurry about to find the coins.

Then, he went to the cart where he found Mary and Josie with George, Lizzie and Ben. They were all mortified by what had happened, especially Mary, whose private life had been made public in a most humiliating way. Everyone was astonished at Connie's behaviour, except for Mary, who knew Connie better than most; her instincts had warned her about Connie the very first day that they'd met.

Tom and Mary said their farewells, and Tom took his new family to the house he had rented. It was a quaint cottage, standing alone on the hillside, about a mile from High House Farm. It had a garden to the front with a low wall and beautiful views of the valley below. Tom helped Mary and Josie down from the cart and saw to the horse while Mary looked around the garden. It had been neglected for some time, but she would enjoy bringing it back to life. A rose climbed up the wall between the window and the door, and a sign on the door lintel read, 'Moorside Cottage'.

Mary noticed that the horseshoe nailed to the door was

fastened the right way up and smiled. The dale's people believed horseshoes had to hang with the points upwards, in a U-shape, so the luck stayed inside. If it was turned upside down, then the luck would fall out. She hoped that it would bring them luck in this lovely little house.

Tom opened the door and effortlessly carried his bride and her infant over the threshold. 'Welcome home, Mrs Milburn.' He set her down inside and kissed her tenderly. 'I am so happy that you're here — and that you're my wife.'

'Are you hungry? Thirsty?' she asked, wanting to take care of her new husband in their new home. She laid Josie down to sleep in the front room.

'No,' replied Tom. 'There's only one thing I want right now and that is you.' He took her hand and led her upstairs.

Chapter 26

Constable Robert Emerson wrote a short article for the press and sketched the gold locket. He placed both pieces of paper in an envelope and addressed it to the 'Durham County Advertiser'.

'A body was found in a remote part of Weardale last Sunday. Police would like to discover the identity of the body which is thought to be that of a young woman. There was evidence of an old injury to the left arm, which had healed. A locket was recovered, a picture of which can be seen below. Anyone knowing of any missing person that fits this description or with any information is to contact PC Robert Emerson of Westgate.'

Robert had several posters printed at St John's Chapel, and he hung them up in the neighbouring villages. Surely, somebody must know who the woman was; somebody must miss her, he thought.

It was two days before the first person came forward. Lizzie

Featherstone knocked at his door.

'Good morning,' said the constable.

'Morning, Mr Emerson. You know our Kate never came back from Durham last year. I just wondered if....'

He had forgotten about the Featherstone girl. 'You'd better come in.'

When they were seated, Lizzie said, 'I don't know anything about the locket, but our Kate did break her arm when she was a bairn.' She rubbed her lower left arm subconsciously. 'She fell out of a tree and broke it. The doctor put a splint on, but it never straightened out quite right.'

Lizzie fiddled with the ribbons on her bonnet.

'Doctor Rutherford?' asked Robert.

'No, the one before him, Doctor Ainsley. He wasn't here long.'

'How old is your daughter, Mrs Featherstone?'

'Twenty-two.'

'And her hair, what colour is it?'

'Very fair, you'd probably call it blonde. She got that from her father's side of the family. The curls as well. I would have loved to have curls like hers, but my hair's always been as straight as a die.'

'And what about her height? How tall is she?'

'She's about the same as me.'

'I see.' Robert paused.

'Do you think it's her? Our Kate?'

The description of the girl was a good fit for the body. Lizzie didn't know anything about the locket, which was a shame, but the girl was a thief, so it wasn't unreasonable to think she could have stolen it. That could explain it. In Robert's mind, all the pieces were falling into place. Something worried him, though. He tapped his fingers on the chair arm.

He remembered that Kate Featherstone had firmly denied the charges against her and had been so shocked when the guilty verdict was pronounced that she had fainted in the courtroom. The dale's people had been as appalled as Kate had been; they couldn't believe that the young Featherstone girl would have stolen anything from the big house.

There was something else that bothered Robert. Nobody had ever found the stolen items, and the police had conducted a thorough search everywhere that Kate could have hidden them — Burnside Hall and its outbuildings, The Moss and its barns, and all the nooks and crannies on the walk between the two.

'You think it's her, don't you?'

He looked into Lizzie's desperate eyes. 'Aye, I'm afraid it could be, she fits the description. Would you recognise her clothes?'

'It depends what she was wearing. She was at Durham for a year and God only knows where she's been since then.'

Robert left the room to fetch the clothes, and he laid them out on the table.

Lizzie lifted her hand to her brow and took a deep breath before saying, 'Aye, it's her. That dress, I made it for myself years ago. It didn't fit me after I had Ben so I give it to our Kate.' Her voice broke as she finished.

Robert took her hand, 'I'm sorry, Mrs Featherstone, so very sorry.'

'Where is she?'

'She's at the undertakers, but I don't think you should go and see her. She was up there a long time.'

Lizzie's face creased up as she imagined how her beautiful

daughter might look now. Holding back tears, she asked, 'Do you know what happened to her? How she died?'

Still holding her hand, he said, 'I'm sorry to have to tell you this, but she was murdered. She was killed by a blow to the head, and then we think her body was taken into the mine to hide it.'

Lizzie was stunned at the news and sat there in silence.

After a few moments, Robert handed her the locket and asked, 'Would you mind taking a look at this, please? Just in case you remember anything.'

Lizzie took the locket and turned it around in her hands. 'I haven't seen it before. I wonder who gave it to her.'

'What makes you think someone gave it to her?'

'Well, it's got her initials engraved on it.'

'Her initials?'

Lizzie pointed at the letters. 'CF — Catherine Featherstone. We've always called her Kate, but it's short for Catherine.'

Kate. Catherine. Why hadn't he thought of that?

Perhaps Kate had been given it, but by whom? A gold locket would have been an expensive gift.

* * *

After Lizzie left Robert Emerson's house, the news of her daughter's death hit her like a hard blow. She stopped by the side of the house, leaned against the stone wall and sobbed her heart out. Kate had often been in her thoughts over the last year, but she had never imagined that something so horrendous could have happened to her.

When the tears finally stopped, Lizzie knew she must look terrible, and she couldn't go home and let Ben see her this way, so she blew her nose and turned towards Moorside Cottage, Mary's new home.

Mary answered the door and was shocked to see her aunt standing there with swollen eyes and dishevelled hair. She'd been crying and was still upset.

'Aunt Lizzie, come in. What's wrong?'

Lizzie perched on a chair by the fireside and rested her head in her hands. 'I've just had some awful news. I went to see Mr Emerson, the policeman, about the body you found. With it being a young woman and not far from here, I just wondered if it might be....'

'Oh, no.' Mary put her hand over her mouth. 'What did he say?'

'He brought out the dress that she was wearing, and it was hers. It was one I made, so there's no question it's her.'

'Aww, I'm so sorry.' Mary reached out and hugged her aunt. 'Does Ben know?'

'No, I came straight here. I couldn't go back home in this state.'

'You must tell him as soon as you get back, before word spreads and he hears it from someone else.'

'I know. He's been so angry at Kate for not coming home to help me. I don't know how he'll take this – his sister being murdered.'

'Murdered?'

'Yes, our Kate was murdered. Mr Emerson said that she'd been hit over the head and then whoever killed her must have dragged her into the mine so she wouldn't be found.'

'Oh my God! I don't know what to say. Do you want me to come back to The Moss with you?'

'No, it's alright. It might be better if it's just me there when

I tell Ben.'

'Alright, if you're sure.'

'Aye, I'm sure. Anyway, you have a husband here to look after. I'm sorry to bother you so soon after the wedding.'

'It's no bother,' said Mary. 'I'll always be here if you need me. Let me know if there's anything we can do.' Mary hugged her again, and then Lizzie set off to share the news with her son.

* * *

Another whole day passed before anyone else contacted Robert about the body. This time he opened his door to Sir Thomas Forster.

'Come in, Sir Thomas. Please sit down.'

'It's about this locket. That's why I've come to see you, Robert.'

'What about it?'

'I recognised it from the picture in the paper. It was my mother's, God rest her soul. Her name was Charlotte Forster and so her initials were CF, as on the locket.'

'I see.' The policeman scratched his head. 'You know the woman we found was Kate Featherstone, don't you?'

'Yes, I heard.'

'Kate must have stolen the locket when she worked for you. Her initials were the same, you see — Catherine Featherstone. So that explains that.'

'I'm afraid it doesn't explain anything.'

'What do you mean?' asked Robert.

'The locket was still at Burnside Hall after Kate was imprisoned. I can vouch for that.'

'So how — what — hmm.' That wasn't possible. How could the girl have had the locket in her possession when she was killed? 'When did you last see the locket?'

'When Henry told us that he intended to propose to Connie Peart, we decided to clear out one of the large bedrooms at the front of the hall. We thought it would be a good room for the newly married couple. My mother was the last to use it and some of her belongings were still in there. I found the locket in a drawer and took it downstairs. That evening, before dinner, I passed it to Henry and remarked that his new bride would have the same initials and suggested that he gave it to her after they were married. He put it in his jacket pocket and that was the last time I saw it.'

'It sounds like I'd better have a chat with Henry. I'd like to know how it got from his jacket pocket into this girl's possession. Do you know where he is?'

'Up in Newcastle, I expect,' said Sir Thomas. 'That's usually where he is when he's not at home. Oh! It didn't say what happened to the girl in the newspaper. How did she die?'

'She was murdered. She was bashed over the head with something heavy enough to kill her, and then her body was hidden in the mine so it wouldn't be found.'

'God Almighty!'

As Henry was not at Burnside Hall, Robert decided that his first call should be on Connie Peart to find out if she had been given the locket by Henry or knew what he had done with it.

The policeman walked up to Springbank Farm and was met in the yard by Tip. He squatted down and stroked the dog's head. 'How are you doing, boy? Missing your master, I'll bet, eh? Good boy.'

Joe was in the barn, and when he heard a voice outside, he came out to see who was there.

'What can we do for you, Robert?' asked Joe. 'Come on in.'

Robert followed Joe into the kitchen, and they sat at the table.

'Well, Joe, it's Connie I'd like to talk to. It's about that body your Tom found in the mine.'

'What would Connie know about that?'

'I have reason to believe she might know something about a locket that was found with the body.'

They heard hoof beats outside and, through the kitchen window, they saw Connie ride into the yard and dismount. Jacob met her and took Star into the stable while Connie walked into the house.

'We have a visitor,' said Joe. 'Robert would like to ask you about something.'

'Oh, what is it?' she asked as she removed her hat.

Robert took the locket from his pocket and placed it on the table. 'Have you seen this before?'

Connie walked over and picked it up. After a quick look, she said, 'No, I haven't.'

'Are you sure?'

'Yes, I'm sure.'

'Sir Thomas gave it to Henry around the time Henry proposed to you because if you had married him your initials would have been CF.'

Connie looked at him blankly.

'So, he didn't give it to you, then?' the constable asked.

'I've already said that I've never seen it. I turned down Henry's proposal so he's hardly likely to have given me a gift, is he? Now, if you'll excuse me, I need to change my clothes.'

Connie left the room, and the men heard her climbing the stairs.

'Well, that's that then. I'd better be on my way.' The policeman got up and made for the door.

It concerned Robert that he didn't know how Kate had got hold of the locket between being released from Durham prison and being killed in Weardale. Where did she go? Who did she meet? As he walked home, he decided that his next visit should be to the prison.

The following day, Robert took the train from Stanhope to Durham. He walked to the prison and went into the office. A large man with ruddy cheeks and a friendly smile sat at the desk.

'Hello, I'm Robert Emerson, the constable from Westgate, up in Weardale.'

'Good day, Constable. I'm Jim Stoker.' He held out his hand, and Robert shook it. 'May I ask why you're here?'

'I've come to ask about a girl that was released last year. Kate Featherstone. She was in for theft.'

'Featherstone. Yes, I remember. A pretty thing. Blonde hair. Said she was innocent, but don't they all?' He laughed. 'Has she been in trouble again?'

'You could say that. She was murdered, probably not long after she got out.'

'Sorry to hear that. So, what can I do for you?'

'Well, I was wondering if she had any visitors while she was here or if she got any letters from anyone. Is there anything you can remember that might help me find out who killed her?'

'Letters. Yes, she got a few. Not many of them do 'cos most

193

of them can't read. Her mother wrote to her regularly. I think she got one letter from a vicar. Then, there was a fella came and left a parcel for her, you know, for us to give to her when she got out.'

'Did you check the parcel? Do you know what was in it?'

'It's not my place to. Once prisoners are released, we don't have any say over what they can and can't have. They're free to do what they want once they're out, but saying that, I did have a sneaky peek.'

'What was in it?'

'There was a letter and — you'll never believe this — a gold locket!'

Well, well! So that's how Kate got it, thought Robert.

'Did you read the letter?' he asked.

'Aye, of course I did. It was from her fella wanting to meet up with her when she got out. Said something like the locket was a token of his love. Asked her to meet him somewhere up in Weardale. Very romantic.'

'Do you remember who sent it? Was it signed?'

'No, there was no name on it. She seemed to know who it was from though. She must have been the only lass in here with just the one lad on the go!' He laughed.

'Thank you. You've been very helpful.'

On the long journey back to Weardale, Robert thought about what Mr Stoker had said. He concluded that the person who wrote the letter and arranged to meet her was likely to be the murderer. So, he needed to know who had Kate been seeing and how had they got the locket.

Chapter 27

Moorside Cottage, Westgate
December 1873

As Mary waited for Tom to return from work, she thought about how well the three of them had fitted together as a family. Tom was kind and considerate to her, and he liked to entertain Josie while Mary cooked and cleaned. Josie adored her new father, and she held out her arms to be picked up by him whenever he was at home. They laughed loudly together as they pulled faces and made noises at each other. Josie's favourite at the moment was sticking out her tongue.

Mary had fallen in love with the cottage and the garden. Being on the hillside, it had the most wonderful views of the dale's landscape, and it was only a twenty-minute walk into the village to visit the shop and the library — much more convenient than anywhere else she had lived. Mary found the domestic work easy compared to what she'd done in the past. The house was small, just two rooms upstairs and two downstairs, and there wasn't much food to prepare, so she found that she had plenty of time to spend with her family. It was only a month since they had moved in, but already it felt like home.

She went to get a clean tablecloth from the drawer in the kitchen table. When she opened it she saw two tiny mice staring wide-eyed at her in surprise, then they suddenly jumped out and scarpered. She couldn't believe that they had been hiding in there all that time.

Ever since they'd moved in, she'd been looking for a nest or hole where the mice had been getting into the kitchen. The pests had been nibbling on any food left uncovered, and they left little black droppings everywhere. Occasionally, she had seen them running across the floor, but the trap in the pantry had remained empty.

As soon as Tom came home, she said, 'Tom, I found the mice!'

'Where were they?'

'You know the drawers in the table?'

Tom burst out laughing. 'We never thought to look in there.'

'They made a nest out of one of my tablecloths,' Mary said, looking affronted. 'It's ruined.'

'Never mind the cloth, we can get another one. Cheer up, at least the mice won't bother you again, not after the fright you must have given them!'

Reluctantly, Mary laughed with him.

'I've got some good news as well. You know it's a long walk to and from work at the moment — it's over an hour each way. Well, just after I rented this house, I asked the manager about getting a transfer to a mine closer to home. Today, he said that I can start at Low Rigg on Monday. It's only about quarter of an hour walk away, so I'll have much more time to spend with you and Josie.'

'That's great. Who will you be working with?'

'Lads I've known for years — Watson Heslop, who was my

best man, and his partners Harry and John from Westgate. There was an older bloke working with them, but he's had to pack it in because of his health — his breathing's bad.'

Mary served out the beef stew she had made for tea, and they sat down at the table to eat.

'If you fancy a walk on Sunday, I'd like to show you where the mine is.'

'Yes, that would be nice.'

On Sunday morning, they set off after breakfast. Tom carried Josie in one strong arm and reached for Mary's hand with the other.

'Low Rigg is one of many workings that cuts into Rigg Vein,' he explained as they walked down the hill. 'In its day, it used to be one of the best mines in the dale but there's not many men working there now. The bosses say that the cost of production has increased almost to the point that it's not worth getting the ore out anymore, but they haven't given up on it altogether. They set a couple of partnerships on at the last bargains to explore working the vein at depth. If there's more ore further down, it might still be worth keeping it open. What me and the lads will be doing is blasting a cross-cut through to the vein that's about twelve yards beyond it. That vein's been worked from the surface before, years ago, but it's never been mined underground.'

'So, you'll be the first to see it?' asked Mary.

'At that depth, yes. It's quite exciting, really. You can predict what minerals and ores should be there, but sometimes you get a surprise.'

'My father said there was silver in the mines. Is that true?'

'There's a little bit, but it's mixed in with the lead ore. They take it out at the smelting mill over at Rookhope.'

'Is there any gold?'

'No, there's not been any gold found in Weardale. Have you seen fool's gold?'

'Yes, me and Annie used to find it when we were looking for bonny bits on the spoil heaps.'

'Underground, in candlelight, it can look like the real thing,' said Tom. 'The older miners like to tease the new lads. Quite a few of them have been fooled into thinking they'd found real gold!'

Mary and Tom laughed.

Near the Middlehope Burn, they walked towards a hole in the ground, protected on three sides by wooden railings. Mary looked down the vertical shaft.

'This is the way in,' said Tom. 'It's 30 fathoms down to the level — that's 180 feet. You'd be surprised how long it'll take us to climb up all them ladders at the end of a shift!'

Mary could see that he was happy with his new job — both the work he would be doing and the men he would be working with, and she was glad for him. She was pleased that he would have more time to spend with her and Josie too.

Mary realised she was standing with her hand on her lower tummy and quickly removed it. She suspected she was pregnant but thought it best not to say anything for a while because she might be wrong and because she knew women could lose babies in the early weeks. Mary wasn't suffering from sickness this time, so her condition was easy to hide from Tom. It would be Christmas soon and, as she didn't have much to give to him, just a hat and a scarf that she had knitted, she decided that she would tell him on Christmas Day.

Chapter 28

Robert Emerson asked the villagers about Kate and whether they knew who she had been courting in the weeks leading up to her trial. Most just shook their heads and said they hadn't seen her with anyone.

He went to Burnside Hall and asked both the family and the staff if they had seen her with anybody. One of the kitchen maids said she thought Kate had met a lad a couple of times, but she didn't know who he was.

Henry Forster had returned from Newcastle, so Robert asked him if he could speak with him alone. They went into the drawing-room and sat in chairs at opposite sides of the fireplace, where a wood fire burned brightly in the grate.

'Mr Forster, I understand your father gave you a locket that belonged to your grandmother. Is that correct?'

'Yes, he did.'

'And he suggested that you should give it to Connie Peart?'

'Yes, that's right. The locket was engraved with my grandmother's initials. If we had married, Connie's initials would have been the same as my grandmother's.'

'Did you give it to Connie Peart?'

'No, I didn't.'

'What did you do with it?'

'I pawned it in Durham.'

'Whatever for?'

'For money, what else?' Henry laughed. 'It was no use to anyone else with those initials engraved on it. The gold was worth something and I wanted the money for it.'

Robert disapproved of what Henry had done, selling a family heirloom, but his story sounded credible. He knew Henry had expensive pastimes — drinking, gambling and whoring — and that he had been in many scrapes over the years. Sir Thomas had called on Robert to appease the local constabularies more times than he cared to remember.

He tried to work out how the locket could have reached Kate. Perhaps it was displayed in a pawn shop window in Durham, and Kate's lad had seen it. Realising the initials were the same as Kate's, he could have bought it for her as a love token. An expensive gift, but people did strange things when they were in love. But, he wondered, if this lad had loved her, why would he have killed her? Jealousy — had she been with another fella? Spurned — did she not return his love? Anger — had she refused his advances?

As Henry walked Robert to the door, he said, 'By the way, you wanted to know if that servant girl was seeing someone. You should talk to the Milburns.'

'Thank you for your time,' Robert inclined his head to him and walked down the drive. He left Burnside Hall with more questions than answers.

On his way home, Robert called into Mr Graham's shop for a

bottle of whisky.

'Good afternoon. I hear tell you've been asking about the Featherstone lass, wanting to know who it was she was seeing.'

Robert kicked himself. He should have come to see Mr Graham first. As the old man spent most of his time in the village shop, gossiping to his customers, he knew most folks' business. He liked to gossip as much as anyone.

'Yes, that's right,' Robert replied. 'Do you happen to know who had an interest in her?'

'As a matter of fact, I do.'

Mr Graham leaned over the counter towards the policeman and, although there was nobody else in the shop, he whispered, 'She came in here with a lad one day, not long afore she was sent to prison. It was Tom Milburn.' He raised his eyebrows and waited for a response.

'Thank you, Mr Graham.'

Robert left without his bottle. Two people had connected the Milburn brothers with Kate Featherstone. He would have to go and talk to them.

Joe was in the yard cleaning off his boots when Robert arrived at Springbank Farm. Tip ran up to greet him and sat by his legs, and Robert reached down and stroked the dog's head.

'Afternoon, Joe. Sorry to bother you again, but could I have a word?'

'Hello, Robert. I'm afraid Connie's not in. She's out riding again.'

'It's you I need to talk to this time.'

'You'd better come in, then.'

When they were seated in the farmhouse kitchen, Robert said, 'Well, I know this might be a bit delicate with you being married now, but I have to ask.'

Joe looked puzzled. 'Go on.'

'Did you know Kate Featherstone?'

'By sight, aye. She was a bonny lass.'

'Did you have any interest in her? Did you ever meet up with her?'

'No, I didn't know her, really. Don't think we ever spoke other than a 'hello' when we passed in the village.'

'You're sure about that? This is very important.'

'Aye, I'm sure. Just what are you getting at?'

'Sorry, Joe, no offence, just doing my job.'

The constable stood up and shook Joe's hand. 'Well, I'll be off.' He walked briskly out of the house and took the path that led across the fields to Moorside Cottage.

About fifteen minutes later, Robert knocked at Tom's door. Mary opened it and smiled brightly at him. 'Hello, Mr Emerson.'

'Hello, Mary. Is Tom in?'

'He's not back from work yet. He shouldn't be long if you'd like to come in and wait for him?'

'No, thank you. It's alright. I heard he's started at Low Rigg. Does he walk back this way?' he asked, pointing towards a stile leading into the field in front of the house.

'Yes, he does.'

'I'll walk down and meet him. Thank you, Mary. It's nice to see you again. I must say you're looking well — marriage must suit you!' He smiled and went to the stile. She watched him climb over and wave from the other side. She waved back and went indoors, wondering what Robert wanted with Tom.

As the constable went down the slope, he saw Tom walking towards him. Robert could see that Tom was feeling uneasy.

'Nice evening, Tom. Do you have a minute?'

'Yes, what's wrong? Is Mary alright?'

'Yes, she's fine.'

'I was worried there when I saw you walking down from the cottage.'

'There's something I need to ask you. You understand I'm just doing my job, don't you? I have to follow up every lead.'

'Aye, of course.'

'Kate Featherstone, did you know her?'

Tom sighed. 'Yes, I did.'

'Were you and her…friends?'

'Aye, I suppose you could say that. I liked her and one day I plucked up the courage to ask her if I could walk her home from work.'

'And did you walk her home?'

Tom nodded. 'I met her by the gate at Burnside Hall and walked her back up to The Moss.'

'Did anyone see you together?'

'I should think a lot of people did,' said Tom. 'We walked through the village and stopped at the shop. She'd just got paid and she wanted to get a few things for her mother.'

'Did you see her again after that?'

'No, it wasn't long before she was arrested and I never saw her again.'

'I see. Did you visit her at the prison, or write to her while she was there?'

'No, I didn't.'

'Now, are you certain about that? You didn't go to the prison and leave something at the desk for her? A gift, perhaps?'

'I've never been to Durham prison, and I've never given Kate a gift.'

'Thank you, Tom. I'll let you get home.'

Robert walked down the hill and back to his home in Westgate, totally unaware of everything he passed on the way. His mind was trying to process all the information he had received that day and work out what had happened to Kate Featherstone.

* * *

By the time Tom got home, Mary's curiosity had got the better of her, and she met him at the door.

'Hello, Tom. What did Robert want?'

'Hello, Mary,' he said as he took off his work boots and placed them just inside the doorway. 'He wanted to ask me about Kate Featherstone. He'd heard that we used to be friends.'

'You knew our Kate?'

'Yes, when she worked at the Hall. I didn't know her well, but I walked her home once. That's all there was to it. Someone must have told Robert that they'd seen us together.'

He went to wash his face and hands, which were covered in pale dust from the mine.

Mary was surprised that she felt jealous thinking about Tom and her cousin together. 'So, you were courting her?'

'No, I just walked her home that one day and I never saw her again after that.'

'But the body….'

'I had no idea that the body we found was her. Maybe I should have recognised her, I don't know, but I didn't. You saw the state of it.'

Mary checked the oven to see if their meal was ready, but

her mind was working overtime. Tom had just told her that he had been interested in Kate. Kate had been killed, and her body had been hidden and left to rot in the old mine. Tom was the one who had found Kate's body in the mine. He had said he hadn't been in that mine before. Was that the truth? She began to wonder just how well she knew the man she had married.

Chapter 29

Durham City
December 1873

A few days later, Robert found himself on the train heading for Durham again. As the train neared the station, he looked out of the window to admire the castle and cathedral that proudly watched over the medieval city like parents, having protected and guided it for centuries.

He disembarked at the station and walked to his destination. On the way, he noticed an old man roasting chestnuts on a street corner, and he was doing a good trade. The streets and the market were crowded with people milling about, carrying boxes and bags. A choir sang Christmas carols and shoppers stopped to listen; some put a coin or two in the collection tin. The butcher's shop in the marketplace had geese and chickens hanging outside its window, ready to be chosen for Christmas dinners. There was a joyful, festive feeling in the air.

Robert's first stop was at the pawnbrokers on Elvet Bridge, where he was greeted by a rotund man in his forties who looked like he enjoyed his ale.

'Good morning, I wonder if you could help me?' asked Robert. 'I believe you may have sold this locket. Do you recognise it?'

The man took the locket from Robert's hand and examined it carefully.

'Sorry, sir, it's not one that's been through my shop. I'd recognise it if it had been.'

'Are you sure? I'm carrying out a police investigation into a serious crime.'

'Yes, I'm absolutely certain.'

Robert took the locket back and placed it in his pocket. He thanked the man for his time and left the shop.

He stopped at another pawnshop on the narrow street leading to the prison. A scruffy couple were arguing behind the counter and seemed oblivious to his presence.

'Excuse me!' boomed Robert. 'I'm Constable Emerson and I'm here on police business. Could I have a moment of your time?'

The man and woman hung their heads like scolded children. 'Yes sir, but we ain't done nothin' wrong,' said the man, with a strong London accent.

'Could you have a look at this locket and tell me if you've seen it before?'

He held it out for them to see.

'I don't think so. What d'you think, Betty? Have you seen it before?'

'No, I ain't never seen it.'

'So you're telling me that you haven't sold this locket in your shop?' asked Robert for clarification.

'No, we've never seen it, never mind sold it.'

'And you're both sure of that?'

'Yes,' they answered in unison.

Robert thought the couple were up to no good but that

they were telling the truth about the locket. Where else could Henry have taken it? Robert didn't know of any more pawnbrokers in the city.

He continued walking up the road until he reached Durham prison. Jim Stoker was in the office, and he stood up as Robert entered. 'Good to see you again,' he said. 'How's the investigation going?'

'So, so,' said Robert, shaking his head. 'The evidence points towards a man, but I'm not convinced he's the killer, so I've come to ask for your help. Would you be able to identify the man you saw at the prison, the one who brought the parcel for Kate?'

'I'm fairly certain I could. I'm good at remembering faces. It's a useful talent in this job.'

'If I arrange a line-up, an identity parade, with a few men, would you be willing to come up to Stanhope and pick the man out? It'll settle things in my mind, you know, whether it's him or not.'

'Aye, I'll do that. I've seen innocent men go down too often. I'd be pleased to help you catch the man that killed that poor lass.'

'Thank you. I'll write to you with the details once I've got it set up.'

'No problem. Season's greetings to you and yours!'

'To you too,' Robert left the office, closing the door behind him.

On his way back to the railway station, he stopped at a jewellery shop in the marketplace. The sales assistant was a young gentleman who looked slightly offended when Robert asked if they bought and sold jewellery, and the assistant assured him that they only dealt in new goods. When Robert

208

explained his mission, the gentleman confirmed that Robert had visited the only two pawnshops in Durham. He had reached a dead end.

* * *

It was the Sunday morning before Christmas. Mary was in her kitchen making mince pies when she heard a knock at the door. Robert Emerson stood there, and she thought that he looked very serious.

'Hello, Mary,' he said. 'I'm sorry to bother you but I need to see Tom. Is he in?'

'He's just out the back. Would you like to come through?'

He followed her through the parlour and the kitchen to the backyard where Tom was chopping firewood.

'Tom, Mr Emerson is here.'

Tom looked up and wiped the sweat from his brow. 'Hello, Robert. I'll come inside, it's a bit nippy out here today.'

He guided the policeman to the kitchen table and invited him to sit down. Mary continued to work around them.

'This is a bit delicate and I'm sorry it's come to this. Would you prefer to talk in private?'

'No, that's not necessary. Anything you have to say to me, you can say in front of Mary.'

'Alright then, if you're sure. It's about Kate Featherstone.' He looked at Tom to make sure he wanted him to continue. Tom nodded.

'We know that a man went to the prison and left a note for Kate. He arranged to meet her when she got out. We were looking for that man and our enquiries led us to you. You are the only man that was seen with Kate before she was convicted, and we haven't been able to find anyone else that she was involved with.'

Tom and Mary looked at one another, both realising at the same time that Tom was a suspect in the murder case.

Looking Robert in the eye, Tom said, 'It wasn't me. I told you the other day that I never went to the prison. You've known me since I was a bairn, Robert. You must know I didn't do it.'

'I don't think you did, lad, but I have to follow the evidence — that's my job. Anyway, the reason I've come today is to ask you to come down to Stanhope police station tomorrow morning. I've organised a line-up. It's just so we can eliminate you from our enquiries, you understand?'

'Aye, I understand. My word's not good enough,' Tom said as he stood up.

'I'm sorry, lad. I'll pick you up at about nine.'

After Robert left, Mary took the seat he had occupied and rested her head in her hands.

'They think you killed her,' she said.

'I know they do — but I didn't. You believe me, don't you?' Mary was silent.

He went over and knelt on the stone floor next to her. Taking her hands in his, he begged, 'Please, Mary, you have to believe me.' He looked up at her pleadingly.

Mary had been thinking about nothing but Tom's involvement in Kate's death since Robert had questioned him a few days earlier. Several things didn't make sense to her.

'I'm not sure what to think, Tom. The police obviously think you had something to do with it or they wouldn't have arranged this line-up.'

'But I....'.

'Please, let me finish,' she said. 'If you had killed her, you would have known her body was in that mine. I don't think you would have taken me in there if you had known. Whoever left her there didn't want anyone to find her, ever.'

'Aye, that's true.'

'I was there with you when you found her. You were as shocked as I was when we realised there was a body down there.'

'Aye, that's true an' all.'

'I've known you for nearly two years, Tom, and I've never known you to tell a lie. So, yes, I believe you.'

'Thank you, Mary.' He put his head in her lap in relief and held her tightly.

Chapter 30

Stanhope, Weardale
December 1873

The next morning, Robert went to collect Tom from Moorside Cottage to take him down to the police house at Stanhope. Tom came out to the cart, and he was followed closely by Mary.

'Good morning. Are you ready?' Robert asked.

'Aye, I'm ready. Mary wants to come as well.'

'I'm afraid she can't, Tom. There are strict rules we have to follow — procedures, like.'

'I don't need to come into the building, I can wait outside,' said Mary. 'I can't stay here not knowing what's going on.'

'I suppose if you stay outside the police house, then there's no reason why you can't have a ride down to Stanhope with us.'

Mary was relieved that Robert had agreed to let her travel with them. She didn't want to wait at Westgate for Tom, or Robert, to return with news. She would hear the outcome much sooner if she went to Stanhope. Mary had risen very early to take Josie over to High House Farm to stay with Tom's mother for the day. Jane enjoyed looking after children, and she had a lovely way with them. Mary had promised that they would collect Josie and tell Jane what had happened as soon as they got home.

It was a blustery day, and the ride wouldn't be pleasant, but Mary wanted to be there to support her husband. She took his hand, and, for the first time that day, he smiled at her. Mary knew that he was worried; he had tossed and turned all night. Even though she trusted her husband and was sure of his innocence, she worried that he could be wrongly identified and end up being tried for murder. Tom was silent for the entire journey and held her hand tightly.

When they pulled up outside the police house, Mary thought the building looked larger and more austere than she remembered. She was afraid of what might happen to Tom if the witness identified him as the man he had seen at the prison or if the police didn't believe him when he said he wasn't the killer. However, she couldn't let him know that she was afraid. She would stand by him and support him because she believed he was innocent. She kissed him and said quietly, 'Don't worry. It'll be fine.'

Mary watched as Robert led Tom inside, and then she waited.

* * *

Robert took Tom into a room at the back of the building, where five men were waiting to take place in the line-up. There were always plenty of volunteers to participate because the pay was a shilling, and all they had to do was stand still for a few minutes and keep their faces straight. They would be home in less than an hour.

Robert explained to the men what they had to do. They could sit and relax until the witness arrived, but they couldn't talk amongst themselves. When they heard a knock at the door, they had to stand in a line and look directly in front of them. They were not to look at the witness or speak to him, and they were not to smile or frown.

The prison officer arrived at precisely ten-thirty and shook Robert's hand warmly.

'Good morning, Constable. It's good to see you again.'

'Good morning, Mr Stoker. Thank you for coming all this way.'

'Think nothing of it. I only hope I can help. Have you got the men ready for me?'

'Yes, they're in the back room.'

Robert knocked loudly at the door and then waited a full minute before he opened it. He was pleased to see the six men standing as he had asked, and he waved Mr Stoker in.

The prison officer walked into the room and glanced down the line. Almost immediately, he shook his head and said, 'He's not here.'

Tom let out the breath he had been holding.

'Don't you want to have a better look at them?'

'I don't need to. He's not here. I saw the man who was at the prison riding up the street about an hour ago. I thought it was strange that he was going the wrong way, but I assumed he would be back in time for the line-up.'

Robert was so pleased that Mr Stoker hadn't picked out Tom. There was no real evidence against him, and he was only a suspect because he was the only man Kate had been seen with. She must have been seeing someone else, though, but who?

Robert took the prison officer into the front room where they could talk privately and said, 'Let me get this straight. You said in there that you've seen the man who brought the parcel to the prison here, at Stanhope, this morning?'

'Aye, I did.'

'Can you give me a description of him?'

'Yes, he was tall, lean, very dark hair, almost black, and cut short, clean shaven, mid to late twenties, I'd say. He was riding a black horse, a smart-looking beast.'

'I see.'

Robert thought for a while — black horse, tall, dark, thin, in his twenties. Good God! Henry Forster.

Henry hadn't pawned the locket as he had said, and that's why the people at the pawnshops hadn't recognised it. Instead, he had taken it to the prison and left it for Kate — but why? Was he the man she was seeing? It seemed very unlikely, with him being gentry and her being a servant, but they had been living under the same roof. If Henry had been taking advantage of the girl, Robert wouldn't have been surprised in the least. It went on in big houses all the time, and everyone turned a blind eye to it. But giving the lass a gold necklace as a token of his love didn't seem like something Henry Forster would do.

'Thank you very much for coming today,' said Robert. 'The description you've given me is very interesting.' He handed the man a bottle of whisky. 'Please, take that for your trouble.'

'It was no trouble at all, but thank you. I hope you get your man.' Jim Stoker left to catch the train back to Durham.

* * *

Mary saw the man she thought was the witness leave the police station carrying a bottle under his arm. She played with the scarf around her neck as she watched him walk down the road towards the railway station. She was getting more and more anxious as time passed. Then, she saw a group of men walk out of the door and she looked for Tom, and he was there amongst them. When he caught her eye, he grinned. Thank God, she thought, as she crossed the road to meet him.

'Well, what happened?'

'He didn't pick anyone out. He said the man that he'd seen at the prison wasn't in the room but that he'd seen him earlier today — here in Stanhope.'

'Tom, that's great news. You're not a suspect anymore.'

Even though they were in the middle of the town, she reached up and kissed him soundly, and he pulled her towards him and gave her a huge hug. When he released her, she said, 'That means it's someone local though that they're looking for, doesn't it?'

'Aye, I suppose it does. I wonder who could do something like that.'

'I don't know. I hope it's not someone we know.'

They waited for Robert to finish his paperwork, and then they travelled back up the dale to Westgate. Robert repeatedly apologised for inconveniencing them so soon after their wedding and so close to Christmas and made it clear that he was just doing his job.

Tom and Mary were just pleased to be going home together, knowing that Tom was no longer in danger.

Chapter 31

Moorside Cottage, Westgate
Christmas 1873

When Christmas Day finally arrived, Tom found Mary in the kitchen cooking breakfast. She was singing, and Tom smiled to himself; it was good to see that she was happy. Mary must have felt his presence because she turned around and looked embarrassed that he'd caught her singing.

'Happy Christmas to my beautiful wife,' he said and kissed Mary on the lips.

'Merry Christmas, Tom. Please get your breakfast before it gets cold.'

'Is Josie still asleep?' he asked.

'Yes, I'll get her up after we've eaten.'

Mary smiled throughout the meal. When they'd finished eating, Tom said, 'What is it? Have I got egg on my face or something?'

Mary laughed. 'No, it's nothing like that. I have something to tell you.' She went to his chair and stood next to him with a massive grin on her face. 'You're going to be a father.'

He looked up at her with wonder in his eyes. 'You're going to have a baby?'

'Yes, we are going to have a baby,' she beamed.

He put his arms around her and held her as though she was the most precious thing in the world, and as far as he was concerned, she was.

Christmas Day was one of the best days of their lives. They swapped gifts in the morning. Mary gave him the scarf and hat that she had knitted, and he loved them. They were useful presents, and he would think of her every time he wore them. Tom had made a wooden rattle and a teething ring for Josie, and Mary had crocheted a beautiful shawl for her.

Tom had made Mary's gift before they were married. It was a practical gift, and he hoped she'd like it. He'd carried it over from High House the night before and hidden it in the shed. He went outside to fetch it. She looked surprised when he carried in a matting frame, but it was no ordinary matting frame; made from polished oak, he'd carved an intricate pattern on three sides, and at the top, he had written 'Tom & Mary Milburn 1873'.

'That's wonderful, Tom.' Running her fingers over the lettering, she said, 'I'll treasure this, always.'

'And that's not all,' he said.

Tom left the house and came back a few minutes later carrying a large cat. 'This is Tabby and he's going to get rid of those pesky mice for you!'

When Tom put the cat down on the ground, it strolled over to Josie, who was sitting on the floor and rubbed around her. She laughed and tried to pull his tail, but he wagged it so quickly that she couldn't catch it, making her laugh even more. Tom and Mary laughed too.

Tom's mother had sent over a plucked chicken and a sack of vegetables, and Mary cooked a tasty roast chicken dinner.

She'd prepared a traditional Christmas pudding for afters, and they spent the rest of the day in front of the fire feeling sated and content.

Chapter 32

Westgate
January 1874

Tom kissed Mary before he picked up his bait bag and left for work. It was a mizzly morning and he would be soaked through before he got to the mine. He walked briskly to the shaft to meet his partners. Harry, John and Watson were waiting by the mine entrance. They exchanged pleasantries before descending the shaft, each of them waiting patiently until it was his turn to enter the dark hole in the ground and climb down the series of slippery wooden ladders into the mine below. They lit their candles to light their way to the cross-cut where they were working.

All morning, the miners worked in pairs to drill shot holes in the rock face. The miners' tools were basic — a long, iron chisel that they called a jumper and a heavy hammer. It was a long, slow process. When the holes were finally ready, deep enough to take a charge, Harry fastened his candle to the rock with a lump of clay and took the gunpowder out of his bag. He carefully placed the powder at the back of the shot hole, laid a fuse and then backfilled the hole with clay. His partners moved to a safe distance from the blast site, back to Rigg vein where the air was better. Harry lit the fuse and walked quickly to where they waited.

The blast was deafening, and the ground shook. The rumble of falling rocks echoed through the tunnels. The air was filled with dust, and the miners couldn't see each other. They heard a groan, and then there was silence.

'Harry, are you alright?' shouted John.

'I'm fine, John. I'm standin' here right beside you.'

'Watson, where are you?' asked John.

'Right here, mate,' replied Watson. 'Me arm got hit with somethin' — it feels like it's bleedin', but it's not bad.'

'Was it you that shouted?'

'No, it wasn't me.'

'Tom, what about you?' asked John.

There was no reply.

All three men started to shout for their missing partner, but their calls were met with silence. The air was thick with dust, and they were unable to see anything. They continued to call Tom's name as they got onto their knees and felt the ground around them in a desperate attempt to find Tom.

'He was stood talkin' to me a few minutes ago,' said Watson. 'He can't be far from here.'

'These rocks shouldn't be here,' said Harry, as he stumbled into a pile of rocks in the tunnel. 'There must have been a fall. Get over here and see if you can find Tom!'

Under his breath, Watson said, 'Dear God!'

The men felt among the rubble to try to find Tom, but they couldn't start to move the rocks until the air cleared. They continued their search for their friend and hoped the dust would settle soon so that they could see where he was.

'I'm goin' out to get help,' said Harry. 'We're goin' to need more men and a stretcher.'

As visibility returned, the size of the rockfall shocked John and Watson. They had seen falls before, but nothing on this scale — the tunnel was almost blocked.

'That's Tom's hat!' exclaimed Watson. He pulled at it to release it from the rocks and held it to his chest. 'Poor Tom, he must be under there.'

They started to remove the rocks carefully, one by one, so as not to cause any more injury to their buried friend.

* * *

Mary was changing Josie's nappy when she heard voices outside the cottage. She recognised two of Jacob's children standing at her door, arguing over who was going to knock. Smiling at their antics, Mary went to the door and opened it. She greeted them with, 'Hello!'

'Hello, Mrs Milburn,' said the boy. 'Harry told me to come and fetch you. He said there's been an accident at the mine and Mr Milburn's missin'.'

Mary couldn't take in the words. Tom had been in a mine accident, she understood, but missing? It didn't make any sense. How could he be missing?

'Mrs Milburn, it's alright,' said his sister. 'Me mother told me to stay here and look after the bairn for you. I look after me baby sister when I'm not at school.'

Mary thought the girl didn't look old enough to care for Josie, but what choice did she have? She had to go to the mine and find out what was going on.

'Thank you. What's your name?' asked Mary.

'I'm Sarah Rowell and I'm nearly eight years old,' the girl

replied with a toothless smile.

'Thank you, Sarah. This is Josie.' Mary grabbed her shawl and rushed out of the house. She ran most of the way to the mine. There were already a few people at the entrance, waiting for news. Mary asked them what going on, and one of the villagers explained that there had been a rockfall in the mine and that Tom was still missing.

That could only mean one thing, that he was buried under the rocks, buried alive and unable to move, or worse still, he could be dead. Please, please, God, let them find him alive, she thought.

'They'll have to bring him out of Grey's Level. They'll never lift him up the shaft,' said an old miner.

The bystanders made their way down the hillside to the water level, and Mary followed. Because of the recent downpours, water gushed from the mine entrance and splashed over the wooden leat that carried the water to the mill.

The morning's mizzle had turned to rain, and there was a cold breeze blowing down the hillside. Mary didn't feel it. She stood with her arms crossed over her chest as though hugging herself. All she wanted was to see Tom.

She remembered the day Tom had come to The Moss to propose to her. Was it just four months ago? She had hardly known him then. He promised her that he would be a good husband and a good father, and he had kept his word.

She and Tom had a perfect marriage of convenience. They liked each other and got on well together. After being with Joe, she didn't think she would like to be intimate with another man. That had worried her before the wedding, but it needn't have. It was clear that Tom desired her; he was a good lover and left her feeling fulfilled. She wanted him more and more as time went by. Mary was sure he cared about her even though he had only married her to make up for Joe's mistreatment of her. When she had told Tom that she was pregnant, he had looked at her and held her as though she was special to him. Please let him live to see his child.

* * *

Harry returned with another team of miners, and the men worked relentlessly to clear the fallen rocks from the dry and dusty tunnel. A couple of boys brought some food and water down for them, for which they were grateful. It was tiring work, but the miners wouldn't rest until they found Tom.

Watson moved a large boulder and saw Tom's twisted leg underneath it. 'Over here!' he shouted. 'I've found him. I've found Tom.'

They all concentrated on the area where Tom was lying. Stones were passed back from one man to another and stacked neatly in piles. The work was efficient and methodical because they were well-practised at it.

As the dust cleared further, Harry realised that just Tom's legs were buried under the pile of rocks. His torso was visible beyond the fall. There was blood on his brow. Harry clambered over the rocks to reach him.

* * *

Mary had been waiting outside the mine most of the day. The boys who had taken the food in for the rescuers returned without news, and Mary continued to wait. She was soaked through to the skin and very cold.

Joe pulled up with his horse and cart and jumped down. He walked straight over to Mary, 'What's happenin'? Have they found him yet?'

'No news,' she replied. She glanced at the cart and realised that Joe had brought it to take Tom home, whatever the outcome, but she couldn't think about that. 'Thanks for coming,' she said.

'Of course, I'd come. He's me brother,' said Joe. Looking at Mary's sodden clothes, he said, 'You're drenched, lass, you'll catch your death. Here, put me cloak on — you're fair nithered.'

Mary stood still while he fastened the cloak around her as if she was a child, and she noticed that the attraction that had once been so strong between them had gone. She felt nothing.

'I dropped me mother off at your place,' he said. 'She'll look after the bairn 'til we get back.'

They stood side by side and waited. Nobody seemed to notice them. All the gossip of the previous year was seemingly forgotten now that there was something serious going on.

As dusk began to fall, someone shouted, 'I think they're comin' out. I can see a light down yonder. Aye, they're on their way out!'

Everyone huddled at the entrance, looking into the tunnel, watching the men's slow progress. Eventually, the miners reached the adit and carried Tom out on a stretcher. There were murmurs from the crowd, and they stepped back to let Mary get to the stretcher. She wasn't sure if Tom was dead or alive. Watson took her hand, 'Mary, he's alive.' She looked up at Watson in disbelief. 'He's in a bad way though. He was knocked out and he hasn't come round yet. His leg's bad an' all. It's broken.'

Harry turned to Joe, 'Best get him home and into a warm bed. I'll let the doctor know to come up.'

The exhausted miners lifted Tom into the back of Joe's cart and threw some blankets over him. Mary climbed in next to him and lifted her husband's head into her lap. Watson climbed up front with Joe to help to carry Tom into the house when they got him home.

Slowly, Joe drove them back to Moorside Cottage — the horse at a gentle walk. He was careful to avoid holes and grooves in the road, which would jostle the cart and cause more injury to his brother. Tom's head rested on Mary's lap, and she held his hand to her face. He looked so still and so pale, and there was blood all over his brow. Were they sure he was alive? His hand felt warm against her cheek, and she could feel the pulse in his wrist. He was alive. Thank God, he was alive.

When they arrived at the cottage, Jane Milburn met them at the door. She saw her son lying in the cart with Mary huddled over him. She clutched her chest as she asked nervously, 'How is he?'

Joe climbed down and shouted, 'He's alive, Mother. He's unconscious and it might be better if he stays that way until the doctor's finished with him. His leg's broken.'

The two men struggled to carry Tom into the house and upstairs to his bed. When they came down, Mary and Jane went up to remove his dirty clothes and to discover the extent of his injuries. Jane washed her son to remove all of the dust and dried blood from his skin. The cut to his head didn't look too bad. It seemed reasonably clean, but there was a big lump. Mary washed the wound and bandaged it.

There were minor cuts all over Tom's body, and bruises were starting to form. His leg was a mess; the lower part twisted at an unnatural angle, the fractured bone almost piercing his skin. As desperate as Mary was to talk to Tom, she hoped for his sake that he wouldn't wake up until the doctor had set it. Joe was right; it would be better if he stayed unconscious for a bit longer.

Doctor Rutherford knocked at the door, and Joe showed him into the cottage, pointing the way to the bedroom. Jane went downstairs to make tea for everyone, but Mary wanted to stay with Tom while the doctor examined him.

The doctor checked the cut to Tom's head first and was happy that Mary had cleaned the wound well. 'He's been out for a while now. Have there been any signs of him waking up? Any movement at all? Has he said anything?' he asked.

'Not since they brought him out of the mine,' replied Mary.

'I think you should prepare yourself, Mary. The longer he's out cold, the less chance of a full recovery,' the doctor said. 'Sometimes people just don't wake up from accidents like this. Sometimes they do, but they aren't right. You understand what I'm saying, don't you?'

Mary was troubled by his words but replied, 'Yes, I understand.'

Doctor Rutherford examined Tom's neck, arms and chest for any signs of damage. His rib cage was bruised, but no ribs were broken. There was no swelling in his abdomen. The examination moved down to his pelvis and legs, where there was more bruising. When he moved down to his leg, he said, 'This is going to be tricky though,' as he looked closely at the broken bone and tried to find the best way to repair it. 'I brought chloroform with me when I heard that he'd had a bad break, but he won't need any if he stays unconscious. I'm going to need Joe's strength to help me though. Thankfully the bone hasn't come through the skin — much less chance of infection getting in that way.'

Mary called for Joe to come upstairs. Doctor Rutherford was setting out everything he would need for the procedure on the chest of drawers. He explained that he would need Joe to pull the lower leg down slightly to make sure that he returned the bone to the right place. Mary couldn't watch. She turned her back while the doctor and Joe manipulated the shin bone back into place. Thank God Tom was asleep, she thought. She couldn't imagine how painful the procedure would have been if he'd been awake.

When she turned back, the doctor was carefully bandaging Tom's lower leg to keep the bones in place. 'He'll have to stay in bed for at least six weeks for this to heal properly. That means he can't get up for anything.'

Mary nodded. She had cared for her mother when she had been bedridden, and she would care for Tom as long as he needed her help.

The doctor finished dressing the broken limb and gathered his things together. Shaking his head, he said, 'I must admit, I'm concerned about this head injury.' He took out his pocket watch and studied the watch face and shook his head. 'He must have been knocked out over six hours ago. Now, I don't need to tell you to keep an eye on him overnight and send someone down for me if you're worried. Otherwise, I'll be back first thing in the morning to check on him.'

Mary walked the doctor to the door and thanked him for coming. Then, she took the cup of tea that Jane offered her and sat down. Her hands were shaking, and the cup rattled in the saucer. How was she going to manage? She had Tom to take care of, as well as Josie. They wouldn't have any wages coming in until Tom could get back to work. What if he didn't wake up? What if he woke up but couldn't move? He had to wake up; he had to be alright because Mary couldn't imagine a future without Tom.

Jane took the cup from Mary's hand and set it down. As if reading her mind, she said, 'Don't worry, lass, I'll stay for a bit until you can manage. It'll be alright.'

The impact of everything that had happened that day suddenly hit Mary, and her pent-up tears started to fall. Jane held her while she sobbed uncontrollably.

As promised, Doctor Rutherford came back early the following day. He was even more concerned when he saw that Tom had still not come round. As he left, he said he would call back later in the day. After the doctor's visit, Jane decided to take Josie for a walk down to Mr Graham's shop to pick up a few things. Mary returned to sit by Tom's bedside, held his hand, and continued to talk to him, as she had done all night.

'Your mother's taken Josie down to the shop this morning,' she told Tom, 'even though it's freezing out there today. I think she wanted to get her out of the house for a bit. Josie's wrapped up well, so she'll be fine. You'll never guess what happened this morning. When Josie was eating her breakfast, she said 'Mama' for the first time. She can say 'Baba' and 'Mama' now, just you watch, her next word will be 'Dada'.'

She noticed Tom's eyelids flicker and then open.

'Oh Tom, thank God! You're awake.'

He looked at her and smiled weakly.

'Me head hurts. What happened?' He lifted his hand to his

head and felt a bandage. He tried to get up and groaned. 'Ow! I hurt all over.'

'You have to stay in bed. You had an accident.'

'An accident?'

'Yes, there was a fall in the mine. You were trapped for hours before they found you and brought you out.'

'I don't remember.'

'You hit your head. You've been unconscious since yesterday.'

Mary offered him a sip of water and then told him more about what had happened and the injuries he had suffered. Tom could remember going to work yesterday morning but had no recollection of the accident at all.

For the rest of the day, he got tired quickly and drifted in and out of sleep. Mary spent most of the time that Tom was awake trying to get him to drink water and eat the mutton broth that his mother had made.

That evening, after Jane retired to Josie's room; Mary went back to her room. She intended to sit by the bed and watch over her husband again.

Tom could see how tired Mary was and said, 'No, you don't. You can hardly keep your eyes open, lass. Get in here.' Tom took her hand and pulled her towards him. She climbed into bed. Despite the pain, Tom put his arm around her and pulled her close. She was careful where she touched him and was pleased when his body relaxed against hers as she snuggled into him.

'I was so frightened I would lose you,' confessed Mary.

'You'll not get rid of me that easily,' said Tom, as he drifted off to sleep.

Chapter 33

Moorside Cottage, Westgate
January 1874

Tom was lying in bed staring out of the window. He didn't see the treetops swaying in the breeze or the robin sitting on the windowsill, and he didn't hear the fire crackling in the grate. He was thinking about the accident and how close he had come to death, how close he had come to leaving Mary and Josie alone to fend for themselves, and how close he had come to never seeing his unborn child.

He thought about Mary and when they had first met. He had liked her ever since he saw her at Killhope that day. She was young and beautiful and bright, and he couldn't imagine a more perfect woman. He cringed when he remembered how he'd talked to her about mining outside the church, but she had been interested, with her father being a miner, and had known more about the subject than he'd expected. She had made him feel comfortable. He had always been shy around girls, but with Mary, it had been different. He'd always found her easy to talk to.

At the dance, she had looked beautiful. Tom had held her in his arms, and they had fitted together just right. He had wanted to kiss her that night, but Joe had come in and whisked her away from him. Tom had been jealous seeing her in Joe's arms, and he had left the hall. He regretted that; he should have stayed at the dance and offered to walk her home. If he had, he was sure that he would have kissed her.

When he saw her at the show, he couldn't let her pass without talking to her and, for some reason, he'd wanted to introduce her to his mother. She had looked so happy that day, walking around the show field with her family.

He had been pleased when she accepted his offer of a ride to Ireshopeburn that morning when she'd been walking home to Fell Top. They were sitting so close on the cart that he had been able to smell the sweet, flowery fragrance in her hair. They had talked about lots of things that day and he had discovered they had many interests in common. He hadn't wanted that journey to end.

For a long time now, he had loved Mary. He wished he had spoken up earlier before she had fallen for Joe. He remembered the night that he had punched his brother. Joe had had a black eye for over a week and still had a small scar on his cheek. Tom wasn't proud of what he had done, he could usually control his anger, but Joe had deserved it for what he had done to Mary. Aye, he certainly had.

When Tom had asked Mary to marry him, he had been so thrilled when she had said 'yes' that he thought his heart would burst. He wasn't sure about her feelings towards him though. He knew he was Mary's second choice, after Joe, and that his brother would always have a place in her heart. But he hoped that she would learn to love him. He knew that she needed time to heal after being hurt so badly. He was a patient man.

Chapter 34

Westgate
March 1874

Mary had hardly left the cottage since Tom's accident and, now that he was improving, she was itching to get outside for some fresh air. His mother was with him, so she knew that he would be well looked after while she went out for a walk. Mary decided to go to the village shop to pick up a few supplies, but that was just an excuse, really. She needed to get her head together and think things through. So much had happened in the four months since their marriage.

Tom had been suspected of murdering her cousin Kate, but Mary hadn't doubted his innocence for long. Once she had considered everything that had happened, she realised that there was no way Tom could have killed Kate. But, still, she'd been worried that the police mightn't believe him or that he could have been wrongly identified as the man who had been seen at the prison. Newspapers were full of stories about people who had been wrongly convicted, and it was only ever discovered when somebody else confessed. Luckily, the prison officer had confirmed that Tom wasn't the man who had delivered the letter to the prison. He wasn't the man they were looking for. She was sure that Robert believed that Tom was innocent too, though she did wonder whether Tom's ordeal with the police would be over completely until the real killer was found.

However, she and Tom had been so relieved that he was no longer a suspect and that they could spend Christmas together. When Tom had heard that she was going to have his baby, he was so happy. Christmas Day had been a special day and one that she would remember forever; it was by far the best Christmas she had ever had.

Then not long after all that, Tom had been seriously injured in the mine accident. He could have been killed. His recovery was taking a long time, but he was getting better, and the doctor was pleased with his progress. She had nearly lost him that day. How did she feel about that?

Voices broke through her thoughts, and she looked ahead. A crowd was gathering around a shaft, one of many ways into Greenfoot mine. She went to find out what was happening. The grass was damp, so she lifted her skirt as she crossed the field and walked towards the restless group. She caught up to an old woman heading in the same direction, and asked her, 'Do you know what's going on?'

'No, but there's somethin' up. Mebbe an accident. Mebbe somebody's taken bad?' She stopped to catch her breath. 'I heard shoutin'. I had to come and see. Me son works here.'

Mary took the woman's arm and walked with her to the shaft top.

People were talking in whispers. Out of respect? She wondered if someone had died.

A loud voice issued orders, 'That's right, pull him up, let's get him out, let's see who it is.' Sir Thomas directed three men lying on the ground with their arms and heads in the hole. They grunted and groaned as they pulled on ropes.

'Sir Thomas is in charge. He'll sort it out, whatever is wrong. He's a good man, he is, just like his father was,' said the old woman breathlessly.

A small man moved through the crowd towards them, 'What are you doing here, Mother? You're supposed to be resting.'

'I had to know what was going on. I couldn't just sit at home waiting for word. Not when you work down there. Tell us, what's happened?'

'Someone fell down the shaft last night. We found him this morning when we went to work.'

'Who is it? Anyone we know?'

'No, I've not seen him afore. He's not from around here.'

As the men continued to pull on the rope, a pair of old, muddy clogs appeared. The thick rope was tied around a pair of skinny ankles. The onlookers gasped and stared at the body being hauled up from the depths of the earth. Coarse trousers covered his thin legs; his lean body was dressed in a grubby shirt, a well-fitted waistcoat and a worn jacket; his grey face was partially covered by a brown beard speckled with white, matching the long hair on his head. His hat was missing — probably lying at the foot of the shaft, thought Mary.

She watched the crowd proceed towards the man, one after another. They glanced at him and shook their heads as they moved away.

Once the crowd dispersed, the constable began to examine the body, and he talked to himself while scribbling in his notebook.

'He doesn't smell of drink. If he wasn't drunk, why did he fall down the hole? Oh, he was beaten up, aye, he was beaten up good and proper — those bruises are from a fist. Aye, I've seen plenty of them before. Mebbe he was killed first and then dumped down there, or mebbe he was knocked out and then chucked down the hole. The fall would've finished him off, all right. No way was this an accident.'

Mary listened to the policeman with morbid fascination. She looked more closely at the body and noticed a slight movement in his chest. 'Mr Emerson! I think he might be alive!'

Robert put his cheek to the man's face to feel for any signs of breathing. He jumped up.

'Good God! Fetch the doctor! Quick!' he shouted at nobody in particular.

A young miner took off at speed in the direction of the doctor's house.

The policeman took off his cloak and placed it over the man. Addressing Mary, he said, 'Thanks, lass. I thought I was dealing with another murder.'

Mary voiced her thoughts, 'I wonder who he is, and what happened to him.'

'Nobody's recognised him. Hopefully the doctor will get him pulled round and he'll be able to tell us himself.'

'He looks so pale. No wonder everyone thought he was dead.'

The doctor ran up the field. With just a brief nod towards Robert and Mary, he got down onto his knees and examined the patient.

'We need to get him over to my place as quickly as possible. He's not going to be with us for long if he doesn't get warmed through.'

Several miners came forward to offer assistance, but one

large man picked him up, put him over his shoulder and walked back to the village like he was carrying no more than a sack of potatoes.

'Mary, my wife is away at her sister's,' said the doctor. 'Are you able to help us for an hour or so?'

'Yes, I can stay for a bit. Jane's up at home with Tom and Josie.'

'Good, thank you.'

When they arrived at the doctor's house, the miner laid the man down on a bed in the front room, and on his way out, he gave his best wishes for the man's recovery. The policeman tended the fire while the doctor attended to the man. Mary stood there waiting for instructions.

'Find some dry clothes. Upstairs, first room on the right, large dresser.' Mary went to fetch them, and she placed them by the bed.

'Robert, give me a hand lifting him, so we can get him undressed. He's cold and wet. We need to get him dried off and warmed up.'

They all worked together to undress and redress the man. The room was hot by now, and the man's colour seemed to be returning.

'A drop of whisky?' the policeman suggested.

'How can you think of drinking at a time like this, Robert?' said the doctor.

'Not for me! For him. Isn't that what you do?'

'Well, it won't do him any harm, I suppose.'

Doctor Rutherford poured a small measure of whisky and handed it to Mary. He lifted the man's head and gestured for her to put the glass to the man's lips. The man spluttered, but some of the liquid went down his throat.

Soon afterwards, he started to thrash about like he was having a nightmare, with incoherent words coming from his mouth.

'He...there...where...off...no...no...away...stop.'

Mary sat by the bedside and took hold of his hand. She talked to him calmly like she would to an upset child, 'Shush there, it's alright. You'll be fine. Don't worry.'

He settled quickly and entered a sound sleep, snoring gently.

Mary said quietly, 'I'll make you a cup of tea before I head back.'

'Thank you, Mary,' said Dr Rutherford. 'That's very good of you. I think there's some gingerbread left in the larder.'

Mary went into the kitchen and came back with a tray of tea and a few slices of cake. They sat around a table by the window, and Mary poured.

'Do you think he'll make it?' asked Robert.

'Yes, now that he's warmed up, I think he will. He's a much better colour. He must have had a bump to his head though, and he's delirious with it. It looks like he's dreaming about what happened to him.'

'Good, I thought he was a goner.'

Mary went back to the man's side. He started to thrash about wildly and shouted, 'No, no, get off me!'

She sat and talked soothingly to him, and he calmed down again. When she took his hand, he opened his eyes and looked up at her.

'Am I dead?' he asked.

'No.' She smiled at him. 'You just had a fall. You'll be fine.'

'Where am I?'

'You're at Westgate. At the doctor's house.'

The doctor came up behind Mary, and he stood in the

background to check on his patient.

'Where is he? Does he know I'm here?' asked the man.

'The doctor's right here,' said Mary, looking puzzled.

'Not him. I mean where's the evil bastard who threw me down that hole? He left me there to die!'

The man grew agitated, and he looked around the room in fear. When he saw Robert, he said, 'Constable, are the doors locked? If he knows I'm here, he'll come and finish me off.'

'Who did this to you?' asked Robert.

'Please, please, lock the doors. Close the windows. I need to get away.'

The man scrabbled to get out of bed, but when he realised how weak he was, he started to shake, and tears rolled down his face. 'Please don't let him kill me,' he repeated over and over again.

Robert asked him, 'Who are you? Who did this to you? Who are you frightened of?' But the man didn't reply.

Mary turned to the men and said quietly, 'Humour him. Lock the doors. If he feels safe, he might talk.'

'Good idea,' said Doctor Rutherford and went to make the place secure.

Mary sat down again and held the man's hand. 'There, there now. You're alright. The doors are locked. You're safe now. The doctor is here, and the constable is here. You're not on your own. They'll keep you safe. I'm Mary. What's your name?'

'Frank,' he said between sobs.

'Hello, Frank. You don't live around here, do you? Where do you come from?'

'Newcastle.'

The policeman looked at the doctor. They both seemed

surprised that Mary's tactic had worked and that she had managed to get him to talk.

'Why did you come to Westgate?'

'To meet someone.'

'I see. You came here to meet someone. Who was that?'

'Forster.'

'Sir Thomas Forster?'

'No — Henry Forster.'

'And did you meet him?'

'Yes.'

'What happened after you met Mr Forster?'

'He did this to me!'

As his words sunk in, everyone looked at each other in horror. Robert asked, 'You're telling us that Henry Forster beat you and dropped you in that shaft?'

'Yes.'

Robert pulled up a chair next to Mary's and said, 'Frank, you'd better tell me exactly what happened last night.'

Chapter 35

Stanhope, Weardale
March 1874

When Frank Collins had finished telling his story, Robert went straight down to the police house at Stanhope to speak with his sergeant. He couldn't arrest the son of Sir Thomas Forster without authorisation from a superior officer.

The sergeant was at his desk writing up reports when Robert arrived. 'What's the rush?' he asked.

Robert took a deep breath, 'Well, there's rather a lot been going on up the dale. I'll fill you in with what's happened, and then I'm going to need your help.'

'Sounds interesting.'

Robert recounted the events of the day and made a case for arresting Henry Forster.

'Yes, you're right. We need to bring him down here for questioning. I'd better come with you, just in case he doesn't come willingly.'

They went to Burnside Hall together to make the arrest. The sergeant stayed with the horse and police carriage, which he strategically placed to block the gateway, while Robert went to the door and asked to see Henry. The housemaid went to fetch him. Sir Thomas had spotted the police constable walking up the drive and, wondering why he was visiting, went to the hallway to find out.

'Good afternoon, Robert. To what do we owe the pleasure?'

'Sir Thomas, it's Henry that I've come to see. Ah, here he is!'

Henry approached the men and said, 'Good afternoon, Constable. What can I do for you?'

'Henry Forster, I'm arresting you for the attempted murder of Francis Collins.'

Henry looked shocked. 'Attempted murder?' he repeated, the colour draining from his face.

'Yes, attempted murder. Mr Collins is alive and well, and he has named you as his attacker.'

'He's lying.'

'Henry, you're going to have to come with me to Stanhope for questioning. If you have anything to say, you can say it there.'

At that moment, Lady Margaret came in from the garden carrying a bunch of cut flowers, the first daffodils of the year. Her smile disappeared when she saw the men's faces and realised that something was seriously wrong. Sir Thomas went over to his wife and took her arm. 'Margaret, dear, our son has been arrested.'

'Our Henry, whatever for?'

'For attempted murder.'

Lady Margaret dropped the flowers, and they scattered all over the hall carpet. She stared, open-mouthed, at her son and eventually said, 'Henry, what have you done?' Her knees gave way as she fell into a faint.

While all eyes were on Lady Margaret, Henry ran past them and out of the front door, and Robert gave chase. The hall had a high-walled garden, and he knew the only way out was through the main gate, and he sprinted in that direction. Before Robert reached it, he saw the sergeant grab Henry as he tried to leave the grounds and, by the time the constable got there, Henry was in handcuffs.

* * *

When they returned to the police house with their prisoner, the policemen explained the charge to Henry. They told him that if he was found guilty, and that was very likely when a victim could testify in court, he would probably spend the rest of his life in a prison cell.

'What can I say or do to stop that from happening? Can my father help?'

'Not this time, I'm afraid you're going to have to stand trial. Your best hope is to confess and hope the judge reduces the sentence. You might be lucky and get off with twenty years.'

Henry had been to the prison at Durham. He had gone with some school friends to watch the last public hanging there back in 1865. What a hash they'd made of that! The rope had snapped, and the poor fellow had fallen to the ground. The prison officers had to find another rope, and they hanged him successfully at the second attempt. Even though the man had been a convicted wife-killer, the crowd had felt sympathy for him.

And Henry had gone back to the prison again to take the locket for Kate. The stench of the prisoners had horrified Henry, and he had been disgusted when he saw them scratching at lice in their hair and urinating in the exercise yard. He couldn't spend a week in there, never mind twenty years.

Twenty years. That would make him nearly fifty by the time he got out — and that's if he got out. If he survived prison, he would be an old man. What life would there be for him after the age of fifty?

A clerk entered the room and said, 'Mr Bainbridge is outside. He says Sir Thomas has instructed him to come and represent Mr Forster.'

'You'd better show him in,' replied the sergeant. He turned to Henry and said, 'You're entitled to see a solicitor. He'll advise you what your best course of action is under the circumstances. Attempted murder is a serious charge, so listen carefully to what he has to say.'

The policemen left the room, and Mr Bainbridge entered.

Without any words of greeting, Henry asked, 'Is it true that I'd get a life sentence for attempted murder?'

'If you're found guilty by the court, then yes, that would be the most probable outcome.'

'What if I was found guilty of murder?'

'Then you would be hanged.'

'Thank you for coming. That's all I need to know. I can't spend the rest of my life in prison.'

'What do you mean?' asked the solicitor.

'I'm going to confess to all of my crimes, and that will get me hanged.' He scoffed. 'I'd rather hang and have a quick death than rot away in that hellhole.'

'I strongly advise you against doing that, Mr Forster.'

'I've made up my mind.'

'Constable!' shouted Henry.

'But Henry, think about your parents....'

The policemen came back into the room, and Mr Bainbridge left without saying another word.

Henry was confident that what he was about to do was for the best. Just the thought of the prison made him feel dirty and itchy. He had heard of men being beaten, and worse, in prisons. Being from a wealthy family and having attended a public school, he was sure he would be targeted. And he would always be looking over his shoulder in case the gentlemen he owed money to had men inside. He would confess everything; he would tell the policemen the whole story, and that way, they would have to hang him.

'Alright, I've decided to confess. I'll tell you what I've done.'

'I'm pleased you listened to Mr Bainbridge. You'll get a lighter sentence with a confession,' said Robert. 'Did he tell you to say that Mr Collins fell down the hole accidentally when you hit him?'

'You don't understand, Constable. I'm not going to confess to the attempted murder charge. I'm going to confess to everything that I've done, all of my crimes.'

'You don't need to do that, Mr Forster. You'll just be on trial for attacking Mr Collins and leaving him to die. Anything else you say may increase your sentence.'

'Yes, I do need to do this. Are you ready?'

The clerk was summoned to the room to take notes, and Henry began his confession. After he had finished, the sergeant asked, 'Is that everything you want to say?'

'Yes,' confirmed Henry.

'Well, well!' said Robert, as he rubbed his hands over his head.

The sergeant read out the charges against Henry and said, 'You will stand trial at Durham. You will spend the night in custody here at Stanhope, and you will be transferred to Durham prison tomorrow where you will stay until your trial.'

'Can't I stay here until the trial?' pleaded Henry.

'I'm afraid not. We only have one cell and it might be needed before then.'

'How long will it be — until the trial?'

'Possibly next month if everything's ready by then, or it could held over until the September sessions.'

'But that's four months away!' Henry exclaimed, with a look of horror on his face. He started to pull at his hair. He hadn't realised he would be imprisoned at Durham until the trial, and all his fears of prison came back to mind.

'Come on, I'll take you to the cell now.'

Henry followed the sergeant to the back of the police station and sat down in the cell as the key was turned in the lock. He put his head in his hands, and for the first time in years, he cried.

* * *

Robert had been shocked at Henry's words, but he thought that everything made sense now. He had caught the right man. Even so, he couldn't gloat. His thoughts were with Sir Thomas and Lady Margaret. He would have to call at Burnside Hall on his way home and tell the couple that their only son and heir had confessed, that he would face a trial at Durham, and that he would probably hang for his crimes.

Chapter 36

After his accident in the mine, Tom had been laid up for nearly two months while his leg healed. When he finally got up, it had taken another couple of months before he could walk properly again. His leg muscles had wasted from not being used for so long. It had been a frustrating time for Tom, but Mary had been by his side, supporting him throughout his recovery. He couldn't thank her enough for everything she had done for him.

During his recovery, he hadn't been idle. He had taken walks twice daily, just short ones at first to get his leg moving and longer ones as he got stronger. He had enjoyed walking with Mary by the burn and searching for 'bonny bits' to build a rockery in the garden. They'd found some lovely pieces of fluorspar and quartz. Mary had enjoyed searching for fossils in the shale and sandstone, too. All their finds had been piled up in the shed until they had plenty to build a rockery.

Tom still walked with a slight limp, which the doctor was confident would improve once his muscles regained their strength, and he had a pink scar on his brow about an inch long. Considering the severity of his injuries, he had recovered very well, although he still hadn't regained his memory of what had happened in the mine that day.

With Mary's help, Tom had also managed to make an oak crib for the baby. It had rounded feet so it could be rocked from side to side. He was very proud of it, and it made him feel as though he had done something useful while he was out of work.

Seeing Mary's body shape change with her pregnancy intrigued Tom. He could imagine the baby growing inside her, and he could feel it moving when he put his hand on her bump. He thought about the accident that had nearly taken his life and robbed him of this experience. He was lucky to be alive and couldn't wait to see his child. It didn't matter to him whether it was a girl or a boy. All he wanted was for Mary and the baby to be well.

Tom was very grateful to his mother for helping them through this difficult time. As well as looking after Josie and doing the housework, Jane had paid their rent and bought food for the family while Tom was unable to work. Joe had helped at High House Farm, freeing up his mother to stay with them for a while after the accident. Jane had continued to call on them regularly ever since, and this morning was no exception. She had popped over from the farm to bring some eggs and milk.

As they chatted in the kitchen, Tom said, 'I think I should go back to work now. I'm feeling much better and I can get around quite well.'

Jane had been expecting this day coming and surprised them both by saying, 'Have you thought about coming back to High House Farm?'

'And work for Joe? I don't think so,' said Tom, folding his arms in front of him.

'Joe and Connie have been living at Springbank Farm since Mr Peart died. Joe's trying to help out as much as he can at home, but he has a lot to do over there as well. He can't keep both farms going indefinitely, even with the lads that work for him. They're stretched too thin.'

'I don't know. I haven't done much farming,' said Tom.

'You know plenty about farming. You've been helping us since you were a little lad,' replied his mother. 'Have a think about it. You could take over the lease when it expires.' She hesitated before adding, 'And I could get a cottage in the village.'

It was clear that Jane had given this a lot of thought, and the least Tom could do was agree to consider it. 'Alright, I'll think about it.'

While Jane was still at the cottage to watch Josie, Tom asked Mary if she would like to go out for a walk and, as soon as they were outside, he asked her, 'What do you think about High House and the farm?'

'I'd rather you were farming than mining, Tom. It's safer,' she replied. 'And High House would be a great place for the bairns to grow up. You loved it there when you were a boy.'

'What about Joe? He'll have to help at High House at hay time and shearing and I'll have to help out at Springbank Farm.'

'I don't care for Joe anymore. Surely you know that. As far as Josie is concerned, you are her father, not him. Don't let Joe stop you from doing this, if it's what you want to do.'

'I must admit, I've been a bit worried about getting a job. The lads couldn't hold me place open until I got better. Watson said they've taken on someone else. You know, there's not much work for lead miners in the dale now. A lot of the mines have closed. There might be work at Boltsburn or Killhope — they seem to be doing alright — but there's nothing near here. Anyway, they've got the pick of the men, so why would they take me on?'

'Tom, you were good at your job, you were just unlucky. There's no reason why they wouldn't take you on. The accident wasn't your fault — and you're getting stronger all the time,' Mary reassured him. 'And I know you love the job inside out.'

Tom thought that the lead industry was dying in Weardale. So many miners were struggling to find work, and he knew of a few men that had moved their families to the east side of County Durham to work in the coal mines there. Some had emigrated to America, Canada and New Zealand to start a new life. Could he leave the dale and take his family abroad?

Wanting at least to make Mary aware of their options, he said, 'There are mines in other places. Tow Law isn't far from the here and there's plenty of work in the coal mines over that way, and it's decent pay. The mining is a bit different though, but I'm sure I'd get used to it. Or there are lead mines in America where the work would be the same as what we do here, but it's expensive to get passage over there now and land is dearer than it used to be.'

Mary could tell by Tom's voice that he wasn't keen on going to the Durham coalfield or to America. She loved the dale and would much prefer to stay here, and she sensed her husband felt the same way.

They continued in silence, each weighing up the options in their minds. They stopped as a peewit walked across the path in front of them, followed by a line of chicks.

Tom turned to Mary. 'With the way the mines are going, farming would give us more security, even a leased farm. And you're right, farming is safer and healthier than working underground. Me parents were happy at High House Farm and it brought in a decent income. If you agree, I think we should take Mother up on her offer.'

'Aye, Tom. I think that's a good choice,' said Mary, smiling at him. 'But I don't want Jane moving into the village. She's helped us out so much. I'd like her to stay at the farm — High House is her home.'

Tom nodded. 'You're right. She'd hate living down in the village after spending most of her life on the hillside.'

Mary took hold of her husband's arm, and they walked back to the cottage, feeling much better for having decided what to do.

As soon as they walked through the door, Jane gave them a questioning look and said, 'Well?'

'We've talked about it,' said Tom, 'and, aye, we'd like to take on the farm. But we've got one condition....'

'What's that?'

'That you stay at the farm with us. We don't want you moving down to Westgate.'

With relief written all over her face, Jane said, 'Aye, lad. I'd like that. Thank you. Thank you very much.'

Chapter 37

High House Farm, Westgate
May 1874

Mary loved their little cottage on the hillside and was sad to be leaving it, but she was excited about moving to High House Farm. The old farmhouse had thick stone walls, a stone-tiled roof, large fireplaces and low ceilings. There were four bedrooms upstairs and a parlour, a large kitchen and a larder downstairs. The garden consisted of flowerbeds at the front of the house and a vegetable patch to one side. At the back of the house was the farmyard with various outbuildings, including a large barn.

Tom and Mary shared a room overlooking the front of the house, which had a fantastic view of the front garden and the valley below. Tom had placed the crib he'd made by their bed, even though it wouldn't be needed for a few months yet. They had moved Josie into the bedroom next door.

A few weeks after they had moved in, Mary heard someone knocking at the door and went to see who was there. She was surprised to see her brother standing on the doorstep.

'Hello, Mary,' said William.

'Come on in. What a nice surprise!' She showed him into the

kitchen, and he took off his boots by the door. She gestured for him to take a seat at the table, then filled the kettle and put it on to boil before sitting down next to him.

'So, what brings you here?' she asked.

'Annie asked me to come down to see you. I've got something to tell you. Father passed away yesterday.'

'I'm sorry,' said Mary.

'It was a blessing in the end, at least that's what Annie says. He'd been bad since that cold spell back in February. That's when he took to his bed. But the last week or so he could hardly breathe. He couldn't eat or talk or anything,' William said. 'Anyway, Annie told me to let you know that the funeral will be on Friday, up at Lanehead Chapel.'

While Mary made a pot of tea for herself and poured a glass of milk and spread some dripping on a thick slice of bread for her brother, she thought about how most of the miners ended up with bad chests, the 'black spit' as they called it. And it wasn't just old men who were affected by it; some young men were too. She was thankful that Tom was no longer working underground. Her thoughts drifted to her sister, Annie, who had looked after their ailing father for months.

'Poor Annie,' said Mary as she handed the plate to William. 'She must have had a hard time of it.'

Misunderstanding what Mary meant, William replied, 'Once Father had stopped drinking, he wasn't so bad. When he'd had a skinful though, that was a different story. Did you know he used to hit us?'

'I knew he'd hit Annie,' said Mary. 'I didn't know he'd hit you though.'

'Aye, Annie got the brunt of it. She used to keep us out of his way most of the time. I hated to see him hit her. Then, there was this one day he was hitting her and I went down and shouted at him to stop. He took his belt off and hit me with it — over and over. I didn't dare say anything after that,' said William, with tears in his eyes.

'Aw, William, that was a very brave thing to do, but you were just a boy, you couldn't have stopped him.'

'Well, I'll not miss him,' said William bitterly. 'There's something else as well. Annie said to tell you the agent's been round and given us notice. We've got to be out of the house by the end of the month. We're not sure what we're going to do.'

'By, he didn't waste any time. Are there any jobs going at Killhope or Burtree? You're nearly twelve now. They might take you on as a washerboy and let you keep the house.'

'You know fine well a washerboy's wages wouldn't pay the rent and I'm too young to go in the mine yet.'

'No, you're right. I'll have a word with Tom when he gets home and see if we can sort anything out.'

'Oh, and another thing — our Annie's courting!' said William grinning.

'Is she now? And who's the lucky lad?'

'Jack Nattrass. He's a miner at Killhope and he seems nice enough. Anyway, I should be getting back. Thanks for the food and milk.'

'Aye, Annie will want you home before dark. Right, we'll come up on Friday and we'll see you then.' Mary stood at the door and watched as William began his long walk back to Fell Top.

Mary hadn't seen much of her father in the last few years. She had never forgiven him for turning her away when she needed him. He had been a good father when she was young, but hard times and losing his wife had turned him to drink, and he had changed with it. Well, her parents would be together again now, she thought.

It was several hours before Tom came home. He smelled strongly of sheep and had bits of wool all over his clothes. 'What have you been doing?' Mary asked as he began to undress by the kitchen sink.

'I've been on with the sheep, trimming the wool on their tails,' he said as he poured water into the sink.

'Wouldn't it be better to wait until you bring them in at clipping time?'

While he washed, he said, 'Not if we want to stop them from getting fly strike. It's starting to warm up now and it's still a few months before we'll be clipping them. When it's warm, flies can lay their eggs in the wool around the tails, especially if they're mucky. Me Dad lost a good ewe once. He hadn't seen the maggots eating away at her flesh 'cos the wound was hidden by her thick tail. By the time he noticed, it was too late to save her. Every year since then, either me or Joe have clipped every single one of them. It's not an easy thing to do but I never want to see that happen again.' Tom put on some clean clothes and sat down at the table.

'Would you like tea, or ale?' asked Mary.

'Some ale would be nice, thank you.'

As she passed him the drink, she said, 'I had a visitor this morning. Our William came down to tell me that Father died yesterday.'

'Aw, Mary, I'm sorry. Are you alright?' said Tom. He stood up and took her into his arms.

'Aye, I'm fine — you know how things were between us.'

'But he was still your father.'

Not wanting to talk about him, she moved away and went over to the range to check on the pie that was in the oven.

'The family's been given notice to leave Fell Top. The agent's been round there already,' she said. Turning back to look at Tom, she asked, 'Is there anything we can do to help them?'

'I could do with a lad to help me here. It would have been a lot easier today if I'd had another pair of hands. Do you think William would take to farm work?'

'Aye, I'm sure he would. He's almost twelve now and he's growing up fast.'

'Alright, that's settled then.' He took a long sup of ale and then continued, 'I heard Mrs Peart is looking for a new girl. I don't know about telling Annie about it, you know, with Connie being there.'

'Beggars can't be choosers. She might have to work there if there's nothing else going. They have to be out of the house by the end of the month.'

After a pause, Tom said, 'We've got plenty of room. They could come here. Annie will find a place soon enough — she's a good worker — and John can stay until he finishes school.'

'Thank you, Tom.' Mary went to his chair and hugged him. 'They'll be so relieved. I can't wait to tell them.'

William wasn't the only visitor to High House Farm that week. When Mary answered the door on the second occasion, she was shocked to see Mrs Peart standing on the step.

'Hello, Mary. I heard about your father and I've come to pay my respects.'

'Mrs Peart, come on in. Would you like a cup of tea?'

'Yes, please, that would be lovely.'

Mary showed Mrs Peart into the rarely-used parlour. It was the best room and only used when they had visitors at the house. 'Sit down in here and I'll bring a tray in.'

Mary hadn't seen Mrs Peart since Connie's wedding day, the day she had run away. She hadn't seen her since Mr Peart's death. Mary had so much that she wanted to say to her, but she'd been too afraid to visit Mrs Peart at Springbank Farm. They were neighbours now, and Mary was pleased that her former employer had come to see her.

When Mary entered the room with the tea tray, Mrs Peart smiled at her. As she set it down on the table, Mary said, 'I'm sorry about what happened.'

'Sorry, what for?'

'I'm sorry for leaving Springbank Farm without saying anything and for making you worry. You and Mr Peart were so good to me, you deserved better. And I'm very sorry for what happened to Mr Peart. He was a lovely man. I went to his funeral…but I didn't go into the church because I didn't think any of you would want me there.'

'Bless you, Mary. You worry enough for all of us. It's all water under the bridge now, as they say. I do miss him though, God rest his soul. And I'm sorry for what our Connie did on your wedding day. I couldn't believe it when Joe told me.'

'It didn't surprise me,' said Mary.

'Well, she shouldn't have gone to High House Chapel and she shouldn't have done what she did, and I told her so.'

They heard the back door close, followed by Jane's voice and Josie's giggles.

'I would love to meet your little girl,' said Mrs Peart. 'There's no sign of our Connie giving us any grandchildren yet. I can't wait to have some little ones around the place.'

Mary smiled and went to fetch Josie.

'What a pretty little thing she is! She looks just like you.' Mrs Peart sat the child on her knee and started to sing to her, much to Josie's delight.

With the air cleared between the two women, they chatted over tea like old friends.

Tom harnessed the horse on Friday morning, and he and Mary set off up the dale road, heading for Lanehead. Josie stayed at home with Jane. As they travelled up the dale, sitting side by side on the cart, Mary was reminded of the first time she had really talked with Tom.

'Do you remember when you gave me a ride up to Ireshope-burn?' said Mary. 'We talked for ages that morning, didn't we?'

'Aye, I didn't want to let you get down off the cart that day,' said Tom. 'If they hadn't been expecting me at the mine office, I would have whisked you away for the day.'

They were met at the chapel by Reverend Hodgson, who presided over George Watson's funeral service. It was brief. Then, his coffin was taken to the churchyard and buried next to the graves of his late wife and their son, George, who'd died as an infant. There were only a dozen mourners in attendance— his family, Lizzie and Ben, his partners from the mine and a couple of neighbours.

Afterwards, Tom and Mary went back to Fell Top, where Annie had laid out some food. They all sat down to eat. 'This tatie cake is delicious,' said Mary. 'You could get a job as a cook.'

'I'm hoping I won't need to,' Annie replied, with a glint in her eye. 'Will you come outside for a minute?'

'Aye, I'd better come now 'cos if I eat any more of this I'll not get through the door,' Mary said laughing.

Once the sisters were outside and could talk privately, Annie told Mary about her new friend. 'I met Jack last year when I was walking back up the dale one day, and we got on like a house on fire. We've been seeing each other as much as we can since then. He asked me to marry him a few months back, but I couldn't leave here, with father being ill.'

'Now that Father's gone, you'll be free to marry Jack,' said Mary.

'Not exactly. There's still the boys.'

'William told me about you having to leave Fell Top next week. Well, me and Tom have been talking and we'd like you all to come and stay with us until you get something else sorted. Tom's going to offer William a job on the farm and he's happy for John to stay with us until he finishes school.'

Annie was so relieved that she rushed to hug her sister. She had been worried about her brothers and, if they were safe with Mary, she would be free to marry Jack. 'Thank you, Mary. You don't know how much this means to me.'

'I think I can guess,' said Mary. 'Are you sure you want to marry him?'

'More than anything,' replied her sister.

'In that case, it looks like there's going to be a wedding to plan!'

'But I'm not twenty-one, and I don't have a parent to give consent. Can I marry him, or will I have to wait until I'm twenty-one?'

'I don't know,' said Mary. 'I'm sure there must be a way. Maybe you should go and talk to Reverend Hodgson. I'm sure he'll know.'

'Yes, I'll do that.' Annie smiled her beautiful smile.

'We'll come up for you on Friday,' said Mary. 'Pack up everything that you'd like to take from the house.'

After they had made the arrangements, Tom and Mary said their farewells to her family and returned home to High House Farm.

Chapter 38

Henry Forster's trial was held in Durham. The courtroom was packed. It wasn't often that someone from such a notable family as the Forsters appeared in court on such serious charges, so the case had received much attention from the press.

The local paper had printed that Henry Forster would be on trial for murder, but everyone assumed it was a misprint because they all knew he'd been arrested for attempted murder. The story about Frank Collins was well-known throughout the dale, and there was widespread surprise that the man had survived his ordeal. Many Weardale people had made the journey to the courthouse, including Tom and Mary, who were attending as witnesses. They had left Josie at home with Jane, but Aunt Lizzie had decided that she would like to accompany them to Durham. As they entered the courtroom, they saw many of their friends and neighbours, including Joe and Connie. Sir Thomas and Lady Margaret were sitting at the far end of the gallery, but Phyllis was not with them. There were rumours that they'd sent their daughter to Yorkshire to stay with relatives.

When the courtroom was full, and the doors had been closed, the clerk stood up and read the charges.

'Henry Forster, you are charged with the murder of Miss Catherine Featherstone. How do you plead?'

A collective gasp of surprise could be heard from the gallery. Lizzie grabbed Mary's hand.

'Guilty.'

'And you are charged with the murder of Mr Jeremiah Peart. How do you plead?'

'Guilty.'

Another louder gasp was heard. Mary looked across at Connie. Joe was holding her tightly, and it was evident that she was distressed.

'And you are charged with the attempted murder of Mr Francis Collins. How do you plead?'

'Guilty.'

'And you are charged with the theft of sheep from the late Mr Jeremiah Peart of Springbank Farm, Mr Joseph Milburn of High House Farm, Mr George Allison of Hope House, Mr John Peart of White Well Farm, Mr Edward Routledge of Wellfield Farm, and Mr Edward Curry of The Cleugh. How do you plead?'

'Guilty.'

People in the courtroom started to chatter.

The judge wielded his gavel and shouted, 'Silence in court.' He proceeded with the questioning and called the witnesses to the stand, one by one. Robert Emerson, the sergeant, Frank Collins, Doctor Rutherford, Mary Milburn, Jim Stoker and several Weardale men who had been on the fell the night Mr Peart was killed told their versions of events as they remembered them.

As Henry was led to the stand, the room fell deathly silent. He took the stand and swore on the Bible that he would tell the truth. Mary thought that the six weeks in prison had changed his appearance. He looked about ten years older, his clothes were creased and seemed too big for him, and his hair was unkempt. He was hardly recognisable as the young man from Burnside Hall.

The judge said, 'Henry Forster, you gave a confession at Stanhope police station on Thursday, the 7th day of May, 1874. This will now be read out for all the court to hear.'

The clerk shuffled some papers on his desk and began to read Henry's confession:

'I needed money. It's as simple as that, really. That's how it started, anyway. At first, they threatened to beat me, but as my debts grew, they threatened to kill me.

'My father bailed me out several times, but he said that if I continued to gamble, he wouldn't help me again. But I couldn't stop. I went to the club every weekend. Sometimes I won, but more often, I lost. I owed over £3,000 and had no way of paying it back.

'I did try. I took a few things from the house and pawned them. Most of them weren't even missed. That silly girl, Kate Featherstone, saw me take a pocket watch. I had to keep her quiet, so I told her that I had liked her for some time and wanted to make her the lady of Burnside Hall. She loved the idea of that. She didn't know that I pointed the finger at her when she was accused of stealing. I told her that if she kept her mouth shut about the pocket watch, I would wait for her to get out of prison and make my intentions plain. I wasn't sure she believed me, but she kept quiet during the trial and went

263

to Durham without any fuss. Then one evening at dinner, Papa told us that the vicar had mentioned receiving a letter from Kate saying that she was innocent and that she knew who the real thief was. Nobody took any notice of her, but I couldn't take any chances.

'When my father gave me my grandmother's locket, I realised the initials on it were the same as Kate's. So, I devised a plan. Kate was due to be released from prison shortly, so I took the locket to the prison with instructions for it to be given to her on her release. There was a letter telling her where to meet me — up at Crooked Folds, above The Shieling. The locket must have been enough to regain her trust in me, and she went straight there to meet me when she returned to the dale. She didn't even go home to see her family first. She was that keen to be my lady!

'It was all a ruse, though. There was no way I could marry someone who had no money, but I couldn't risk her telling anyone about me either. I had no choice — I had to kill her. I hit her on the head with a stone. The noise was dreadful, and blood splattered everywhere. I pulled her into the mine and left her there. I didn't think anyone would ever find her — not with all that 'Owd Man' nonsense that the miners believe.

'Pawning those few items didn't help much to pay off my debts, so I had to find another way. I was riding down the dale one day and noticed sheep grazing in the fields all around me. They were everywhere. Only that morning, I'd overheard my father talk about the value of the stock. I remember thinking to myself that there was money in those fields just waiting to be taken. I started with just one or two sheep at a time, and I sold them to a dealer. He didn't ask any questions. But once I began to pay back the debts, they demanded more and more until I was so desperate that I took larger numbers of sheep to stop them from hounding me.

'That's when the farmers took the thefts seriously and started to look for the culprit. I was lucky to get away with shooting Mr Peart that night. I had hoped to get away unseen, but he was right there in front of me. He saw me and recognised me too. I saw the look of shock on his face when he knew who I was and that I was going to shoot him. I lifted my pistol to his chest and pulled the trigger, and then I ran. That bloody dog caught me at the bottom of the bank and grabbed me by the ankle. I couldn't risk getting caught, so I shot it to get it off me, and I climbed onto the barn roof to hide. I waited there for hours until everyone had gone before I climbed down and went home.

'And then there's Frank Collins, the man that was found down the shaft. He's the dealer that fenced all those sheep for me. When he heard about Mr Peart being shot, he wanted out and threatened to tell the whole story to the police. He tried to blackmail me! I hit him in the face, and he didn't get up. He was lying so close to the mine shaft that I couldn't stop myself from dragging him to the edge and pushing him over. I expected the fall would kill him, but obviously, it didn't—my mistake.

'And what else am I guilty of, let me think. Oh, yes. Connie Peart. Dearest Connie. I proposed to her. After all, she was the richest heiress hereabouts, the sole heir to Springbank Farm. Joe Milburn did very well for himself. I did my best to court her, and her father was all for the match, but Connie was one of the few people who saw me for what I am. She wasn't taken in by my family name or my good looks. I never cared for her really, she was a spoilt bitch, but I have to admit that I did respect her for that. That didn't stop me from spoiling her good name though. Well, what did she expect after refusing to marry me!'

When the clerk stopped speaking, there were muffled sounds of astonishment from the gallery, and the people started chattering. Mary still held her aunt's hand.

'Henry Forster, was this the confession made by you on Thursday, the 7th day of May, 1874, to Sergeant Parsons and Constable Emerson?' asked the judge.

'Yes, it was.' Henry replied.

'And was it made of your own free will?'

'Yes.'

'Is there anything you would like to add?'

'No.'

The judge summed up the case, and the jurors huddled together for a discussion. After just five minutes, they had reached a verdict.

The jury's foreman indicated to the judge that they had made their decision, and the courtroom fell silent once more. The judge asked for the jury's verdict, and the foreman stood up and said, 'Guilty — on all counts!'

The judge made his pronouncement to the packed court-room.

'Henry Forster, we have heard the evidence against you and it is condemning. Through your habitual gambling habit, you accrued large debts which you were unable to repay. These debts led you to commit a series of crimes whereby you stole from your neighbours and, in so doing, you shot a man dead. You planned and executed the false imprisonment and the murder of a young woman. You beat a man, pushed him into a mine shaft, and left him there to die. Henry Forster, you have shown no remorse for your actions.'

The judge put on his black cap and black gloves. 'You have been found guilty of murder, attempted murder and theft. The sentence of this court is that you be taken from here to the place from whence you came and there be kept in close confinement until Friday, the 19th day of June, 1874, and upon that day and date you are to be taken to the place of execution and that you there be hanged by the neck until you are dead. May God have mercy upon your soul.'

Henry smiled as he was led from the courtroom by two guards. He had got the sentence he wanted. Just two more nights to endure in prison, and then he wouldn't have to suffer anymore.

Sir Thomas ushered Lady Margaret out of the courtroom, their faces devoid of emotion or colour. They had lost their only son and heir.

On the journey home, Mary thought about everything that she had heard that day. Who would have thought Henry Forster could have done all those horrendous things? She had been aware of everything that had happened: Kate going to prison, the sheep going missing, Mr Peart being shot, Kate's murder, and she had heard the accusation made by Frank Collins, who he had beaten and left for dead. But even so, Henry was the last person Mary would have suspected of doing any of those things. Had she missed any clues? Could she have guessed it was him? Then, she thought that was unlikely because nobody had suspected Henry of anything until Frank Collins had named him as his attacker. If Frank had died from his fall that night, Henry might never have been brought to justice.

Mary felt so sorry for her aunt having to sit through Henry's confession and hear how he had manipulated and murdered her daughter.

'Aunt Lizzie, I'm so sorry for what happened to Kate. To be killed because she'd seen Henry take a watch - it's dreadful. Henry is an evil, twisted man and he's going to get what he deserves.'

'At least her name's been cleared,' said Lizzie. 'Now everyone knows it wasn't our Kate that did the stealing at Burnside Hall.'

'But you must feel angry about what happened?

'Well, yes, of course I do. I wish she'd never gone to work at Burnside Hall, and I wish none of it had happened and that she was still with us, but you forget that for over a year now I haven't known what to think. She didn't come back from Durham, that's as much as I knew. I didn't know why she hadn't come home, I didn't know where she'd gone, I didn't know if she was happy or not, or even if she was alive. At least now I know where she is, and I can visit her grave.'

Chapter 39

High House Farm, Westgate
August 1874

Mary finished kneading the bread and left it by the range to prove. She would put it in the oven in an hour or so. The baby she was carrying had been restless all morning, and Mary's back and feet were aching. It was hot working in the kitchen, so she decided to go outside. Josie was playing with a rag doll. Mary took her hand, and they walked out into the garden together, leaving the door open.

It wasn't often that she and Josie had the place to themselves. Everyone had gone over to Springbank Farm for the day, where the men were gathering the last of the hay. The women would lend a hand where they could and provide refreshments for the workers.

The sun shone brightly, even this early in the day. There was a slight breeze that would stop it from becoming too hot. Part of the garden wall was in the shade, so Mary sat down on it, lifted her skirt above her knees and took off her boots. She lifted her legs onto the garden wall and leaned back against the wall of the house. It was surprisingly comfortable, and the cold stone helped cool her down. Josie sat on the path, pretending to feed her doll with a spoon.

The garden looked beautiful. All the time that Mary had spent tidying it and pruning plants had paid off. There were shrubs and flowers on both sides of the flagstone path and not a weed in sight.

Mary watched a red admiral butterfly flutter from one flower to another; it seemed to favour the blue cornflowers over all the rest. A bumblebee buzzed lazily around the white roses that climbed up the house wall. She felt so relaxed and at peace that she didn't want to get up and do anything. So, she sat there and enjoyed doing nothing for a change.

She remembered that she needed to put the bread in the oven. She had stiffened up sitting on the wall, so she stretched and put her boots back on — not an easy task when her baby was due in a week or so.

Once the bread was in the oven, she made dinner for Josie and herself, although she hadn't much appetite. Once they had eaten, she laid Josie down for her nap. Mary was tired as well; she was struggling to keep her eyes open. Josie was sleeping peacefully, so she decided to lie down with her and rest for a while.

When she woke, Josie was still asleep. Mary checked the oven and found the bread was slightly overdone, but thankfully, she'd caught it in time.

Mary felt much better, so she decided to launder everything in preparation for the arrival of her new baby. She washed the sheets for the crib, baby clothes and nappies. Then, she hung everything out to dry on the washing line in the garden. It was a perfect day for drying clothes. While they were drying, she prepared tea, played with Josie when she woke and set the iron by the fire to warm. She had all the laundry ironed and put away before the rest of the household got back.

Tom looked tired when he came in, and Mary noticed that his limp was more pronounced than usual.

'Are you alright?' she asked.

'Yes, I'm fine. It's just me leg, it's hurting a bit,' said Tom. 'You're looking well today. How are you feeling?'

'Great, thank you. I've got loads done this afternoon,' Mary said, proud of her work. 'Tea's ready. I'll serve it out while you're having a wash.'

'I'll give you a hand,' offered Jane. Looking around, she said, 'You've been feathering your nest all day. It won't be long until the little one arrives.' She turned to William and John and said, 'You boys, go and wash your hands before you sit down to eat.'

Tom reappeared wearing clean clothes, and they all sat down at the kitchen table for tea. Mary chopped Josie's food into small pieces so that she could eat it herself with a spoon.

'How did it go today?' Mary asked.

'I couldn't do as much as I wanted because of me leg, but I had to go and show willing after they've done most of the hay-making over here. William did a good job though. Anyway, all the hay's inside now and the barns couldn't be any fuller.'

Mary shifted uncomfortably in her chair.

'Are you alright, Mary?' asked Jane.

'Me back's aching a bit. I think I might have overdone it this afternoon.'

'Why don't you sit yourself down and maybe do a bit of reading? I'll clear up tonight.' Jane cleared the table and carried the dishes over to the sink.

Mary stood up to move to a more comfortable chair, but a painful cramp gripped her belly and made her cry out. Tom took her into his arms and held her. When the pain subsided, Mary said, 'I think our baby's ready to meet us.'

Tom sat her down and held her hand. The pains started to come regularly, and Mary got back to her feet.

'It's going to be a while yet and I'm more comfortable walking around. I'll put Josie to bed and make up the crib.'

'You'll do no such thing,' said Jane. 'Stay here with Tom and I'll see to everything. Don't you worry about anything except this baby. William, take John up to your room and read him a story. We're going to be busy tonight, so make sure he stays in bed.'

'Alright, Mrs Milburn, I'll look after him. We won't get in the way,' William replied. He took his brother's hand, and they headed for the staircase. He turned back to Jane and said, 'I remember when our John was born, and Mother died. Mary won't die, will she?'

Jane went over to the boys and knelt down next to them and said in a quiet voice, 'I'm sorry your mother died. Mary is young and healthy, and she's already had one baby. She'll be fine. I'll take good care of Mary, if you take good care of John. How does that sound?'

William put his arms around Jane and hugged her tightly, and then he helped his brother up the stairs.

* * *

Tom wanted Mary to sit down and rest. Even though she said she was more comfortable pottering about, he thought she should save her strength for the birth. She was obviously in pain, and he wished he could do something to help. When the pains came, he held her, and she squeezed him tightly or gripped his hand.

Tom had helped cows and sheep with difficult births; he knew what was involved, and he knew the risks. Most births were straightforward, but sometimes things went wrong. Sometimes the mother died, sometimes the baby died, and sometimes both were lost. Childbirth was a dangerous business.

When Jane came back down, she looked at her son and said, 'We'd better get her upstairs.'

Tom waited until a contraction ended before helping her climb the stairs. He wanted to stay with her, but his mother shooed him back down. He was worried that Mary would tire herself out and not be able to manage the birth. He was worried for Mary. Yes, he wanted a child, but not at the risk of losing his wife. What if something went wrong? What would he do without her?

He hadn't realised he was pacing up and down until Jane said, 'Sit down and relax, lad. You'll have us all worked up. It's going to take some time yet. You could go over to Joe's if you want?'

'I'm not leaving her, Mother. I need to be here.'

'Well calm yourself down. I'd like a cup of tea; can you see to that?'

Tom got up and put the kettle on. He realised his mother had given him something to do just to keep him busy, but focusing on doing something was helping him to relax a little, so perhaps she knew what she was doing, after all.

He took a cup of tea and a glass of water up to the bedroom, for his mother and Mary, and then settled down in front of the fire. He started to think about Mary and how much he loved her. He had decided Mary was the woman for him long ago on that journey to Ireshopeburn. He had never found a lass as interesting as Mary was that day. Nobody knew that he'd had his eye on her, but he had intended to ask her out. Then, she had gone missing from the Pearts' farm, and he found out she was pregnant. It tore him apart, wondering who the father was and the circumstances between him and Mary. When they had gone to the wrestling at Newcastle and Joe had told him everything that had happened — that he had been meeting Mary, got her pregnant, and then abandoned her — Tom had been furious. He had hit his brother that day, but he could have strangled Joe for what he'd done.

When Tom had told his family that he would marry Mary, they thought he was marrying her because he felt terrible about what Joe had done, and he'd never put them right. But he'd loved her even then. Tom knew Mary had only accepted his proposal because she wanted Josie to have a father. He knew she didn't love him when they married. He hadn't minded though; it was enough that she had agreed to be his wife.

Jane brought her cup down and washed it at the sink. She asked again, 'Are you sure you want to stay?'

Tom knew his mother wanted him out of the way and that if he went to Springbank, he might stand a chance of getting some sleep, but there was no way he could leave. He had to be here for Mary, and he wouldn't be able to sleep while his wife was in labour wherever he was; he'd be too worried about her. So he sat in the kitchen feeling useless while Jane busied herself preparing everything she needed for the birth.

Four hours later, Tom wished he had left the house. It was dreadful listening to Mary's cries, and he wondered how Josie could sleep through the noise in the next room.

At one point, when he thought he could stand it no longer, he had gone upstairs, but his mother had chased him out of the bedroom. He'd returned to his seat by the fire with a mug of ale. The noises became more frequent and louder, and then suddenly he heard a baby cry — but he couldn't hear Mary anymore.

Jane shouted downstairs, 'You've got a son. He's a big, strong lad.'

'Is Mary… is Mary alright?' His voice faltered.

'Mary's fine. You can come up and see them in a minute.'

Tom hadn't realised that he'd been holding his breath, and he breathed deeply and relaxed. They were both alive, and they were both well, and he had a son. He smiled as he listened to his mother walking around upstairs. It wasn't long before she came down and said, 'You can go up now.'

He climbed the stairs two at a time and rushed into the room. He saw Mary lying in bed, propped up with pillows. She held their baby in her arms and looked lovingly into his eyes. Tom went over and sat on the edge of the bed and looked at their tiny boy. With tears in his eyes, he kissed them both and wrapped them gently in his arms.

Their son was christened Thomas Watson Milburn at Westgate Wesleyan Methodist Church when he was six weeks old. He was named Thomas after his father and Watson after Mary's family name and their friend, Watson Heslop. To avoid any confusion between father and son, they decided to call him Tommy.

Chapter 40

High House Farm, Westgate
Christmas Eve 1874

'It's early for snow! It's not often we get any before Christmas. It looks like there's more on the way as well,' said Tom, looking out of the kitchen window. 'The wind's picking up and the sky's dark. There's a decent covering already, and it's knee-high where it's drifting.'

'I hope Jane and the bairns got over to Springbank Farm alright,' said Mary, who was clearing up after their meal.

'They should have got there before it started to drift. There was just a dusting when they set off and it didn't look like it would come to much.'

'If I'd thought it was going to get worse, I wouldn't have let her take the little ones. I couldn't have stopped your mother from going though. She was determined to take the Christmas presents over for Joe and Connie.'

'William's been wanting to go to the farm to see the stock over there ever since he came here, and you know she can't go anywhere without John and Josie tagging along. They love going off on adventures with her,' Tom smiled as he thought of some of the stories his mother had told.

'Do you think they'll get back alright?'

'It's hard to say. It's drifting now, and it doesn't take much to block the road. Maybe I should have a ride over and see what's happening. I know you won't settle until you know they're all safe.'

As he finished speaking, he saw Joe ride past the window and dismount in the farmyard. 'Here's our Joe now,' he said as he went to open the door. His brother came in covered in snow.

'How do! I was just saying to Mary that I should ride over and see what's going on.'

'Aye, this was a surprise, wasn't it? We don't expect snow as early as this. Anyway, I thought I'd better let you know that Mother and the bairns are over at the farm. She didn't want to bring them back in this weather and we can't get the cart through the drift at the bottom of our bank. So, she's decided they'll have to stay with us until the snow clears. Mind you, she's upset because she wanted to be here for Christmas and she knows that you'd want the bairns here for Christmas as well. They might get back over tomorrow if it clears up a bit.'

'At least we know they're safe, that's the main thing,' said Tom, although he was disappointed. 'Thanks for letting us know. We'd have been worried sick about them, not knowing if they'd set off for home or not.'

'They're excited about staying over. When I left, the bairns were deciding which beds they wanted to sleep in,' said Joe, smiling.

'Did you come the road way?'

'No, I came across the fields. It wasn't bad that way because the snow's blowing off the hills. It's the valley bottom and the dyke backs where it's building up. Anyway, I'd better be getting back.'

'Merry Christmas,' said Tom, out of tradition rather than sentiment.

'Merry Christmas. And don't worry about the bairns; they'll be fine,' said Joe looking at Mary before turning to leave.

When Joe was back on his horse and riding away, Mary went to Tom and put her arms around him. They'd been looking forward to Christmas with the children, but now it would just be them and baby Tommy.

The wind howled outside and, despite the fire burning in the grate, Mary shivered.

'It's going to be a bad storm,' said Tom.

'Aye, but we're well stocked. We've got plenty of food for us, and for the animals, so we'll be fine,' said Mary, with more conviction than she felt. As far as Mary was concerned, the snow had its good points and bad. She loved to see children playing in it, and she had fond memories of playing with Annie in the snow. They had loved to walk in soft snow because it stuck to the bottom of their clogs, and it felt like they were walking on stilts. The Weardale landscape looked even better than usual when it was covered with a fresh coat of glistening snow — it was breathtaking.

But on the other hand, snow could be deadly. Just last winter, a woman from Wearhead had gone missing in a snowstorm on her way home from her sister's house in the village. Her body had been found three days later, only a hundred yards from her door.

'Yes, we'll be fine,' agreed Tom. 'There's plenty of logs and peat in the shed to last all winter. We'll be warm enough.' Tom had concerns too. He had twenty-two ewes up on the fell. If the snowfalls were heavy and he couldn't get hay up to them, they could starve up there with no grass to eat. He couldn't afford to lose any sheep. The ewes were all in lamb as well. Yes, they were well stocked with food and fuel for the winter, but money was still tight, and he wanted their farming venture to work. If he could bring the sheep down to the lower ground, he would be able to feed them through the bad weather and keep them safe.

'You know, I think I should go and bring those sheep down off the fell. If I put them in the back pasture, I'll be able to throw hay over the wall to feed them. If they stay up there and it gets really bad, we could lose some of them.'

'Well, if you're going to go, go now before the snow starts again. It'll take you a good couple of hours to round them up and fetch them down.'

Tom dressed in lots of layers of warm clothing, including the hat and scarf Mary had given him for Christmas last year. Mary went to him and put her arms around him. 'Please be careful, Tom.'

'I won't be long,' he said, with a smile. He kissed her first on her brow and then on her lips. As he opened the door to leave, a gust of wind blew in and chilled the room. Mary heard him shout for Floss and the black and white collie ran out from the barn. Mary watched Tom set off up the hillside, trudging through the snow with Floss by his side.

She turned and wondered what she should do until he got back. They would need food for over Christmas, so she decided she would do some baking. She liked baking, and it would keep her busy and take her mind off the weather. She glanced out of the window and saw a few fine flakes of snow falling to the ground. She took her mixing bowl, scales and weights out of the cupboard and set them on the table. Mince pies first, she decided. Christmas and snow always made her think of mince pies, and she was sure Tom would love some when he returned.

Two hours later, the snow was falling fast; fine, powdery snow that was lifted again by the constant wind as soon as it had fallen. The windows were coated with it, and Mary could no longer see out; the kitchen was dark. She lit the lamps and then went to the door and opened it. Snow was swirling around the yard. It stung her face as it hit her, and the frosty air caught her breath. It was bitterly cold. She closed the door and went straight to the fire to put on more peat. She had only been outside for a minute or two, and her hands were cold. Tom would be frozen when he got back. She thought she should go out and milk the cows for him so that when he returned, he could stay inside and get warmed through. Mary checked on Tommy, who was sleeping peacefully, wrapped herself up and went out to the barn.

It was dark outside by the time she had finished milking, and Tom had still not returned. Mary was worried; he should have been home. Yes, it would take longer than usual to bring the sheep down because he would have to walk through the snow, and that was hard work when the snow was deep but, even so, he should have been back by now. At least another foot of snow had fallen since she'd gone out. It was about three feet deep, and she could see where the snow had blown up against the barn wall to about her height. She wasn't one for praying very often, but she was certainly going to pray for her husband's safe return tonight. It was as bad a night as she could ever remember.

The snow had piled up against the door again, and it fell into the room as she opened it and went inside. She was grateful to be back in the warmth. She fed Tommy and put him to bed and then returned to the kitchen and continued to bake.

After another hour or so, she looked at the mass of pies and scones that filled the table. Tom hadn't come home. He had been outside in this blizzard for five hours. God only knew what state he would be in when he got back. She went to the door and, when she opened it, more snow fell into the kitchen. Outside, the snow was falling so thickly that she could no longer see the barn across the yard. Everything was white. How would Tom find his way back? Maybe Floss would lead him home; she had heard of dogs doing some wonderful things.

In a state of despair, she called out Tom's name and listened. It truly was a silent night. She could hear nothing; the snow deadened any sounds. When she went back inside, she couldn't decide whether to bank up the fire for the night and go to bed or find a book to read and sit by the fire until Tom returned. There was no way that she would sleep until he got back, so she decided to sit by the fire and read, and that way, she could tend the fire and keep the house warm for when he came in.

Mary woke with a start. The chiming clock must have woken her. She saw it was seven o'clock in the morning and remembered that it was Christmas Day. She must have fallen asleep sometime during the night. Her book was on the floor by her chair. The fire was out, and the house was cold. Tom. Where was Tom? She looked around the house to see if he had come home. He wasn't there. With a feeling of despair, she realised that he must have spent the night outside in the storm.

Even though she was worried, she had to pull herself

together because there were things she had to do. She fed Tommy and changed his clothes before going out. She went to the door and opened it. The snow had blown against the door, almost to its full height, and she could hardly see any daylight. She got the fire shovel and started to dig and, as she worked, she couldn't stop thinking about the lady from Wearhead and how close to home she had perished. What if Tom had almost reached the house and was lying under the snow in the yard?

Mary was exhausted. She had cleared a path from the house to the barn so that she could get to the animals there. The snow was about four feet deep in the yard, but it had drifted up against the buildings. There were still a few flurries of snow coming down, and the sky promised to yield more. When she had reached the barn, all was peaceful. The animals were well — Bobby, the cows, the geese and the chickens. Tabby met her at the door with a huge, dead rat in his mouth, which he dropped at her feet. 'Thank you, Tabby. Good boy! You earn your keep, don't you?' She threw the dead rat onto the snow-covered midden and fed the cat first. Then, she fed all of the other animals, broke the ice on the water troughs, milked the cows and went back indoors to warm up and check on her baby.

On her way back inside, Mary looked up at the hillside. Snow stowered across the fields and swirled to form drifts. The path she had dug was already filling with freshly fallen snow, and the wind howled menacingly.

Before clearing a path to the barn, she had thought she should try to get help, and the obvious place to go would be Springbank Farm. If Joe knew that his brother had been out all night, he would get a search party together. But now, she realised the idea was futile. It had taken her such a long time just to get across the yard, she would never make it through the snow and the drifts to Springbank Farm. All she could do was wait and pray.

She hadn't eaten breakfast, and it was now dinner time. She should be hungry. She tried to eat a mince pie, but her stomach was so unsettled that she only managed one bite. Thoughts of last Christmas came to mind. It had been such a wonderful day, and she remembered it as if it was yesterday. She could still see Tom's face when she had told him that she was pregnant. He'd been so excited about becoming a father. They'd swapped gifts, shared a lovely meal and enjoyed each other's company. The only Christmas present she wanted this year was for her husband to come home to her.

She built up the fire and then fed and changed Tommy. Thinking about Christmas had given her an idea. She needed something to do to fill the hours between feeding the animals and milking the cows, or she would go mad with worry. She decided to start making a clippy mat. Jane had an old chest where she stored old clothes and pieces of fabric for making things. Mary took them out and sorted them into different materials. She left all the woollen items on the table and returned the cotton and linen ones to the chest for making a quilt another time. She started to cut the clothes up into small, rectangular strips of equal size. When she had finished, piles of different coloured fabrics were on the table, ready to be used.

She brought out the wooden matting frame that Tom had made and fastened a piece of hessian onto it, stretching it tightly. She started to push the navy pieces through it, around the edges. It was a slow and monotonous process but one that kept her mind off Tom, but all of the time she was listening intently for the sound of the door latch.

By nightfall, Tom had still not returned. Mary fed Tommy and settled him for the night, banked down the fire and went to bed alone. Sleep didn't come, and the longer she stayed in bed trying to sleep, the more elusive sleep became. The wind was howling outside, and snow was still falling. There was a small pile of snow on the bedroom windowsill where it had found a gap between the panes of glass.

Mary was cold and anxious. Now that her mind was no longer occupied, she worried more and more about Tom. Could he have sheltered somewhere? There were no farms or cottages above them on the hillside. Could he have made his way back down and have been stuck at Springbank Farm? That was possible. She strongly hoped that he was safe and warm and that they would laugh about how worried she had been in the future. But what if he was outside in the freezing wind and snow? This would be his second night outdoors — without food, water or warmth. Oh, Tom! Please be safe.

She wished she had tried to get help today. Perhaps she should have saddled Bobby and ridden him through the fields to Springbank Farm. Joe had said that it wasn't too bad that way — but that had been yesterday before most of the snow had fallen. Would it have been passable today? She didn't think so. Anyway, she couldn't have left Tommy at the farm by himself, in case she couldn't get back to him, and she wouldn't have risked her baby's life by taking him out in this weather.

Wondering what else she could have done, Mary remembered something her mother had said years ago. 'If you're ever in need of help, hang a sheet out the window. It'll attract attention. Someone will see it and come to help.' She vowed to do that at first light and to pray that there was someone out there to see it.

In her mind, she replayed the conversation that she and Tom had had after his accident when he'd wanted to go back to the mine. They had discussed whether mining or farming was the better option, and she had said that farming was safer. If he died out there trying to save their sheep, she would regret saying that for the rest of her life. If he died, what would they do without him? How would she manage without him?

Her childhood dream of finding a handsome man and of falling in love seemed fanciful now, her girlish crush on Joe meaningless. What she and Tom had together was real, and she couldn't ask for any more in a man. She realised she didn't want anyone else ever — there was only Tom for her.

Mary prayed that he was still alive and would come home to her. She needed to tell him how she felt. She needed to tell him that she loved him — and she desperately hoped that she hadn't left it too late.

For warmth and comfort, she hugged herself, wishing that the arms wrapped around her were Tom's. As she wondered if she would ever feel his embrace again, she began to cry. When sleep finally came, it was restless. Mary dreamed of being frozen and unable to move. All she could see was white everywhere, then her back began to feel warm, and she thawed out. She woke up to find Tabby lying stretched out along her back, and the slight warmth he provided was welcome.

Frost formed a beautiful, intricate pattern on the inside of the bedroom window. Mary couldn't see out, but she could tell it was still dark. She undid the latch and opened the sash window. She took the sheet off the bed and tied a knot in one corner. Pushing most of it out through the opening, she secured the last part by closing the window onto it. From outside, the sheet would look like a flag billowing in the wind. Hopefully, it would draw attention to her plight.

Mary went downstairs and lit the fire, tending it until it was burning well. All she could hear was the crackling sound of wood burning in the grate. When the day dawned, the sky was clear and blue. Mary cleaned and fed Tommy and then went out to the barn, grateful that there wasn't snow blasting into her face today. She tended to the animals and was pleased that they were all well. When she returned to the house, the fire was low, so she added some wood and stoked it; she watched the flames until the fire came back to life. She felt hungry for the first time in days, so she put some oats and milk into a pan to make porridge.

While breakfast was cooking, she went to the door and was surprised at how still and quiet it was outside — so peaceful. The white snow glistened in the sunlight, and it was so bright that Mary had to squint to look out across the fields. Something caught her eye in the distance; she tried to see what it was. Something was moving on the fell. She watched for several minutes before she was sure somebody was walking along the fell, heading towards the gate. When he came through into the top pasture, she saw a man walking with a limp and there was a black and white dog beside him. It had to be Tom.

'Thank God!' said Mary, unable to believe her eyes. How could he be walking down the hill after spending two nights out in the storm? Was she seeing things? Was it his ghost?

The man got closer and he waved at her. It was Tom - and he was alive!

Mary moved as quickly as she could through the snow to

meet him in the pasture. When she reached him, she said, 'Tom, oh Tom!'

Tom picked her up and swung her around, and they laughed. He placed her back on the ground and held her tightly. He said, 'I've missed you, lass.'

'Thank God, you're safe,' said Mary. 'I can't tell you how pleased I am to see you. Come on, let's get you back to the house.'

They walked to the farm, hand in hand. Floss ran into the barn and went straight to her empty food dish. Mary gave the dog something to eat, and she wolfed it down. Then, she curled up on the straw. 'Good girl, Floss,' Tom said, stroking her head.

The kitchen was warm, and the porridge on the stove was ready. Tom took off his coat and sat at the table to eat. He finished his bowl quickly and said, 'I've been so hungry.'

Mary refilled the bowl. When Tom had finished eating and was sitting comfortably by the fire, Mary sat on his knee and wrapped her arms around his shoulders.

'I was so worried you wouldn't come back,' she said. 'You were out for two nights in that awful storm. I can't believe that you survived. What happened up there?'

'Well, by the time I'd got up onto the fell, the snow was coming down quite heavily. I couldn't see more than a yard or two in front of me and I was walking through snow up to me knees — that was tough going for me, but Floss was finding it hard running through that depth of snow an' all. We found a couple of sheep, but I knew we wouldn't find the rest in time to bring them down before dark. I couldn't see very well, me bad leg was aching, and the snow was biting into me face. To be honest, if I'd known it was going to get that bad so quickly,

I would never have set off.'

'I wish you hadn't,' Mary said, putting her hand on his cheek. She leaned forward and kissed him tenderly.

'Anyway, you asked how come I'm alright. That's down to me Granda Milburn. When me and Joe were little, he told us what to do if the snow closed in and we couldn't see where we were going. He said we should find a deep drift at the back of a dyke and dig a hole into the snow — you know, like a little cave — and huddle up in there until the weather clears. Stay out of the wind and stay dry. So that's what I did. Floss came in and stayed with me the whole time. It was surprising how warm it was out of the wind. I remember him telling us that the worst thing you can do is carry on until you're exhausted or blinded by the snow. You don't stand a chance then.'

'I felt so helpless here, not being able to get out and get help. Thank God your Granda told you what to do. He saved your life! If it had been me up there, I wouldn't have known what to do.'

'I would never have let you go up there in the first place. I love you too much to let you risk your life for a few sheep.'

There, he had said it. He did love her. Mary looked into his eyes, and she could see that he meant it, 'Oh Tom,' she replied. 'I love you so much.'

* * *

Those were the words that Tom had longed to hear. She loved him too. At last, he had heard the words from her lips, he could feel it in her touch, and he could see it in her eyes. He held her close and kissed her passionately.

Epilogue

High House Farm, Westgate
July 1875

'Come on Josie, run faster, you're supposed to catch me!' called John as he ran through the newly cut hayfield.

Josie replied in a sulky voice, 'Can't catch you, you run too fast.' She tried to copy her young uncle, who was jumping over the cut grass, pretending he was riding a horse, but she tripped and fell. 'Ow, my knee hurts!'

'Come here,' said Tom. Without getting up from the blanket he shared with Mary, he held out his arms to Josie.

Josie ran over to him with a slight limp, 'Dada, Dada, make it better.'

The grass stubble had grazed her knee slightly, but she wasn't badly hurt.

Tom bent down and kissed it and said, 'All better now.'

Josie immediately got up and started running again, trying to catch John.

'It's nice having an afternoon off and being able to spend a bit of time with you,' Tom said to Mary as he lay down next to her. 'The grass will be to turn tomorrow and if it stays dry like this,' he said, shielding his eyes to look up into the sky, 'it should be dry enough to build pikes the day after. It looks like we'll have plenty of hay to see us through the winter, even if it's another bad one.'

'Let's hope it not as bad as last year,' replied Mary.

'Last year wasn't all bad. I remember it did have its good points — and there are some advantages to the long winter nights,' said Tom, with a seductive smile.

Mary nudged him with her elbow and laughed. The children were playing nearby, so she changed the subject.

'William knows all of the cows by name and he recognises most of the sheep as well.'

'He likes farming and he's good at it.' Tom looked across the field to where William was training a new dog to herd the geese. 'He's a good help around the place.'

'John loves playing with Josie,' said Mary. 'Watching them, you'd think they were brother and sister.'

They heard the sound of horses' hooves and raised voices in the distance. Joe and Connie came into view, riding along the road at the bottom of the field. Even though they were over three hundred yards away, it was apparent that they were arguing.

'Joe and Connie at it again,' said Tom. He felt sorry for his brother stuck in a loveless marriage, but it had been Joe's choice to marry Connie. Tom was pleased that he had because that meant Mary had been free to marry him. She was the only woman he had ever wanted, and he still couldn't believe that she was his. Things had worked out very well. They hadn't had an easy start to their marriage with Mary's relationship with Joe, the murder enquiry, his accident at the mine and then the snowstorm last year. The storm hadn't worried him too much, but Mary had gone through hell thinking that he'd perished in the snow and that she'd lost him. He had waited such a long time for her to love him and had been so glad when she finally said that she did.

'I'm so pleased we took on the farm. How much better is this than working underground? Just look around us — blue sky over our heads, sun on our faces, fresh air to breathe, being able to watch the bairns playing around us and the best of all is being able to lie next to you, my beautiful wife. I love you so much.' He leaned over and kissed her on the lips. 'I'm a lucky man — a hell of a lucky man. What more could I possibly want?'

Then, without waiting for an answer, he asked, 'And what about you, lass? I hope you're as happy as I am. You should be now that you've got the house full of bairns you always wanted!'

* * *

Mary thought about her life since she had married Tom. She had married him because he had offered a solution to her problems. When she thought she had lost him in the snowstorm, Mary realised that she truly loved him, and now she had no doubt whatsoever about her feelings for him. She loved him more than anything.

'Aye, I'm happy - and I love you too,' she said sincerely. Then, she added with a cheeky smile, 'I hope there's room for one more in this full house....'

'Why's that?'

'Because another baby will be joining us in the New Year.'

Tom rolled over and, holding her close, whispered in her ear, 'That's perfect, just perfect.'

Author's Historical Note

In the 1870s, the primary industry in Weardale was lead mining. Miners worked in small groups, called partnerships, and the partnership entered into a bargain, or contract, with the mining company. They would agree where in the mine they would work and negotiate the price for lead ore by weight or dead work by distance. Dead work was cutting tunnels through rock to reach the mineral veins which contain lead ore. They were paid every six months, and they received subsistence money to live on in the meantime. There was no such thing as a steady wage. If the miners brought out more ore than expected, they earned a good wage, but if there was less ore than expected, they received little or no wages.

Lead mining was a dangerous occupation, and accidents were a common occurrence, usually in the form of rock falls or explosions involving black powder, an early explosive used to blast rock.

Miners in remote parts of the dales lived in smallholdings belonging to the mining company. They relied on this land to provide for their families. In the census returns, occupations in these areas were often recorded as miner/farmer.

In the Durham dales, hill farming was dominated by sheep but included dairy and beef cattle, pigs and poultry. Farmers in northern England used a traditional method of counting sheep, using words derived from an ancient Celtic language.

By the 20th century, the practice had almost fallen out of use, but the author's mother and others brought up on rural farms could still recite them.

The highlight of the year for the dale's residents was the agricultural shows that took place in late summer. There are three annual shows held in Weardale at the time of writing. St John's Chapel began in 1869, whereas Wolsingham and Stanhope have longer histories stretching back to the 18th century.

Cumberland wrestling was a popular sport in the 19th century, and men from Weardale competed in regional competitions. The author's ancestor, Robert Adamson from Rookhope, is listed as a competitor at the annual Easter competition at Newcastle in the 1850s.

The first 'real' character in *The Lead Miner's Daughter* is George Steadman, a notable wrestler who won at least sixty cups, hundreds of metals and seventeen heavyweight championships. His highest monetary prize was £200 in 1892 (worth £25,000 today). At five foot eleven inches tall and a weight of eighteen-and-a-half stones, he wrestled internationally and won more often than not.

The other is Matthew Atkinson, who was the last person to be publicly executed at Durham on 16 March 1865. He was sentenced to death for murdering his wife. He was hanged, but the rope snapped, and it is rumoured that he talked to people in the crowd while a new rope was found. He was successfully hanged on the second attempt.

The Weardale Association for the Prosecution of Felons was formed on 29 July 1820, with its members clubbing together to share the cost of prosecuting the neighbourhood's felons. Every district had its own association up to the 1850s when the police took on a more active role in prosecuting criminals. *The Weardale Association for the Prosecution of Felons*, known locally as *The Felons,* still exists and meets regularly, although it is now merely a social event.

Methodism was very strong in Weardale, and John Wesley regularly visited the dale to preach. High House Chapel at Ireshopeburn, built 1760, was the oldest purpose-built chapel in continuous weekly use. Unfortunately, its last service took place in 2019, as the building required extensive repairs. The Weardale Museum has purchased it. The Primitive Methodist Chapel at Westgate is in the care of the Historic Chapels Trust.

In 1788, a small group of dales people founded a 'sixpenny' subscription library with forty books – most of which had been written about Methodism by John Wesley. It had one hundred and fifty members and three thousand books housed in Library House in Westgate in its heyday. The library closed in 2002. The books were given to the Weardale Museum and its records to the National Archives. Library House is now a private dwelling.

The year 1872 was exceptionally wet, and it held the record for the wettest 12 months in England and Wales until the 21st century. The autumn was particularly stormy, and many ships were wrecked around the coasts of Britain. December 1874 was the 6th coldest December ever recorded, with an average temperature of -2.9°C between Christmas and New Year.

Many years ago, the author studied the population census data for upper Weardale. The surnames and given names used in *The Lead Miner's Daughter* are typical of the area at that time. The surname Peart was very dominant, being shared by 25% of the population in upper Weardale in 1891. John, Joseph, Thomas and William were the most common boys' names, and Mary and Ann (with the variants Hannah and Annie) were the most popular girls' names. There was a strong tradition of naming boys with surnames, often the mother's maiden name, e.g. Watson Heslop. Children were usually named after a parent or close relative.

About the Author

Margaret Manchester lives in County Durham, England, with her husband and two sons. She was born in Weardale and spent her childhood there.

Research into Margaret's family history discovered that many branches of her family had lived and worked in the area for centuries, either as lead miners, smelters or farmers. This sparked her interest in local history.

Whilst she studied local history and archaeology, Margaret worked as a guide at Killhope Lead Mining Museum. She was awarded a Masters degree in Archaeology from the University of Durham and taught archaeology, local history and genealogy.

As well as writing, Margaret is currently the managing director of a multiple award-winning business. She is the chair of a charity that supports industrial heritage. She also enjoys spending time in her garden and with her dogs.

You can connect with me on:

🌐 https://www.margaretmanchester.com

🐦 https://twitter.com/m_r_manchester

📘 https://www.facebook.com/margaretmanchesterauthor

Also by Margaret Manchester

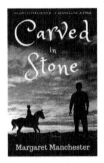

Carved in Stone

Northern England, 1881. Sent away during her brother's trial, Phyllis Forster returns home seven years later to find Weardale and its people have changed. They've turned against her family name and Phyllis desperately wants to win back their respect.

At twenty-eight years old, she has almost given up hope of love and marriage, and throws herself into the management of the family estate, until two very different men come into her life.

Ben, troubled by the past and full of anger and distrust, is a shepherd who shuns the company of others until his new boss arrives at Burnside Hall.

Timothy, the new vicar, is preoccupied with the ancient past, but he takes a keen interest in Phyllis.

Will she settle for just a husband? Or will she defy convention and follow her heart?

Fractured Crystal

Northern England, 1895. Josie Milburn meets Elliott Dawson, a man who shares her interest in collecting crystals. Defying an age-old superstition, Elliott takes Josie into a lead mine, an action that sets off a sequence of dramatic events, beginning with a miner's death that same day.

Elliott and Josie face a series of trials involving tragic loss and the unveiling of family secrets, which change their lives and fortunes in ways that they could never have imagined.

Will these traumatic circumstances bind them together or tear them apart?

Printed in Great Britain
by Amazon

11589125R00181